PRAISE FOR HANNA PARK

Reading *Resurrection* reminded me of Sarah J. Maas's *A Court of Thorns and Roses*, but with a sharper mythological backbone and a darker and more haunting atmosphere rooted in Irish folklore. What struck me was the writing itself. Park has a way of spinning language that feels alive, almost like it breathes.

— LITERARY TITAN

Author Hanna Parks begins 'Resurrection'—the extraordinary follow-up to her jaw-dropping debut 'The Scald Crow'—in an overloaded explosion to my senses. I didn't simply slide into the tactile, aural, visual, and scent of the narrative; I was launched, landing fully submerged in the fantastical worlds only Ms Parks can deliver. THIS IS SUCH A GREAT BOOK!

— MORALLY GRAY NOLA

PRAISE FOR HANNA PARK

From ancient gods to a host of otherworldly magical creatures, Resurrection has everything to make it an absolute treat for fantasy lovers. The lore of this world is simply fascinating. The plot is fast-paced and features twists and turns that keep pulling the rug out from under your feet.

— READERS' FAVORITE

I wish I could visit the worlds Hanna Park brought to life

— BOOKSIREN'S READER

RESURRECTION

BEYOND THE FAERIE RATH
BOOK 2

HANNA PARK

BAISONG PRESS

Resurrection

Copyright © 2025 by Hanna Park

All rights reserved.

This novel is a work of fiction. While some characters are inspired by Irish mythology and historical figures from the 1500s, they have been adapted and fictionalized for the purposes of storytelling. Any historical references have been interpreted creatively, and this book is not intended to be a factual or scholarly representation of history or mythology.

All characters, events, and settings are either purely fictional or used fictitiously. Any resemblance to actual persons, living or dead, is entirely coincidental.

No part of this book may be used or reproduced in any manner whatsoever, including the purpose of training artificial intelligence technologies in accordance with Article 4(3) of the Digital Single Market Directive 2019/790. Baisong Press expressly reserves this work from the text and data mining exception. Only brief quotations embodied in critical articles or reviews may be allowed.

Cover Art by *Niki White* www.nikiawhiteart.com

Visit Hanna Park at www.hannapark.ca

Baisong Press, Box 291, Port Carling, ON P0B1J0

First Edition, 2025

Digital ISBN, 978-1-0696340-0-9

Paperback ISBN, 978-1-0689975-8-7

Published in Canada

HUMAN
AUTHORED™
THE Authors Guild
3352988

to those who believe

Author's Note

Resurrection is a tale woven with threads of magic, love, and ancient power—but even in Faerie, darkness finds a way in.

Within these pages, you'll find a scene depicting a graphic attempted sexual assault. It is a key part of Calla's journey and is handled thoughtfully, but I understand that some moments have a lasting impact.

If this is a sensitive subject for you, please read with care or consider skipping the scene altogether. Your well-being is more important than any story.

Thank you for walking between worlds with me,

—Hanna Park

CONTENTS

1

---

alla

Fog clung to the earth, drifting in a circular formation, shielding me from whatever dangers lived within the dark wood. I lifted my hand and extended my fingers. The mist responded, flowing backward, then drifting closer, playing a game of cat and mouse. The haar lived and breathed and had a purpose. The life breath of a being unknown within the mortal realm, called upon to collect and bring me here, to this unknown land, this Otherworld, the one the Irish whispered of in hushed tones.

I scoured the darkness for any entity accountable and found none, neither ghostly nor human. I was alone, and yet I was not.

I stared upward into a lacy green veil, tried to piece together the last few moments, and came to one conclusion—this was a different Ireland, untouched by the hand of man, by civilization. Lush ferns captured the forest's spirit, and emerald fronds wafted in a still breeze.

Red squirrels chittered overhead, leaping from one gnarled branch to another, rustling the broad leaf canopy.

Colm—the copper-haired Celt who had promised me forever. His fingertips leaving mine were the last thing I remembered.

The sky shivered, and thunderbolts had struck the sea. Ice pellets shot down, and balls of hail battered the sand, striking everything in its path.

I turned away from Colm's anguish, from his love. A greater force had called to me, and I was helpless against it. No, that was a lie. I wanted to know. I needed to know. Who I was. What I was.

The haar wrapped me in warmth and swallowed me whole, the whorling sea giving me up to the sky. The needle bounced out of the groove and, everywhere, became elsewhere. One moment I was grounded—the next, I found myself thrown into a sparkling abyss, like a fly caught on a gust of wind. I had fallen from the sky, landing in superhero fashion—crouched on my heels, fists flailing. How far I had traveled, I could not say—this place was that and so much more. The aroma hit me first —damp earth touched by a faraway sea.

I stood, taking stock of my current condition, running my hands over my bones and finding none broken. My leggings had ripped at the knees. I gazed at my bare feet, toes curling into the soft earth. The oversized caramel-colored work shirt had held up. My silver link bracelet— still dangling from my wrist, not a single sapphire out of place from the dangling horseshoe. But where were my shoes? I ran my fingers through my hair, trying to tame the Kraken, realizing I had lost my hair scrunchie, leaving me no choice but to let my hair fall naturally, untamed in all its snake-like glory.

When I was young, I would chase the wind, leaping into the air and relishing the sensation of flight. Arms outstretched, I would soar high above the tall grass, unafraid of where I might land. I would lie on my back, lost in the rolling skies, at one with the universe. The earth would whisper, and I would listen.

What happened on the strand in Ardara brought back those same sensations.

My gaze followed the moving shadows and the stray sunbeam illuminating a man in its path. Dressed in soft leathers, with an archer's bow slung over his broad shoulders, stood a man—Finvarra, the King of the Faeries.

I rubbed my eyes and looked again. He was the man from Ériu's vision—my biological mother, the Princess of the Dead. The thought of opening that door filled me with dread.

I held my head high, anticipating the moment our paths would cross. This meeting was inevitable. Orlaith had confirmed the impossible—this immortal being was my natural father. Was it only yesterday that the older woman served tea to Colm and me in her sister's flat in Dublin and, in no uncertain terms, revealed the truth? I had sisters. I was the progeny of a Faerie King.

He stood taller than any mortal man, thick-limbed and broad-shouldered. His nose was straight, and his lips were full. But his eyes—nothing could prepare me for those. Shimmering silver streams circled dark pupils of a crushed velvet hue. Banded in smoke and framed by long lashes, those lustrous orbs held me captive.

His jet-black hair swept away from his face with a leather thong, revealing the sharp, chiseled features of a respected king. A golden diadem adorned with blood-red rubies rested upon his regal head.

I folded my arms across my chest and swallowed the rock lodged in my throat.

"Rioghain, may I have a word?" He called me by my middle name, Ree-an, his golden voice piercing the silence. Even the squirrels listened—they sat at attention, twitching their tufted ears, awaiting his royal command. Leaving the footpath, he joined me among the ferns and, with a slight bow, presented himself. He seemed ageless.

I found myself caught in his silver-eyed gaze. I wanted to laugh and cry at the same time. He should be dead if he ever existed at all: myth, legend, the Faerie Folk. This Other Crowd, this Otherworld the Irish whispered of, existed. I recalled the words of a believer—what is faith but belief in the unseen?

In the twelfth century, in an act of revenge, the Milesians invaded Ireland and defeated the *Tuatha Dé Danaan*. Many *Tuatha* left, but some, led by Finvarra, stayed. The man standing before me negotiated a truce with the Milesian High King, Érimón. The *Tuatha* would inhabit the world beneath the ground, building cities, kingdoms, and palaces of gold. More than that, they would instill fear in the hearts of men. Finvarra became King of the *Daoine Sidhe* of Western Ireland.

Yeah, I looked him up.

"What are you?" I hesitated at each word, rage coating

my tongue. How dare he enter my life uninvited? How dare he take me from mine?

"I am Finvarra, and I am your father." Simple, gentle words that spoke to my heart. He held my gaze. He saw right through me.

Huh. He could lure the unsuspecting away, trusting his languid expression and ethereal beauty. And yet, the idea of family wrenched my heart in a million directions. I crossed my arms over my chest and swallowed my last breath, acknowledging the awe flowing over me.

I had lived a happy and privileged life, sent away from Ireland as a babe to an unsuspecting family across the seas in Canada. My adoptive parents did not know the oddities I exhibited as a child were because I was not human. They passed away in a plane crash, oblivious that I was the halfling daughter of a Faerie King.

Twenty-nine years after my birth, a letter arrived. Dermot Sweet, a man with the same name as mine, had left his estate in the town of Ardara, Donegal County, Ireland, to me. I left in a heartbeat, thrilled to escape the nightmare my life had become, but the nightmares only worsened and the visions intensified. The last few weeks have weighed on my mind—those I had met and touched.

Saoirse, the young witch, grieved the loss of her beloved.

Colm, the man I wanted more than anything.

And Ciarán, the one they both missed, was taken by the Faeries many years ago.

Those I encountered brought the truth closer—their horrors were connected with mine.

"I asked what you are, not who. And my name is not Ree-an. It's Calla, but you already know that." I dropped my arms and stretched my fingers, cracking each knuckle, and then turned my gaze to the cloud-capped mountains, hugging this green vale to avoid confronting my past.

My visions began with Orlaith and ended with Ériu and the man standing before me—my ability to foresee was not a curse. It was something else.

Finvarra stole Ériu from the mortal realm, taking her from Dermot Sweet on their wedding day. Orlaith was there when Ériu delivered three daughters: one light, one dark, and one touched, and when Ériu died in the arms of her Faerie lover. A bad birth, Orlaith had said—were we to blame, my sisters and I? My thoughts spun. Ériu had called herself Princess of the Dead. What did that make me? I had so many questions.

The ferns parted as I circled the man, the mossy undergrowth soft beneath my feet. The aura surrounding him was imperceptible—one might almost believe him mortal. And now I stood face to face with the man who could answer my questions. It was almost a relief.

Colm's voice screamed in my head, filled with such pain, demanding retribution. I stared at the man responsible for tearing me away from the man I loved, setting our connection aside for now. I looked with my heart and knew I would return. I would hold Colm in my arms again.

A waterfall ran down a rock face into a shimmering pool. Bluebells draped the forest floor, wood sorrel, archangel, and creeping underfoot, a carpet of golden saxifrage. Birds chirped, singing a song I had always known. A rhapsody filled my ears, the angelic strains of a harp. I shut Finvarra out, breathing in the sweet fragrance of wildflowers.

"We are the *Aós Sí*, and this is our world." He extended his gloved hand toward the ancient wood.

The threads loosened, and the knots unraveled. This moment had to come, and I didn't know what to do with it. Family. Kith and kin. Bloodline. Ties that bind. Ériu sent me away from all of this. Why?

"What does that mean? Am I dead?" I looked at him, unbelieving.

"I would speak with you, Rioghain." He lifted one side of his mouth in a thoughtful manner, as if this meeting were but a brief pause from his idyllic day, not one engineered by him.

"You've been spying on me, haven't you? From the very beginning. Are you Seamus? How did you do it? How did you change into a different being?" I remembered the little man in the threaded red vest, short navy pants, and buckled brogues who welcomed me to Seldom Inn, the property left to me by Dermott Sweet. He had bent at the waist, sweeping his felt hat in a wide arc, his pert lips lifting. *"Your father wishes to meet you. Would you come with?"* He had offered his hand, his amber eyes reflecting a kingdom of dense woods and lush green fields.

It seemed so long ago.

"Seamus is in my employ. He is always with you, Rioghain. To keep you safe." He motioned toward the forest.

I followed his gaze and beheld the little man concealed in the shadows of an old-growth pine. He seemed to step right out of the tree. Had he been there all that time?

"Lord King." Seamus tipped his felted head in my direction.

"What is this? Who are you people? You don't get to spy on me. Steal me away from my world. This isn't right. Send me back." I breathed through my nose, throwing Seamus a dirty look. He smiled back—his shimmering eyes filled with laughter. Then he dipped his head and was gone. I stared, open-mouthed.

"There are things you must know before you give your gift to a mere mortal." His gaze did not leave mine— black pupils surrounded by a silver iris flecked with hard steel.

"Excuse me?" If he were a king, then I would be a princess. All those fairy tales rushed back to me, and then the pages of that storybook slammed shut. No fairy tale prince was coming to my rescue. I planted my feet in the lush forest and took on his regal persona.

His glamor flickered in the subdued light, exposing the true horror of Faerie.

The ever-changing eyes of a wolf-like creature, with fur as black as the darkest night, held its massive head low, yellowed fangs glistening in the half-light, ready to rip me to shreds. Its authoritative gaze demanded submission—the king of the glen in more ways than one. Go figure.

"A Dire Wolf? Huh. You're quite the trickster, Fin. You don't mind if I call you Fin, do you?" I maintained my position, refusing to blink or show any sign of fear. That would not do. I held the wolf's gaze.

Still, that he transformed into another form in the blink of an eye? I was more than impressed.

The shapeshifting bastard lifted his lips, revealing a hint of a snarl.

I willed myself to think. The *Tuatha Dé* traveled to Ireland from four mythical cities, bringing mystical treasures and magical abilities. They were a force to be reckoned with. He had just proved it.

The air shivered, and the beast vanished, replaced by the archer in the hood. His tanned skin was almost too beautiful to gaze upon. This ancient had lived in the underworld for millennia. God only knew what persona he preferred: man or wolf. Both were dangerous beings, predators in their own right.

"You did well, dear one. You possess your mother's bravery." He nodded.

"Ériu?" My palms tingled as silver scales formed and vanished in the dappled light. My heart stuttered. Did I possess those same abilities? I gazed at my palms, smooth-skinned and devoid of any reptilian scales. If his familiar was a wolf, then what was mine?

I looked into those silver orbs, willing him to share his secrets.

"Let me be clear. Our people revel in pleasure, but pleasure is one thing—union is another. A king, a proud warrior, or at the very least a prince, awaits you, my dear.

I didn't know what to do with that.

I left him staring after me and circled the thick tree

trunk from which Seamus had emerged. I tapped the rough bark. No one answered.

"Are you referring to sex? The birds and the bees? Listen up, Fin. That conversation should have happened ages ago." I ignored his sudden intake of breath and focused on this Otherworld, losing myself in the enchanted forest, a fairyland. "All right, I'll play your game. What did you do with Colm? And what is this place?"

"Some would call this the land of the young, the land of pleasure. You need not worry. You will be safe within our world." He gave me a look, lifting a single eyebrow.

"Safe from what? And how did I get here?" My thoughts returned to the one left behind. Showing weakness would not do, not in a place like this.

"You are referring to the *féth fíada*. One of many skills you will learn to call upon." He cracked a smile, bewitching me with those shimmering eyes.

"*Tables turned*," a voice whispered. Those eyes were mine.

"What is this *féth fíada*?" I tilted my head, giving him an appraising glance.

Damn, he didn't look a day over thirty-six.

"It is how we travel unseen within other worlds. We call upon the mist. This—" He twirled his fingers, bending the air with a magician's ease.

All that stood before me were moss-covered trees and ferns dancing in the dappled light.

"Are you serious?" I scanned the standing trees, the shimmering pool, and the tumbling waterfall. No Faerie King. No wolf.

"Daughter." He appeared behind me in all his immortal glory, his voice a quiet melody of soothing bass notes.

"No fucking way. Magic mist?" I twirled my hands in front of my face. Once. Twice. Nothing.

"We have much to speak of—your future and role in our kingdom. Let us continue." He looked skyward and then walked away, leaving me staring at his broad shoulders.

"Excuse me? I'm not staying here. This is your world, not mine." I tagged after him, my thoughts spinning in six directions, and that would not do. Stay here? For how long? I fought to keep my emotions steady. Showing my hand to the trickster of tricksters would not help my cause. Not one bit.

"You were taken from us, Rioghain." He followed the footpath deeper into the forest.

"Wait. My clothes? My shoes?" I stopped in my tracks, my thoughts turning to my ragged appearance, the torn leggings, and bare feet.

He glanced over his shoulder and waved his hand, sending magic my way. The air shivered, hardly noticeable, yet it affected me in a way I had never expected. The rippling shadow zipped and reformed, transforming my torn clothing into something different.

"What is this? A wedding cake?" I fiddled with the double-puffed sleeves of a pearly-white gown: one gathered above my elbow, and the other secured my wrist. The square neckline, adorned with numerous gathers, and the high waist pleated with more. A ruffled hem embroidered with silver threads fell just below my knees.

Pockets—at least it had pockets. "It's very whimsical. How about a parasol? That would make it sing."

"And now you are returned." He lifted his hands and shrugged.

"Returned? More like taken, wouldn't you say?" I touched my hair, threaded and swept back with silk ribbons.

I did not question the magic he swirled my way. That would mean accepting my predicament.

"Where are we going? Are you going to explain why I'm here?" Pointed-toe leather pumps in a rich burgundy hue hugged my feet, the delicate open-work cutouts showcasing the contrasting ivory of my stockings. I lifted my skirt, extended my stride, and swished through the ferns—power-walking through the glen with the greatest jester the world had known.

"When your dear mother passed. When you and your sisters were born, you were taken." He gestured far into the distance, where the stone spires of a castle rose against a blue sky speckled with cotton-like clouds. The man lived in a castle. Well, of course he did.

"It's true then? Everything Orlaith said?" I gave him the same wide-eyed, pointed stare he had given me.

"The midwife followed Ériu's wishes. I hold the woman no harm. I trust your mother had her reasons." He halted before the shimmering lake where a waterfall cascaded down a steep rock face. Brambles sprawled beside the water's edge, each stalk teeming with fat blackberries.

"You forced Ériu to be with you." I planted my hands on my hips and stated what I believed.

"I did no such thing." He tilted his head, his piercing gaze meeting mine.

"Oh? That's not what I saw." Conflicting memories filled my mind. I replayed my vision of Ériu and Finvarra just before she was stolen from the mortal realm.

"You would deny your rightful place amongst our people? You would deny your king?" He released her and paced back and forth, his deer-skin riding boots silent on the stone floor—a king in every way.

And of how Ériu stood up to this immortal being, her voice surging with conviction.

"They are not my people. And you are not my king. You are Tuatha, banished beneath the mounds by my people. My people. Remember who I am. I am Ériu, Princess of the Dead." She clenched her fists, her eyes flashing dark swords.

"Ériu had her mind. She made her choice." He huffed, but then smiled with a boyish charm.

"Excuse me?" I lifted my voice over the tumbling roar of the waterfall, determined to prove him wrong. I knew what I saw.

"Your mother was a complicated being. Whatever you think you know, you are mistaken." He reached into the gnarled branches, selecting only the ripest berries and filling the leather pouch attached to his waistcoat.

"She was a human being whom you stole from the mortal realm." Or was she? What had Orlaith told me? *"Ériu was from away. Not one of us."* I pinned my lips into a tight line, unwilling to accept or admit I might be wrong.

"You know not of what you speak." His tone softened, and he turned toward me. His eyes carried the distant look of a man longing for the one he loved.

Oh yeah, we were having this conversation.

"She died giving birth." My eyes welled up for the woman I never knew. Who, rumor had it, was my mother.

"Yes. That happened. Yet Ériu left me with two beautiful daughters, your sisters, Nemain and Macha. Had I known you existed, Rioghain, I would have come for you sooner. For that, I apologize." He lifted his palm, offering a handful of lush berries as black as the night.

"Don't change the subject." I steeled my gaze. "Why did Ériu die if this is the land of the young?"

"All women bear the risk of childbirth. No one is ensured immortality. Our kind dies, just like anyone else." He stared with deep intent, forcing me to believe or to look away.

I chose the latter, absorbing his words and reliving Orlaith's. I lost myself in the rippling waters of the inland lake, bathed in the most extraordinary magenta hue. Disturbed by our presence, the water undulated toward the mossy banks and then stilled, the glassy surface becoming an artist's canvas of dancing leaves and cotton ball clouds.

"Did you see that?" I looked again at the still surface.

He smiled, giving no hint of what lay beneath the shimmering waters.

I left that nightmare alone.

"Would you like one?" He motioned at the blackberry bush.

"Is this a trick?" I peered at him and then forgot my fear. I dove right in, drawn to the last purple jewel. Wild canes grabbed my sleeve, and one sharp thorn stabbed deep, ripping open the pad of my thumb.

"Ow." I stared at the ichor oozing from my flesh. The droplet of blood reflected the sky and the color of the sea. "What is this? What does this mean?" My knees buckled. It was all I could do not to stumble into his arms.

"You are one of us, Rioghain. In this world, your blood is ours." His silver eyes twinkled, his slight nod acknowledging my surprise.

"It's true, then." My mouth dried at the blue rivulet staining my palm. "I'm one of the Other Crowd, an immortal." I mumbled to the trees, Ériu's last words ringing through my mind. "Is this the land of the dead?"

"We exist unseen by others. This gives our people an advantage. Advantages you must learn." He droned on and on, not answering my question.

All around me, honeybees hummed—buzzing, buzzing, buzzing. The hum intensified, taking on a life of its own. The transition from Middle-earth to the world under the ground took my breath away.

"How did you find me? How did you know of my existence?" I kicked the soft dirt with one leathered foot.

"The bees shared their knowledge with me." He shrugged, looking oh-so-smug.

"What?" I stared at my reflection in the shimmering pool. A different Calla Sweet stared back. My eyes were no longer grey. They were shining silver orbs like his. Well, of course.

"Honeybees are messengers from the spirit world." He motioned at the buzzing swarm.

"And the bees told you about me?" I considered this revelation, looking at the bees with new interest.

"Once I discovered your presence, finding you was

easy. The midwife had a loose tongue, and the sheep farmer swayed. The poor man was under Ériu's influence too long." He shook his head in pity.

"Ériu's influence?" My words sounded hollow. Everything I thought I knew crashed around me. Everything.

"She was perplexing, your mother, like no other." A muscle in his jaw feathered.

"But she was human, right?" I turned from my reflection, my thoughts returning to the self-avowed Princess of the Dead. I refused to accept that. What would that make me?

"Do you see how the bees gather around you?" He motioned, distracting me from my mother's memory.

The way his eyes shimmered. The way his voice soothed.

I turned my head away from his bewitching gaze and followed the flight of the little creatures.

"The bees? Well, I never thought of that, but you're right. They have since I arrived in this land. Well, not this one. The other one, the real one. Oh, God." I threw my hands against my face while the bees whirred, so many never far away.

"They're drawn to you. Darkness hums beneath your skin." He lifted his hand in an outward gesture. One bee hovered and then landed on his gloved index finger. "Try it." He looked at me, his lips curving into a smile.

"Maybe later." I had almost agreed with him. Instead, I gave him the floor, and he took it.

"I fear you have aroused suspicion within the mortal village. Our meeting should have occurred days ago." His dark gaze left me wondering if he was reading my thoughts.

And just like that, somewhere else found me, as it had so many times before—blinded by the light, touched by the darkness. The air shivered, and Colm's voice echoed, calling me home—Colm—a battle-scarred guardian of the people, warrior enough for me. Thick roots clawed through the underbrush, a spiderweb oxygenating the world beneath this one. That realization had me tripping over the moss-covered tendrils. Colm reached for me, his face stricken with fear. I barely caught myself from falling.

"You mother bestowed your name upon you to honor the great queen, the phantom Goddess—the Morrigan." Finvarra offered his hand, amusement dancing in his silver gaze.

Uh-huh. No way. Touching meant visions, and I had encountered enough otherworldliness for one day— visions I had fought to stay away from my entire life. I turned my thoughts in another direction.

"What are they like, Nevan and Macka?" When I was a child, I would beg my adoptive parents for a sibling, how I had envied those with brothers and sisters—the big family dinners, the teasing, the fun.

"Nemain reigns chaos. Macha instills fury." He spoke with clear pride, his gaze lingering as if he sensed my true feelings. "And you, Rioghain, complete the Triskele. You are the foreteller of doom."

And there it was, the song I sang. That same sensation gripped my soul: a tightening in my chest, an acute awareness of every breathing and living thing. I could best describe it as being sucked into a swirling vortex of kaleidoscopic, blinding colors. A breeze lifted, brushing my face, and for a brief second, I floated on a rising current, then spiraled downward, landing in an ancient wood.

"What's the Triskele?" I met his curious gaze, my throat aching and my voice rasping.

"The maiden, the mother, and the wise woman." He looked wise.

I stared through the looking glass, and my stomach turned. This was not where I belonged. Or was it?

"Three times the charm, huh? You're mistaken, Fin." I swallowed hard, trying to grasp the meaning of his words.

An ancient oak tree stood in the path, its girth wider than six long-armed men. Energy exuded from her. She was the magnificent mother of all things—a myth, a legend. I turned away from him, drawn to the old one.

At another time, the *Tuatha Dé* ruled the upper earth. It was a time of gods and goddesses, kings and queens. Finvarra told a tale of make-believe, yet it was real. All of this was real. I had to wrap my head around the impossible because I was part of it. This wasn't a dream.

I detected sadness in his mellow tone.

"So, what are you saying? Do the three of us serve some magical purpose? For whose gain?" I placed both hands on the hollowed trunk, and my heart stuttered. An energy prowled beneath my skin, her energy. I could have stayed there all day.

"You are young, Rioghain, a mere child in our years. Your gifts will blossom with time. This land will make you all-powerful." He studied me, his dark brows furrowed.

"Do you know what this gift has done to me, Fin? It's ruined my life. I had a career. I had friends." Okay, so I pushed the truth. The friends who abandoned me at the first sign of trouble. The trouble? Me...it was me. I was the trouble...the troubled. The girl who scared the living bejesus out of everyone I touched. It seemed like a long time ago.

I turned from the old one and faced Finvarra, the legendary being from the time before man. He was real. This was real.

"Mortals fear what they don't understand. Embrace your gift, Rioghain. As one, you are forbidding. As three, you will sway worlds." Finvarra spoke of a future only he could see. Leaving the beaten path, he ventured deeper into the dark woods.

"Look, Fin. I'm quite happy on my side of the fence. If you don't mind, I'd like to go home." I bid silent thanks to the Tree of Life and left the canopy of the ancients behind. I followed Fin along a rough, narrow track where ferns brushed against my feet, where the bare branches of a hazel tree hung with yellow catkins, and walked right into a wall of cobwebs.

Spiders—almost as horrible as the visions of death I had endured my whole life. Not that I was scared—scared is a strong word.

"Ew. You're telling me there are spiders? Could you not have banished them to another realm?" I swept my hands over my hair, searching for the eight-legged arachnid who had spun the intricate web, but found none.

"You are home, child. I have known of your existence for quite some time. I owe you what every father owes his child." He lifted his hands, removing wispy silks from one golden ribbon.

I flinched but stood my ground. I would not run, not from the spiders, not from him.

"I ask you for time, Rioghain. That is all. You are welcome to come and go as you please. I make you that promise." He tucked his hands together, continuing in the same melodic voice. "There are dangers in your world —dangers you are unaware of. Here, we live in the shelter of each other. Not so in the middle plane." He removed his glove and put two fingers between his lips, whistling three snappy tones through the dark wood.

The underbrush rustled, and a hairy beast pounced toward his master, its pink tongue lolling from its mouth. The dog, the size of a small deer, sat on its haunches, its head cocked, looking at me.

"His name is Bran. He once belonged to an adversary of mine—a worthy adversary. Some believe Bran drowned, but as you can see, he is alive and well." He motioned toward the piebald dog, his coat mottled with white and blue patches. The dog gazed at me through one lake-blue eye and one disconcerting white one. He seemed to understand Finvarra's words. But of course, he would. Legends were made of this stuff. I searched my mind for that legend and came up empty.

"Let's get something straight, Fin. My name is Calla. I'm not Ree-an, and I don't intend to continue this legacy, or whatever it is you call it. I'm not the doom-bringer. I don't want to be the doom-bringer. Thank you very much." I looked from the dog to Finvarra but extended my hand toward the dog, who sidled beside me and rubbed his giant head in my palm.

"Rioghain is your given name, and someone stole you from us." The light caught Finvarra's eyes, making the silver tones shimmer.

"No one stole me. Ériu gave me to Orlaith. Why would she do that, Fin?" I refused to be drawn under his spell. How often had he used his allure for that purpose, bewitching innocents with those flashing eyes? I reminded myself that this supernatural being was a myth of Irish lore. I glanced into the forest, losing myself in the many shades of green.

Bran whined, nudging his wiry head against my hip.

"I don't have an answer to that question." Finvarra's smooth voice jarred me from my wonderment.

I lifted the hem of my dress and sat back on my heels. I patted the dog; his mottled fur was rough, while his undercoat felt silky. I held his colossal head and gazed into his all-seeing eye. A bond flowed between us, which I found odd. I glanced at Finvarra, this mythical being, capable of transforming into a wolf. It was too much— too overwhelming. I longed to return home to the thatched-roof cottage on the Glengesh Pass and Colm, to pick up where we had left off, moments away from losing the V-Card. Goddammit.

Finvarra pinched his brows together and studied me right back—so very human.

"Just say I believe this wild tale, and I'm not saying I

do. We will bargain for my cooperation. I'll stay on one condition." I lifted my eyes and stared at him.

Bran licked my fingers, encouraging me to strike the bargain percolating in my mind—one that would make so many people happy in the mortal realm. It was a good plan. It made sense. I could do something great here. For Colm. For Saoirse. I had to try. Like, why not? I had nothing to lose.

"And what, pray tell, would that be?" The muscles in Finvarra's face twitched, his grin lighting up the world. He thought he had won.

I saw then how he had become a king. He lacked none of the prerequisites: intelligence, charm, wit, and good luck.

"You have someone within your world who doesn't want to be here. Set him free, and I will go with you. That's the deal." I willed my voice to exude the same confidence he portrayed.

"The humans who live amongst us have chosen their path." His voice filled with an animosity I wasn't used to hearing. It was cold and cruel.

"Well, I think you're mistaken—his name is Ciarán O'Donnell, and he wants to return to his home, to the people he belongs with." I pressed for more than a vague promise.

"I know not of this man." His eyes flickered, revealing the ages of time. Something in the way the shadows deepened and refracted the light. "You have your mother's quick mind. We agree. We will release this Ciarán you speak of." He nodded his crowned head once, pleased with our arrangement.

"Not good enough, Fin. I need a commitment. Right now. As we speak. Free him, send him back. Before I go wherever it is, you're taking me." If he could bend the air, he could do that. I searched the wood for Seamus, the spy—Finvarra's messenger. Where was the little man? I peered at the hairy dog...no, Bran was something different.

"My word is my bond, as is yours." He held out his hand, demanding agreement.

From somewhere above, a dove cried out, its wailing screech piercing the sky. An icy hand tightened its grip on my mind, a cold chill licking the length of my spine. My throat closed.

"I don't shake hands." I swallowed hard, knowing that whatever my life was, for better or worse, was mine and mine alone, but the future dared me to accept the unknown. "Adapt or die," a voice whispered. I turned on my heels, searching the enchanted wood, and saw nothing.

"There is no room for doubt, Rioghain. Not anymore." His gaze narrowed, his lips curling into a smile.

Oh yeah, Finvarra was aware of the torment I had inflicted in the living realm.

"No. No, I can't. I see things I don't want to see." Clouds drifted across the sky. Daylight became darkness.

"Embrace your gift, Rioghain. You are safe here." His voice soothed.

The dog nudged my hand, spreading warmth through my veins.

Ciarán's freedom for mine. I imagined Saoirse, her eyes brimming with happy tears. I saw Colm and the guilt he carried. Finvarra could send Ciarán back. Their troubles would end. And me? My blood was blue. Holy fucking god.

I took his hand, sealing the deal—Ciarán's life for my time in this realm. How bad could it be?

I stared into Finvarra's eyes—oh God, his eyes—were luminous, shimmering particles of light, like a waterfall flowing with liquid silver.

This wasn't the same as my other visions. This wasn't a premonition of death. This was something different.

The wind picked up, buffeting my body yet caressing my soul, teasing me with strains of music—high notes of promise and low notes of desire. I was home. My mind floated in the hereafter.

The doom-bringer. Was that what I was?

The vision enveloped me in shades of blood-soaked crimson, but it wasn't a vision—it was a time and place, and I was part of it. I could taste it.

The skies darkened, and the air swirled with black clouds. Below me lay a valley, resplendent with trees, where two groups of men, spears at the ready, faced each other. The golden-haired men, striking in appearance and strong in build, confronted a monstrous horde of dark-haired, swarthy warriors, towering in height. So many surged into battle that I couldn't count them.

My presence foretold their death, and my mournful cry predicted doom. I embodied the spirit world and all its darkness. Another, a glossy grey-breasted crow, flew overhead of one golden-haired man, feeding his blood lust, wreaking havoc in another way.

The skies screamed, and the earth split open,

unleashing a demonic host I had always known—phantom beings pouring from each fracture. I had picked a side. I had conjured a mystical force to assist the golden-haired band.

Satyrs, half-human creatures with cloven hooves and human faces, surged from the tree line, shouting coarse obscenities and hurling spears with tremendous force. The dark-skinned men yelled in defiance as they fell, one by one.

I swooped low and became one with the creeping mist, undulating into a nightmare of nightmares. Fairy sprites took form, swirling over the earth's edge and soaring among swarthy giants, one-eyed megaliths who flailed spiked clubs, stoking fear with their ghoulish cries.

Their savage wails fueled my hunger.

I ripped the sky open with one shriek.

Goblins, grotesque creatures from another dimension, trailed behind the fairy sprites, hissing venom through yellowed fangs, wielding blood-soaked cleavers. Bones cracked. The fallen begged.

All I could hear was my rasping breath.

With a fleeting thought, I called the witches into the fray. I soared with them through dark clouds, cackling amid hell's storm.

The dark horde was powerless against the ethereal beings. The haar crept through the ancient growth, claiming each soul as they fell.

They were all I could see. The only sound was my rasping breath.

"Open your eyes, child. Tell me, what did you see?" Finvarra's voice sliced through the whispers haunting my mind. I returned to him, to this place of the pine forest and soft earth. I sighed, a final breath, the metallic scent of blood tainting my thoughts.

The shaggy dog licked my fingertips with a warm, sloppy tongue.

"I saw death—men falling onto themselves—a slaughter. There were...things, beings. What was it?" My eyes grew hot as I woke to the tumultuous vision.

"You saw the past, one of many great battles the *Tuatha* faced. You will learn much more from the deeds of our people, and when you're ready, you will see the future. The future of all men. Not just those you touch. You will become the greatest seer in all of eternity. This makes you vulnerable, Rioghain. You will learn how to protect yourself from the world of men. How to become one with the wind. How to stay safe." He helped me to my feet.

He believed what he said. Of course, he did. With the twirl of his hand, this man summoned me to another plane of existence.

"How? No. This is crazy." My stomach flip-flopped. A shaman predicting the future? A simple psychic gift? No, this was way beyond. When did the human species ever learn from past wrongs? Keep your mouth shut, Calla Sweet. Wasn't that my mantra?

"There are many forms you can take. This one, you have already mastered." He produced a feather—a black tail feather from a hooded crow. "You dropped this."

"You're saying I changed into a bird? Shifted? Is that what you're saying? No. That can't be." I slipped through the crack and relived those familiar sensations—the scratchy throat and raw voice—holy mother of God.

"Not just a bird, Rioghain. The scald crow. She is the omen of death," his reverent gaze reflected my horror.

"Great. That's just what I wanted to hear." I bent forward, leaning on my knees, my eyes shut tight. Shapeshifting. How many times had I become one with the wind? And what of the silver scales that formed on my palms? What was that?

"Rioghain?" He touched my fingers, his voice gentle.

The confusion cleared. I squared my shoulders, gazing into those eyes like mine.

"I have seventeen sons but only three daughters—Ériu's beautiful daughters." Turning my wrist, he traced the red blotch marring the palm of my hand. "Do you see this teardrop?"

"A teardrop?" I gazed upon the blood-red blotch, seeing the tear stain as if for the first time. "They have the same mark?"

"Aye." He tilted his head, his expression filled with warmth.

"What does it mean?" I swallowed hard. I had agreed to this. There was no going back, not now.

"The magic of the goddess runs through your veins. You are the oracle, Rioghain. Together with Nemain, with Macha, you are the Morrigan reborn." He held my gaze with no uncertainty.

"Huh, sounds like all hell broke loose to me." I traced the red stain with my thumb, envisioning myself standing on some street corner many years from now, a grey-haired hag shrieking warnings of nightmares to come. And of someone throwing away the key.

"You must speak of this to no one outside of me and your sisters. Tell me you understand." His expression showed concern.

"Oh, don't worry. I won't tell anyone." I rolled my eyes, stepped back, and bumped into Bran, who wagged his long tail.

"Good." Finvarra moved away from me with an ethereal grace, surefooted along the narrow path.

I followed more leisurely, awed by the overhanging branches, the moss, the ferns, and the wild thickets. I lost sight of him among a stand of beech trees. My eyes adjusted, revealing a crevice, a cleft in the limestone face. So easy to miss, even here in this Otherworld.

"So, where do we go from here?" I stood at the entrance to Fairyland, a path burrowing deep within the limestone walls. The blue sky above was barely visible. This was where the spirits lived.

Bran whined.

"Home." Finvarra appeared beside me. How, I did not know. It was one of those things I had to learn. He offered his hand, and this time, I took it.

2

iarán

The frigid waters of the North Atlantic Ocean rose by the minute, the seawater gnawing at the walls of the underground cave with a hunger intent on claiming another soul. The swirling currents tugged at my calves, pushing against my thighs. I had lost sight of the entrance long ago and now stared into an endless black void, hoping against all hope that the way out would materialize. The shifting sands made walking difficult, and the rock stacks beneath the water slowed my progress. Yet the promise of freedom urged me on, but was it a trick? Was I still a captive in the Faerie realm, or had they released me from their grasp, as Cian had said? "Leave now and don't come back."

The ocean's roar played tricks on my mind. The tidewaters gurgled and popped, reaching my fingertips. My clothes clung to me, drenched in salt and brine. Time was running out.

Relief washed over me as the black pitch transformed, an arrow of light bathing the walls in a deep purple hue. The water shimmered, reflecting the afternoon sky of the middle realm—home. My heart burst as I found myself in a familiar place—the strand below Clonmara, where rugged limestone formations rose and fell, stretching from shore into the sea. I lifted my face to the howling wind, a just welcome for a lost soul—angry gusts battering my body with hell's fury.

"Bloody hell." I covered my eyes, blinded by the moody sky. I hesitated, taking in an extraordinary scene. A man raced back and forth, arms outstretched, his tortured lips screaming into the cloudless sky. Wet hair clung to his face, blood seeping from a gash on his forehead.

I waded through waist-deep water, determined to meet my brother. How often had I stood before him, yet he couldn't see? I neared the moment of truth, my heart filled with fear. Had the glamour left me? Was I mortal once more? Or was I still lost to those I loved?

"Where is she? Where is she?" Colm staggered away from me, toward the largest of the sea caves. "What did you do with her?" He screamed into the sky, his voice hinting at a hysteria I had never witnessed before. Colm was the stoic one, always holding his emotions in check.

"What in bloody hell is wrong with you, bro? Are you possessed?" I sloshed through the swirling eddies, speaking to him as I often had. I held my breath, hoping for some sign of recognition. Could he see me, or was I still invisible within the mortal realm? I waited for the answer and received none. I watched him. Stared at him. I reached for him, my grip missing him by mere inches. "Colm? It's me, it's Ciarán."

"You're not Ciarán. Who are you? What are you?" He struggled to his feet and then charged at me, pushing his hands against my chest and knocking me into the sand.

I gasped for breath, one hand gripping the ground as I fell. What a fantastic feeling to be alive and to sense my brother's anger. It had been far too long.

"Hey bro, it's me." Pulling myself up and onto my feet, I grinned—couldn't stop. I took stock of his condition, his bruised and bloodied face, his torn clothing. "You don't look so good, mate."

His eyes glazed. Wary. Hesitant.

"No, this can't be happening. Not like this. Not like this. How did he do it? Where is she? Where's Calla?" He fell to the sand, a guttural moan rising from his throat. His pain howled, echoing off the basalt cliffs, hugging the cove.

"I don't know what you're talking about. There's no one here." I looked to the horizon, searching the distant dunes, and scratched my head, trying to understand—Calla—the girl who could see. Was that what this was about?

"I know she's not here. Do you think I'm a fool?" He struggled to articulate, his eyes darting. The ivory jumper he wore brought back memories of the ones Mam knitted that Christmas before I left—that day etched in my mind like indelible ink. How foolish I was.

I reflected on the moment they freed me from the

Faerie realm and—even before that, the rumblings from Finvarra's court—talk of the Morrigan, the warrior goddess, the phantom queen, returning, and what it would mean for the Tuatha. When I asked Cian why they set me free, he said, "My sister has returned to the Kingdom." He wasn't talking about Nemain or Macha. No, he was talking about the other—the dark-haired girl Colm called Calla.

"I heard rumors. They spoke of the Morrigna, the Triskele. Who is she to you, Colm? Who is this woman?"

"She is everything." His hair fell over his face, hiding his pain.

"The Tuatha Dé took her, Colm." I knelt before my brother and spoke in a quiet voice. "Cian told me his sister had returned to the kingdom. I don't think he meant it of her own accord. Who is this Calla to you?"

"What? No. No. It can't be." He held his head in his hands. "Hamstead. It had to be Hamstead. I have to find her. I failed. Oh God, I failed to protect her."

"She's the sister Cian was talking about. That's what Cian meant," I voiced my thoughts. I should have avoided recalling those memories now that I was in the mortal realm. It didn't matter when they couldn't hear me or when I was invisible to them, but now? The reality hit me hard—I had survived seven years in the Otherworld. I was free. But were they listening? Were they always listening?

"No. No. It had to be him." His eyes shone, and his lips were blue, with sand embedded in his hair. "He must have followed us here."

"Who is this Hamstead?" I looked at him, unsure how

to process his distress. This girl meant something to him, yet he blamed the wrong enemy. I knew who had taken the Calla-girl.

"The bastard's after Calla. Oh, gods and the boy. The wee lad in Malin Head. He's been missing too long." He clenched his hands together and rocked back and forth. "I've failed Eamon, I failed Calla."

"What wee lad? What does this have to do with the Other Crowd?" I shook my head. His assessment was incorrect. Cian, Finvarra's halfling son, had confirmed the truth. This Calla was one of Them; halfling or not, she belonged to the *Tuatha Dé.* "It was Finvarra. I'm sure of it. That's what Cian meant." I could see where this was going. I bent down and hauled him to his feet.

"Finvarra?" He leaned into me, gripping my shoulders. "What? Who is..."

"Finvarra is the King of..." He didn't let me finish.

"I know who Finvarra is. He abducts women from the mortal world." Colm squared his shoulders and stood tall. For the first time, I noticed how thin my brother had become—muscular but thin.

"Aye, and more than that. Who is this Calla to you?" I gazed upon my brother, shaken by his distress.

"She's lost to me. I failed her." He paced back and forth, a man possessed. "What have I done? God, what have I done?"

"What can I do, man? How can I help?" The anguish I endured was nothing compared to the hurt I had inflicted on my family. This was not the calm and collected Colm I remembered. This was a man lost to his demons.

"You said Finvarra took her? How? How did he do it?" He gripped my wrist, his eyes crazed. "Take me to her."

"I can't. I can't go back there. The immortals would not take kindly to my return." I faced my brother, Cian's warning echoing in my mind, "Do not return. It would not bode well."

"That's where you were, alive and well, living with the fucking Faeries? While we mourned you? For seven fucking years?" His bitter words ripped at my heart, and I deserved every rash word for the years of pain I had inflicted. Unforgivable pain.

"The gateway opens on festival day." It was the only avenue I could think of. "We can try then." Even on that day, when the veil thinned and souls wandered, entering the faerie realm came with risks. To proceed uninvited was just plain foolish. But...

"No. Not good enough." He stomped away, his shoulders heaving. Broken. Colm, broken.

"There's no other way," I swallowed hard and whispered to myself more than anyone. A gust of wind blew in from the ocean, and my blood ran cold. I accepted the warning for what it was.

Cian had entered my tower room without knocking, his footsteps heavy on the circular steps. The sun shone through the lancet window as I lifted my gaze from the ancient tome of spells I had lifted from the King's library when heads turned elsewhere—the grand hall adorned in black, the strains of a harp whispering through the ancient stones as I returned to my room with the book concealed beneath the folds of my cloak. I clung to the faint hope I would find my escape in those yellowed pages. Months I stared at those pages, at words written in an almost illegible hand—indecipherable, at least to my eyes. When I looked at Cian, my heart seized.

"Pack your things. You're free to go. Father's instructions." Dressed in riding leathers, Finvarra's youngest son leaned against the doorway, his blue eyes piercing. Watching. Calculating. I wondered if he was a step ahead of everyone, even Finvarra.

I gathered my meager belongings into the leather satchel given to me before that first hurling match: the purple cloak—my lifeline to the mortal realm. I slipped the leather tome between the star-studded folds that Saoirse had meticulously sewn to prepare for that Hallowed Eve celebration. It seemed like the right thing to do.

Cian led me down the circular stairs to the castle courtyard, where two horses stood, saddled and waiting. We rode side by side through the glade, the shadowed forest, and then toward the ocean, where he pointed to a vertical stone column surrounded by sand, accessible only at low tide. "Be quick. You're running out of time."

Freedom. He offered me freedom. I didn't question it.

I walked through the endless foam toward the sea stack, unsure what I would find. On the dark side, a fissure appeared. I turned for one last look and found Cian staring after me, sadness in his gaze. I had thought nothing of it.

"Where did you come from? How did you get here?" Colm grabbed my arm, his gaze tortured, his voice filled with fury.

"I've been with the Other Crowd—the *Tuatha Dé.*

They exist, Colm, in a realm parallel to this." I gestured with my hands. "Everything Da said was true. Everything. Cian sent me through a sea cave—a portal from there to here." My heart thudded in my chest, my mind reliving the journey to freedom.

The fissure had twisted downward into a black abyss, narrowing as the sea floor leveled. I had walked for what seemed like hours through knee-deep water. How much time remained before the tides flooded the underground cavern? Dark thoughts overwhelmed me, and when I thought death was inevitable, the floor sloped upward, and a shimmering light appeared at the crest of the rise—rainbow shades pulsing with life. I stepped into the time warp and emerged on the other side, still buried beneath the ground but on the right side of the world—my world. One step closer to freedom.

"Who the fuck is this Cian you're on about?" His head snapped back, and he looked at me.

"Finvarra's youngest son." I envisioned the young prince—a striking lad with a tousled mane of chestnut hair, one of the king's many bastards, his blue-eyed gaze an anomaly among the Otherworldly. Tones of silver, shimmering iron ore, and white gold were to be expected, not blue. Never blue.

"Ciarán? Brother. It's you. Is it you?" He grappled both my arms, the shadows in his eyes lifting. "You're here. Ciarán, good gods. You're alive."

"They released me. They let me go." My voice cracked.

"After all these years, you appear? How did this

happen? Why? Why now?" His tone sharpened, and he stared through me as if I didn't exist.

"I'm not sure. I don't know what to make of it." I turned away, gazing at the two horses, my father's horses, my heart flirting with happiness. My wish—granted. I owed someone big time. "What's wrong with that horse?" I reached for the white mare while Colm corralled the crazed stallion.

"Whoa, boy. It's all right." He crooned. He soothed. The black stallion reared onto his hind legs, foam flying from his mouth. "He's Calla's horse now. He belongs to her." The stallion pawed the hard sand, his ears twitching at the mention of her name.

"Who is Calla? To you?" I asked again. Who was this woman who caused such confusion in both realms?

"She is everything, Ciarán. Everything." He threw his hand on the saddle horn, leaping onto the dancing horse. Without a backward glance, he urged the horse into a gallop, sand flying with each pounding hoof.

"Then we'll get her back, mate." I urged the mare toward home—the home I had missed and the woman I longed to see.

Gathering the reins in one hand, I followed Colm's horse along the water's edge. He slowed his mount, navigating through the many boulders, then urged the stallion upward and over the steep bank, taking a shortcut that led toward Clonmara.

Home. More than a word. Family. A white house with paned windows, bathed in the afternoon sun, stood surrounded by sea and meadow. A woman raised her hand to shield her eyes. She wore a yellow dress, its skirts dancing in the breeze, cradling a basket overflowing with red roses in her arms—my mother.

The horses thundered across the meadow, with Colm in the lead.

I feared the worst. What would she think? Her long-lost son returned from the dead. I pulled back on the reins, bringing the mare to a sudden stop.

"Mam." Jumping from the saddle, I rushed toward my mother, gathering her into my arms. How could I ask for forgiveness?

"Ciarán. My boy. Is it you?" My mother placed her hands on both sides of my face, her black eyes wide.

"It's me, Mam. I'm back." I could have wept.

"Sweet Jaysus, Mother Mary. A miracle has happened. But how? How?" Tears fell, wetting her soft cheeks.

"It is, Mam. That it is." I held her close, tucking her into my arms.

"I don't understand. Where have you been?" Her gaze met mine, her forehead creased.

Colm stood beside his horse. He looked toward the driveway and then back at me.

"It's been a long journey, Mam, but I'm home now." I didn't know where to begin. Would the truth set me free?

"Dear gods, I can't believe it. My baby. My baby." She kissed my cheek, holding my hands, willing me to stay.

"Mam, I know this is a lot. I can't explain right now." I smiled. This woman had been through so much.

"Aye. Aye. It doesn't matter. Nothing matters, but you're here. You're here. Dear gods. Are you hungry, laddie? Should I fix you something to eat? Look at you. You're wasting away. Did they not feed you where you were?" Seven years of worry lines surrounded her mouth. Seven years.

The house where I was born stood weathered and gray, in need of a fresh coat of paint. The distant mountains glowed red in the setting sun, while the ocean breeze bent every blade of grass. This place held my soul. I caught Colm's anxious look. Two sons wandering worlds apart—seven years lost.

"I'd like that, Mam, but... Saoirse. I have to see her." I squeezed her fingers. There would be time, Gods willing, for the truth.

"Aye. Aye. Of course. Aye. You go to that girl, luv. What a happy day this is! Oh, dear Ciarán. Your da. You must know your da passed, luv. We lost him. He's no longer with us." She gripped my elbow.

"Aye, Mam. I know. Colm told me." I held her then, pressing my face into her shining hair for a moment longer. I owed all of them more than just a mere explanation.

The boy, James, gathered the horses from Colm, his bony face pale. His fear was palpable.

I had returned from the Otherworld. There would be questions.

Colm threw me a pointed glare, silencing my confession.

No explanation could mend the damage done.

"I'm sorry I couldn't be there for you, for everyone." My heart broke for all we had lost.

"Ach, now, no sense crying over spilled milk. I can't believe my eyes. This is a happy day, Ciarán—a happy day. Go on with you now. Go to the girl." She broke away from our embrace and hugged herself. Her eyes beamed sunshine.

The years I had wasted, the pain I had caused. What would they think of me when the shock wore off, and they realized where my wandering soul had taken me? My father died a broken man. What part did I play in his death?

"I'll drive. Get in." Colm's long strides took him toward the red truck parked in the drive—Da's truck. He motioned to the passenger seat, his gaze rife with discontent. He slammed the door behind me as I got in.

"Colm. I'd rather meet with Saoirse alone, if you don't mind." Facing my brother after so many years. What my disappearance did to him, I could only guess.

"I needed answers five minutes ago." He settled into the driver's seat, leaned over, and yanked the passenger door as if I might disappear again.

"Aye. What would you like to know?" I grazed the cracked dashboard with my fingertips, the memory rising in my mind of Colm's fist smashing the surface so many years ago. I inhaled the sweet aroma of the past.

"Everything. What happened the night you disappeared?" He gunned the motor and drove down the long driveway, leaving a trail of dust wafting in the rearview mirror.

"It was All Hallows Eve. I was out for a smoke, aye? I was there for the craic. You know how it was, Colm. I heard music coming from behind the bushes. It was Them. Jaysus, I wish I could take it all back." My stomach dropped as the rear tire bounced off a deep pothole.

"Never mind now. Where were you?" He tapped his

fingers on the steering wheel, his lips pinned into a straight line. I knew that look.

"Inside their world." I slipped my hand through the window, my fingers playing with the wind currents.

"The *Sidhe*? The *Na Daoine Maithe*?" A muscle ticked in his jaw, his eyes accepting of the Otherworldly race.

"Yes." My mind wandered. I used to play this game as a child, crammed into this same truck with Colm, Pádraig, Killian, and Tadgh. The open window was my escape from their jeers and taunting. I could see the Other Crowd and talk to Themselves when I was a wee lad. With my eyes shut and my arm hanging out the window, the breeze slipped through my fingers, and I caught the wind, riding the roller coaster into town. But I was no longer a child. I had wasted so much time.

"There's a palace in this other realm, this faerie realm?" Anger sparked in his eyes. No fear, just rage.

"That's what it is, Colm. A world within this world. They found me useful. They wouldn't let me leave." Any other man would have flinched. Colm was a powerful force. The quiet ones were.

Saoirse understood. We were childhood sweethearts. We were lovers. What would she think of me now? She loved me, of that I was certain. But was it only grief she clung to? She had moved on without me—a successful woman with a future. What could I offer?

"Useful? For what?" He bristled, his eyes expressing confusion.

"Hurling. Tournament play." I thought back to the championship match that had been held two weeks ago. The Faerie King took winning to heart.

"I don't have time for jokes, Ciarán." He gripped the steering wheel, his knuckles whitening.

"Do you think I wanted to stay? I cursed myself every day. They cast a glamour over me. I couldn't escape." I chewed on my words. How impossible it sounded.

"What do you mean? Couldn't?" He let out a sigh and then ran his fingers through his hair, sand trickling onto his shoulders.

"I could come and go, but you couldn't see or hear me. I tried Colm. Believe me, I tried. Even Saoirse, with all her magic spells, couldn't see me." The wind ripped through the window. The world never smelled so good.

"So, what happened? You're here now." He took the forest road and then coasted through a long valley toward town, toward Saoirse.

"I walked through a portal. The next thing I knew, I was on the strand, and you were in the sea, the riptide pulling you away from shore." I shivered and then laughed at the state we were in. We left the comfort of Clonmara without a care, our clothes sodden and drenched by the sea—two drowned men in more ways than one.

"How do I get inside this 'world'?" Colm punched the brakes, stopping the truck in front of Donegal Castle. "Damn it. She's not here."

"Who?" I lifted my gaze, lost in my wonderings.

"Calla, goddammit. That's her car." He pointed to a green coupe parked on the wrong side of the road. "I was hoping I would find her safe. This makes little sense. Where is she?"

"Cian mentioned his sister has come back to the

Kingdom. Colm, I believe he was referring to Calla. I doubt you'll locate her at Donegal Castle." He was clutching at straws. I lacked the heart to inform him that any hope of discovering her in Donegal County, on this side of the ground, would be futile.

"You don't know that." He sped down the narrow road to Ardara, tearing around every corner like a man on a mission.

"I haven't seen her since Da's burial." A hollow moaning rang in my ears. I convinced myself it was only the wind.

We arrived on the main street in time to see Joe, the barber, hanging the closed sign in his shop window. I looked down the sidewalk at the Wild Horse Pub, and my heart lifted. Behind those rubble-stone walls, I would find Saoirse.

"It's true then. All of it. She spoke to you at the wake... she could see you when we couldn't. This isn't over, Ciarán. I will find her, and you will help me." He leaned over me, shoving the passenger door open, his blue eyes screaming his pain.

"Tomorrow is Bealtaine Eve. Only then can mortals enter their kingdom uninvited." I climbed from the truck, resting my hand on the open window, and looking at him.

"Where is this portal? Tell me where it is." He gave me a long look, one that would frighten most people.

"There's one on the edge of Eamon's field, beyond the barn." I wondered if leaving him alone was the wisest choice, but my heart ached to see her once again—Saoirse, her auburn curls framing her heart-shaped face, the fire dancing in her amber eyes—the love of my life.

"Eamon?" His eyes widened at the mention of the elder's name, Eamon, who left bread and milk for the Good Folk in his barn every night without fail. Eamon knew how to keep the Faerie's wrath at bay.

"I'll take you there, bro—tomorrow. Now, go home. Get some sleep." I ignored Cian's dire warning. Whatever lay ahead, I wouldn't let Colm face it alone.

3

____

C olm

I left Ciarán standing on the sidewalk in front of the Black Horse Pub. Within moments, he would embrace Saoirse, and she would take him back, forgiving his indiscretions because that's what love is.

Ciarán. How long had we mourned him? Melancholia. How long had I wallowed and wasted in it? Happiness flickered in my heart—Ciarán was alive. He was home. Loss eclipsed the celebratory moment.

Whatever took Calla from me possessed a supernatural force unseen in the mortal realm. It was outrageous and unbelievable, yet Ciarán confirmed it—Finvarra, the High King of the *Daoine Sidhe*, was the mastermind behind this scheme. Not Hamstead. Not the psychopath who hunted my halfling princess. Calla was safe if Ciarán spoke the truth, far removed from the machinations of Hamstead's diabolical mind. It should have been a relief. Yet my heart told a different story. I wouldn't rest until I found her, until I saw her with my own eyes, until I was certain.

Ciarán's fear was palpable. Whatever he had experienced over the last seven years had scarred my little brother. I could see it in his eyes. My thoughts percolated, and a plan formed in my mind as I weighed the pros and cons of a deal made long ago with my ancestors. I had no reservations. For Calla, I would go to hell and back.

Few civilizations honored their dead like the Irish, and my father prized the family. In troubled times, his first response was to call on our ancestors for strength and guidance.

"Blood is blood. Laddie. There is nothing stronger." My father's voice swept through my mind, a whisper from the heavens, or perhaps the underworld.

I clung to his words now more than ever. One of Da's favorite sayings, before he shuffled off to bed, "The night is for the dead. The day is for the living."

It was a night like no other—All Souls Eve—the night spirits walked among us. We would dim the lights and gather around the hearth, and my father would speak the invocation, summoning our ancestors by name. Their souls would rise from everlasting sleep and join us, sharing stories of the land, love, and loss. There was no black and white—it just was.

On one particular Samhain night, long after my father had retired, my brothers and I had sat outdoors, huddled around the raging fire, telling lies and, one might say, building castles in the sky. The moon cast an eerie glow, and a hush had fallen over the glade.

"I call upon the O'Donnell lost. Leave your endless slumber. Break the chains and walk once more." Cillian, the most spiritual among us, rose to his feet, holding the hilt of a dagger in his hand, the blade reflecting the moon's glow.

We guffawed and howled when he sliced his palm and poured his blood on the fire. His incantation wasn't graceful, but it was effective.

The fire erupted into extraordinary flames, and from the azure spirals, the warrior sons of the O'Donnell clan joined the circle—three copper-haired youths clad in saffron-colored belted tunics edged with emerald silks, heavy woven woolen brats pinned with gilded brooches that shielded their shoulders.

Wise beyond their years, they spoke of noble deeds, rebellion, and war, their fiery words igniting our young hearts. They offered what no adventurous lad could refuse—a chance to step back in time and walk in their bloody footsteps—for a price. No blood oath was ever innocent.

We raised our cups in unison, acknowledging our pact. In times of need, we would summon our illustrious ancestors, and they would respond to our call. This seemed like a one-sided victory.

Their mother, the Dark Lady, her face hidden beneath a heavy satin hood, accompanied them. Dressed in a satin gown of midnight blue—an exquisite creation adorned with lace overlays, wide flowing sleeves, and waterfall cuffs cinched with ribbons—she looked on in approving silence. We crossed the fires—a pact made with the dead—except for Ciarán. He was untouchable.

He was touched. Even the dead held a healthy respect for the Other Crowd.

The currents shifted as we rode the pale horse beyond the veil, from this world into theirs.

A black shroud covered the land as we walked in their footsteps, witnessing the horror through their eyes: villages torched, women and children bludgeoned and put to the sword.

Bile burned in my throat, and yet I had to know.

The sickening, sweet stench of rotting flesh had hung in the air, the pine forest smoking with the pungent aroma of exploding shot. Fallen men stared through empty eyes, their lips curled in the throes of death. Carrion crows blackened the skies. Talons extended, they ripped the flesh of the slain while wolves devoured the entrails, cracking bones, and tearing limbs. Maggots feasted on what remained.

It was a pivotal time in Irish history that the country would never forget.

Their spirits live deep within our hearts, and that sliver of time—those moments in their lives—carved into our souls a blood oath binding the O'Donnell clan for the rest of our lives.

I had raised The O'Donnell more than once, each time easier than the last. Calling his spirit left my hands shaking and my blood running hot—a shared transformation of body. One being, with two minds, and the young prince commanded freely, his heart hardened by suffering and his hatred razor-sharp. Exalted to clan chieftain as a mere boy, he persuaded those around him with an eloquent tongue.

The drums pounded for the true Gael.

I found banishing his spirit a hellish task—the fire in his blood unquenched. Each time his spirit waned, I lost more of myself. I wondered if that was the Dark Lady's intention: the rebirth of a better man. We gave our souls away that night, even though we would never admit it.

I clenched the steering wheel tighter, urging The O'Donnell to join my mission. There seemed to be no other option. How could I confront the invisible as an ordinary human? I had already failed once; I refused to fail again.

My heartbeat slowed as his rage infused my flesh with bloodlust. Each surge, each contraction triggered an electrical current, awakening every blood vessel. As the fog lifted, I saw through the eyes of The O'Donnell. I became one with my warring ancestor, a sworn enemy of the Saxons of the Pale.

"What did I fight for?" the wind whispered.

"Calla." Her name flowed over my lips. She was the bane of my existence—she was my life.

The day we met, Calla had asked what I dreamt of. Shadows stirred in her eyes, leaving me without words. Ruairi would have spoken without hesitation—The O'Donnell had no filter—he looked at the world through a clear lens.

Vengeance should have been my answer.

I graduated secondary school by the skin of my teeth—schoolyard battles were my forte. I joined the army, and that institution provided me with what I needed most: discipline and the opportunity to hone my skills in hand-to-hand combat. "He's a natural,"

Eamon would tell my folks. "A born scrapper, if there ever was one."

Orange flames danced across the western sky as I veered off the road, guiding the truck down a quiet lane toward a quaint cottage on the outskirts of town.

No one knew Eamon's role in the Irish Secret Service. A shuffling old man who relied on a walking stick and peered through dust-covered glasses in charge of the Republic's covert operations? My gaze wandered to Eamon's command center, a medieval dovecote made of parged rubble stone, where monitors and fiber optic cables transmitted data at the speed of light. To an outsider, it was a pigeon coop.

I had little idea of where life would lead me.

The clouds drifted, and the skies darkened, yet through Ruairi's eyes, I saw a land scorched by fire. In the final transformation, my muscles tightened, leaving my shirt stretched across my chest and my biceps more defined.

I swore by the sea surrounding the shores, by the earth beneath my feet, and by the skies above, I would find her and bring her back.

When I met Calla, I told her half the truth: that I was a tree farmer living in the Maritimes, Canada, rather than an independent contractor working for the Irish government. I was a man who moved with the shadows, hiding in plain sight. I went where Eamon sent me. I asked no questions.

My latest contract—protecting Calla Sweet from a madman named Sean Hamstead, bent on proving the *Tuatha Dé* exists.

Eamon's conversation floated through my mind.

"Your girl sent away for her DNA. Her genetics confused a lot of people. The results were flagged, but before we could investigate, the file disappeared. Likely taken by someone on his payroll. This whole DNA business, ripe for the picking by fanatics like him." His breath had rasped, heavy in his chest.

I was in love with her before then.

A plume of smoke drifted from Eamon's chimney. Honeysuckle climbed the whitewashed walls, wild and untamed, the windows shuttered. Beyond the cottage, a small barn stood, surrounded by a rocky meadow and bordered by stone hedges.

How many hours had I spent with the old man? Yet he had never mentioned the Other Crowd visiting his property. I followed the beaten path past the barn, searching for the Faerie rath that Ciarán had described.

A blue twilight descended over the fields, leaving the long grass basking in a milky hue. I glanced over my shoulder, sensing movement, and scanned the whispering grasses but saw nothing.

I came across an ancient burial site: a circular mound on the very corner of Eamon's property. A hollowed-out oak trunk, with gnarled, bent branches, grew from the ground. I moved toward the rocky hillock, searching for the entrance, but a stone hedge crossing the field blocked my way. I climbed onto the stones. It was eerie and quiet, and the wind whistled low. The hairs on the back of my neck raised, and yet a sense of calm washed over me. One magnificent whitethorn shrub encompassed the entire barrow. Thick with angry thorns, the branches hummed with soldier bees guarding their queen—an added defense against intruders.

I nodded, approving of their defensive tactics—any attempted invasion would cause a world of hurt.

A dog barked, and a gruff voice called out.

"Hallo! You there. Stop." He waved his shillelagh, the polished horn glowing like a beacon in the night.

"Eamon, it's Colm. Colm O'Donnell." I jumped down from the stones. Tomorrow could not come soon enough. "Is it you, laddie?" His gaze darkened. In his flat cap, knit jumper, and muck boots, he looked like a gent out for an evening stroll.

The red border collie, called Finnigan, bounded up to me. The dog wagged its tail in recognition.

"It is. Eamon." I stepped into his path, acknowledging my trespass on his lands. Pulling the wool over Eamon's eyes was something few would dare.

"Laddie?" He searched my face.

"This place. The undergrowth must be centuries old. It's incredible." I avoided his scrutiny, gazing at the tumulus in awe of its magnificence.

"Aye, it's been here since my granda's time. That's close enough, ye hear. They don't take to visitors." He drew the shillelagh through the air, like a sword, stopping me in my tracks.

I detected fear in his voice.

"What are you doing here, Colm? Does this have something to do with Hamstead? And the girl? Are ye all right?" He was right on point, as usual.

"I'm counting on you to keep the girl from harm's way. I expect you're up for the job?"

And I failed.

"Ciarán's back, Eamon. He told me about this place." I searched the rocky hillock for a way in.

Even basked in shadows, the rath hummed with bees. Blackbirds perched on the upper branches of the oak tree, observing our every move. The whispering wind invoked a mystical force.

I tipped my head, acknowledging Ciarán and giving him the credit he deserved. He, more than anyone, knew the ways of the Other Crowd. Venturing uninvited into their kingdom would be unwise. As much as I wanted to tear the fairy fort apart, it would be a fool's quest.

"Is he sound?" Eamon tapped his stick on my shoulder, taking me from my musings.

"What's that?" I looked his way.

"His mind. Is he in a sound state? It's not often our kind returns unscathed." He glanced at the tumulus, his voice a whisper.

His concern worried me. I reflected on my brother's actions and his demeanor.

"He seemed fine to me, Eamon." I scratched my head, realizing I had given no thought to Ciarán's well-being. I was so consumed by despair. Did I even ask the question?

"It's a strange thing, Colm. A strange thing. Your mam's pleased?" He looked at the moon, his brows furrowed.

"Aye." I followed his gaze.

"It's getting on, Colm. We should leave Themselves to their doings." He turned as if to abandon this place for good.

"To their doings?" I stood stock-still, enraptured by

the whistling wind, but it wasn't the wind—strains of fiddle music reached my ears from a faraway place. And laughter, the joyful sounds of laughter. It drew me in.

"C'mere to me, Colm, back to the house. The tea is wet. You'll have a cuppa?" He extended his arm, touching my elbow and breaking the spell.

"Is the boy still missing, then?" His image drifted into my mind, a young child taken by the faeries, a parent's worst nightmare come to life. Eamon's conversation faded from my mind. I gazed into the moon's face, expecting nothing. "Tomorrow is Bealtaine Eve."

"Aye, that it is, and Themselves will move on from these parts. Taking up residence in the south." He shuffled away, his voice a low, muffled drone.

"Excuse me?" I followed behind him.

"Ye have doubts, Colm? After what Ciarán endured? There's something ye need to see." He supported himself on his walking stick, taking slow steps toward the barn. He gestured toward the barn door.

"What is it, Eamon?" I stepped onto the path and opened the barn door. The welcoming aroma of sweet hay and fresh straw greeted me.

"Have a look-see." He lifted his chin at the brown mare, sharing a box stall with a white-faced donkey. He left his walking stick leaning on a hay bale and limped past me into the stall. Both animals nickered, welcoming the older man.

"She's beautiful, Eamon." I admired the mare's perfect proportions and her lively eyes.

"Aye, she's of excellent stock." He snapped a rope on the horse's halter, turning her toward me.

The mare tossed her head, letting out a loud whinny. The donkey sidled up beside her and bared its teeth.

"Themselves like to ride at night. Betty's a favorite." He fed the horse an apple and then gave another to the donkey.

"I don't understand." I ran my hand along the muscled crest of the horse's neck and across her withers.

"Have ye ever seen anything of the like? The Good Folk did that, marking her as one of their own." He motioned toward the horse's mane, knotted into a slew of tiny braids. "Aye, believe ye me, laddie. Ye couldn't comb it out if you tried."

Eamon's smile reminded me of the younger man he once was.

"I'm way past not believing, Eamon. I'm here because I need to enter their world." I closed the stall door behind the pretty mare and her donkey pal.

"I'm not saying you're a fool, laddie, but that's a fool-hardy decision." His lips tightened, and a muscle ticked in his jaw.

"Sir, I failed. The girl is gone." I met his gaze, recalling the moment I lost her. "I have to get her back."

"Was it Hamstead?" He turned toward me, his question demanding a detailed answer.

"No. No, it wasn't. It was the *Tuatha Dé*." I shared with him the course of today's events, from start to finish.

He listened in silence, nodding every so often.

"I failed, sir." My anguish turned into fury, and Ruairi's wrath demanded succor. I turned away and punched the wall with my fist. Dust wafted through the air from the loft above.

"You've roused him, I see. Is it wise to wake The O'Donnell so soon after your da's passing?" Worry lines etched his forehead, revealing grave concern. "Your tattoo, Colm." He jutted his chin, gesturing toward the Triquetra inked into the side of my skull.

The same tattoo I shared with my brothers symbolized life, death, and rebirth. The throbbing stopped when I acknowledged Ruairi's presence.

"I could see no other way." My voice rasped, deeper and more throaty than I was used to hearing.

"Ye have your reasons, I'm sure." He acknowledged my decision with a nod, his silence reassuring.

"Is it obvious, Eamon?" I wore a path on the dirt floor, my father's memory passing over me. What would he have done?

"Aye, it is, laddie. Is it the young prince? He took a liking to you right from the start." He smiled, his eyes warm.

"I can't fight what I can't see. Not without help." My knuckles whitened, ready to squash the life force from any being who would harm her.

"You can't fight them, laddie. They're not of this world." The tea forgotten, Eamon settled onto a stool in the aisle.

"I lost her, Eamon. The tides ripped her from my arms. The next thing I knew, Ciarán was there." I planted my hand on my forehead and closed my eyes.

"It sounds like a deal was struck. 'Tis their way." Eamon rubbed his chin with his thumb.

"What say you, O'Donnell? Is that what this is?" Ruairi

made his presence known, his voice resonating and penetrating my mind—analyzing my thoughts.

I detected disapproval.

"Do you know your mind, laddie? Who am I speaking with?" Eamon's hand trembled as he stared into my eyes.

"I will find her. I will get her back." I spoke to both men.

"*'Tis the dead walk there, mo chara. Ye won't make it out alive*," Ruairi huffed, then chuckled.

My heart raced, and then, in a rare moment of quiet, I sensed Ruairi O'Donnell's indecision lifting. We agreed.

"A deal? What kind of deal?" My mind raced with conflicting emotions. The unthinkable had become a reality because it made sense. Everything Eamon said made sense. Calla vanished, and moments later, my brother appeared.

"Your Faerie girl bargained with Himself for Ciarán's freedom. She's a sharp one, aye, that she is. I don't see Himself letting her go. No, not anytime soon." He clucked his tongue and shook his head.

Eamon's prediction cut me to the core.

"They took her against her will." I replayed my conversation with Ciarán. He had mentioned another, a Faerie Prince, who spoke of his sister returning to their kingdom.

I imagined Calla standing her ground, her voice filled with fury as she faced the Faerie King. It was a bold move to bargain for my brother's release. My admiration grew, but unease filled my mind, and I dreaded the worst. She was no match for their kind and knew nothing of their vengeful ways.

"*Trickery is their way*," Ruairi drilled into my mind. "*Three years I languished behind Saxon prison walls. I learned their ways, mo chara. The Tuatha are no different. The same treacherous beings. If you want this maiden, let us waste no further time.*"

I tamed his vengeful roar for the moment.

"'Tis their world. You would do well to get on, Colm. Do not speak of it again." Eamon's face was noticeably pale.

"Eamon, have you ever talked with Them? Have you seen Them?" I prodded. Anything he could share would help.

"I do my best to avoid Themselves, laddie. I leave an offering every night, and in the morning, it's gone. That's proof enough for me." He leaned on his stick, rising from the stool.

"Are you all right, Eamon?" I stepped toward him, offering my hand.

"These bones get wearier with every day that passes. Will you have that cuppa, laddie?" He shuffled toward the door.

"Thanks, Eamon, but I'll pass, but I'll return tomorrow if ye don't mind?" I nodded toward the Faerie rath.

"Aye, laddie, if it must be so. You're in excellent hands with that one." He tipped his cap, acknowledging the young prince.

I left Eamon inside his home, my mind clinging to one last hope: Calla's cottage. What were the chances she would return, and I would find her safe and sound? Would she not call? I checked my phone for messages.

I turned and climbed into the truck. The engine coughed and then roared to life. My heart raced with each curve on the desolate road. I swerved, avoiding a pothole.

"Why are we waiting, man?" Ruairi made his presence known or was that my thought?

Deserted homesteads and the skeletal structures of dilapidated barns haunted the night. Drifting clouds hid the moon, accompanied by a wet drizzle. I flicked on the wipers, the blades sliding across the windshield.

"Tomorrow is Bealtaine Eve. We will enter then. Preparation and strategy are of the utmost concern. First, we will check Calla's cottage," I answered without hesitation. Good God, I was talking to him like a crazed man. "God dammit." I slammed the brakes, skidding sideways on the wet road.

"Bamboozled by a dumb flock of sheep? This would never happen in my day. Our beasts were wild—feral even. They would scatter. Smart buggers, they were. Do you have a stick?" His voice drummed inside my head.

"No, I don't have a stick. We have to wait." I tapped the wheel, tension building. Time was wasting.

My phone beeped, the call display showing a message from Saoirse Dunne, the witch—the love of Ciarán's life.

—Colm? It's Ciarán. I'm with Saoirse. Something's happened. Call me, bro, call me back.—

I hit the callback button. Ciarán picked up on the first ring.

"Colm. Where are you?" He sounded hurried and almost out of breath. I wondered if I caught him at a bad time.

"I'm on my way to Calla's." I punched the accelerator, the wheels spitting gravel. "She might be there. I have to check."

"Colm, listen to me. Saoirse had visitors. Two guys looking for Calla came to the pub this morning. Something about her DNA." His voice stuttered, fading in volume with each hairpin turn. "Hold on. Saoirse wants to chat."

"Colm? Are you there? I can't hear him. It's an awful line," Saoirse shouted through my phone's speaker.

"I'm here. I'm listening, Saoirse. What happened?" I held the steering wheel with one hand and raised the phone's volume to the max with the other.

"The guy said he was a biologist from Oxford. I checked. I called the university. They've never heard of him. I'm scared, Colm. What do they want with Calla? Colm? Colm?" Her voice squeaked, her words garbled.

Her fear added another dimension to my already heightened anxiety. Hamstead. It could be no other. Eamon's warning rang in my head. Keep her safe. Keep her close. For the first time in my life, I tasted the meaning of fear.

Hamstead was close—too close.

"Saoirse, I hear you. Can you hear me?" I tapped my phone's screen. The call failed.

Calla had arrived in Ireland alone, with no one to turn to, ostracized from the only life she had ever known because of her ability to foresee death. It wasn't a gift or a curse. No, it was genetic. She was one of Them. Sweet Jesus.

I swung into the driveway of the old Sweet place, speeding past the stone gates, the trees whipping past. I took the single-lane bridge at breakneck speed, the truck flying through the air, landing in the soft muck with a thud of spinning tires.

"Sounds like your lady friend has raised the alarms." Ruairi offered his opinion from the back of my mind.

In hindsight, I should have told Calla everything I knew about the man, Sean Hamstead. She had no idea of the threat she faced. The *Tuatha* were one thing, crazed psychopaths another.

Calla's cottage loomed ahead, yellow lights shining from every window.

"She's home. Thank Gods." Relief washed over me, hope blinding me to all rational thought.

"Slow down, mate. We don't want to approach this battle head-on. Hide this iron horse in the bushes." He tried to dampen my spirits.

"She's here. She has to be here." I hit the brakes, grinding to a halt in the cobblestoned courtyard.

"The left flank, mate. The shadows will hide us from view. That's our approach." He directed the attack from a commander's point of view.

I shut him out and leaped from the truck. I barely noticed the wee bird squawking a hellstorm from the eaves.

"Calla? Calla? Are you here?" I pushed the door open. An eerie silence greeted me, broken by the tick-tock of the grandfather clock. A cold, dark hearth taunted my empty heart.

I scanned the reception room, my gaze resting on a chessboard—the pieces engaged in play. My thoughts drifted, wondering what opponent she faced.

Calla's voice echoed, her eyes shining, her laughter tinkling. *"You're in danger, my love."*

The floorboards creaked behind me. My muscles tensed as I realized my mistake too late.

A dark shape loomed in the shadows. My assailant struck with brutal force, his aim precise. A direct blow from a hard object to my forehead sent me reeling backward against an unforgiving pine wall. The boards shuddered as white lights danced behind my eyelids. My knees buckled, and I dropped onto the stone floor with a thud. I struggled to rise, rivulets of warmth streaming over my eyelids, and a metallic taste of blood flooding into my mouth.

Taught to kill, to move without sound, my hands a weapon of lethal force capable of inflicting serious damage on a human body: a simple hand strike to the throat would crush a windpipe, a proper chokehold cutting blood flow to the brain. Bones could be broken. And thumbs pushed eyeballs into the brain. But then there was the element of surprise—the candlestick—and a simple blow to the head.

From somewhere above, footsteps pounded across the floor, coming closer. Voices rose; one was low and rumbling, the other a nasal pitch. Two men flung words back and forth.

The man wielding the silver candlestick curled his fingers into my hair, lifting my head. "We will find her,

O'Donnell. Don't think we won't." His twisted smile emanated malevolent hate.

The last thing I remembered before the final blow struck was the haunting laughter of the man Eamon was hunting—the pretender, Sean Hamstead.

4

———

Calla

The haar rose from the ground, white fog swirling around me. I focused on the sensations—this *féth fíada*, this magic mist. My breath became an echo, my flesh a million water droplets running down the mountain's face, my bones melting into cotton clouds drifting through a vast blue sky, my thoughts one with the swirling wind. I was weightless—an essence—particles of stardust. This was a magic created before Earth was even born.

"Where is she? What did you do with her?" Colm staggered and fell onto his knees, the tide washing over the sand.

His need called to me, and my essence changed direction, a free-fall through space and time toward Colm, the man I loved.

"Stay with me, Rioghain. Allow me to take you home to your sisters." Finvarra's voice engulfed the cosmos. The bargain. The deal I made. Was it a deal with the devil?

How was this possible? What magic could transform physical form into particles of mist? The tornado touched down and then dissipated as if it had never existed. I gasped, inhaling a sharp breath, my chest heaving beneath the frilly gown, my toes curled in those sensible shoes. At least I had landed upright.

This home Finvarra spoke of was like none other.

Light streamed through three lancet windows, draped in purple velvet. I craned my neck upward. The ceiling glimmered like unripened gold.

I gazed out the window, tracking my escape route back to Colm: the fissure in the cliffs, the shimmering lake. But what then?

I turned away from the window, aware of two beautiful women. Finvarra was nowhere to be seen.

A redhead lounged on a macrame swing. Ringlets framed her heart-shaped face, cascading down the back of a sheer jumpsuit that flowed to her feet. She was barefoot, her toes painted a brilliant shade of purple.

A snow-white cat lounged on her lap—not just any cat, but one twice the size of any I had ever seen. The feline bristled, greeting me with a fierce hiss, its blue eyes wide and round in a pointed face. The redhead stroked its long fur with delicate fingers, oblivious to the cat's agitation. I wondered what demonic spirit possessed it.

Another woman stood tall and straight before a blazing fireplace. Gazing down a straight nose, her red-painted lips curved into a curious smile. Blonde hair cascaded over her shoulders in lustrous waves, reaching her lower back.

I examined the sky-blue mini-dress, which highlighted the woman's upper thighs, emphasizing her long, shapely legs. I wondered how she came across the sparkling silver closed-toe stilettos. The designer's face appeared in my mind. We had played tennis just last month—but that was then.

White gold eyes, crushed with silver, met mine. It was unsettling.

I turned, drawn to the embroidered tapestries adorning the interior wall, each one telling a wondrous tale. I moved with sheer determination, running my finger along the fine threads that depicted extraordinary scenes. A satyr, a man with pointed ears, a long tail, and goat-like hooves, fought air demons with a long sword. Witches soared through the night sky, while hellhounds pursued them. Sprites, ethereal in the mist, played tricks with the human mind. Friend or foe? I shut out their frenzied cries, unaware of the tears streaming down my cheeks.

The final tapestry depicted the horrors of battle. Soldiers lay upon their swords, the river flowing red with their blood. The hooded crow fluttering among them had sparked their rage. Was she to blame for the carnage? I covered my ears, her maddening cry awakening the monsters.

Those tapestries revealed the battle from my vision with Finvarra when I had held his hand, and time fell away. More than that, I transformed into another form —a black crow with mottled gray feathers, the scald crow of mythic lore; not just a crow, but an omen of death.

"It's her." The blonde tossed her hair, staring with

eyes like mine. Disdain filled her gaze as she caught the redhead's glance.

"Who are ye?" The redhead chewed on the end of a pencil and then jumped off the swing, the cat pouncing along with her. She removed the thick frames, squinted, and then blinked. She took one step closer, trailing her painted fingertips along the curve of my jaw. "Ye look like Father. Doesn't she, Nemain?"

"Who are you?" My mind crashed all at once. Orlaith's tale rang true—one light, one touched, and me, the dark one. I wiped the tears from my face and met their curiosity with my own.

"I am Macha, and that's Nemain. We're twins, although ye wouldn't know it." Macha's eyes widened, awaiting my response.

"Maka? Nevin?" I glanced at the two otherworldly beings.

"Aye, that's right. Can I help you up?" She reached out, curling her fingertips around mine. Her grip was strong and sure. No hesitation. No fear.

I shut my eyelids and saw nothing. When I opened them, Macha was still holding my hand.

"My name is Calla." I scrambled to my feet and squared my shoulders. Brushing my hands over the ruffled skirt, I faced them. "Fin brought me here."

"Fin?" Nemain covered her mouth, her eyes widening.

"Do you mean Father?" Macha's auburn brows lifted.

"That's who I mean." It was safer not to commit. Who knew what these two girls were aware of? I imagined their lives: two fairy princesses living in a golden tower, so far removed from my reality that I couldn't even grasp it.

Macha twirled the pencil between her fingers. "How did you come to know our father?"

"Oh, my God. That's Ériu." I left them, crossing the marble floor, drawn to the portrait hanging over a walnut credenza—Finvarra, dressed in navy blue finery, stood beside a smiling blonde woman seated in a matching velvet chair.

"How do you know, Mother?" Nemain's chin dropped. She gaped at me.

Nemain reminded me of the queen of the Elven people, with her translucent skin, wide eyes, and willowy frame. She stood posture perfect. Macha was right. There was no resemblance between the two of them or the three of us.

I stared at the painting. Ériu's wide smile exuded happiness. She looked young, her golden hair styled into a sophisticated updo, wispy ringlets framing her delicate features. This was not an angry woman.

"Whatever you think you saw, you are mistaken." Fin's voice echoed. The pain shining in his eyes was real. He loved her.

I grasped at straws I couldn't find, the mystery only deepening.

"When was this portrait done?" I gazed into Ériu's blue eyes, lifted my hand, and touched her dewy skin. Would she speak to me?

"What do you think you're doing?" Nemain's voice rang in my ears, breaking the spell.

"That's Father and Mother when they were young," Macha said in a whisper.

"When they were young?" I asked, repeating her words.

"Yes." They both answered.

"You know our mother?" Macha whispered, as if she already knew I had a story to tell.

"I have visions. I met a lady who knew her." Was this the time for full disclosure?

"Visions? Of our mother?" Macha's voice filled with curiosity. She tilted her head and lifted her chin. A faint sensation flowed through my thoughts, a soft touch like satin on silk or the brush of a feather. I had the powerful impression that she was reading my mind.

"Who are you speaking of?" Nemain demanded clarification. "And why are you dressed like that? You look ridiculous."

"Nemain." Macha chastised her sister. My sister.

"What? Where did you come from? Knockma?" Nemain sized me up with a smirk.

"Where? No." I stared at the double-puffed sleeves and ruffled hem. Ridiculous was an understatement.

"Let's back up." Macha calmed her sister's impatience. "Nemain, why don't you pour the wine? Come, let's sit where we can talk." She gestured toward a grand fireplace and two oversized sofas covered in fine brocade.

Nemain turned away, obeying the quiet sister's order. She placed a crystal carafe and three globe-shaped goblets on a silver tray while Macha looked on.

"Chocolate, Nemain. Don't forget the chocolate." Macha pointed her chin toward a silver canister with an ivory lid.

"All right. All right." She used silver tongs to transfer half a dozen rough chocolate slabs to a crystal plate.

"That's perfect." Macha smiled and then looked more at the dress than at me. "Did you come from a wedding?"

"A wedding? Um, no." I sat on the sofa, crossing my ankles beneath the full skirt and folding my hands in my lap.

"It's not often we have visitors." Nemain gave me a sidelong glance as she walked across the shining floor, holding the silver tray in one hand. She set the glistening display on the marble coffee table between the sofas. She poured the wine from the carafe into the gilded goblets, offering me the first one.

"Thank you." I had so many questions. Where should I start?

"*Sláinte.*" Nemain raised her glass, and Macha did the same.

The red elixir swirled in the stemmed crystal. What did I know of these people, my sisters? Doubt filled my thoughts. What if the tales were true? How many mortals had the *Tuatha Dé* bewitched with this very wine? How many remained enraptured by their spells?

"What magical journey brought you here?" Macha gazed over the rim of her glass.

"Pardon?" I placed my untouched wine on the shiny table. Better safe than sorry.

"Do you wander in the guise of another? Who are you?" Nemain set her glass beside mine.

"Nemain!" Macha glanced at her sister.

Nemain's lips tightened, and she looked away.

"Um... No. I don't know how to wander, as you call it.

At least, I don't think I do." That dizzy feeling returned, and then I remembered. I had proof. I was not crazy. I slipped my fingers into the side pocket of the flowy dress, retrieved the black feather, and held it in my hand—a peace offering of sorts.

"What is that?" Nemain's eyes flashed.

"A feather?" Macha smiled.

I studied them, not sure how to answer their question. My past flashed before me. How many times had I predicted death? I lost my job because of that Otherworldly ability. But that was then, and this was now. Since arriving in Ireland, something had changed.

"*The power in this land will seep into your bones, Rioghain.*"

Isn't that what Finvarra had said?

"You could not journey here without aid from another. Magical spells, a glamor of sorts, keep us safe from intruders." Macha nibbled a purple fingernail.

"A glamor? Are you trapped inside these walls?" I searched the spacious room with a furtive gaze.

"No, why would you think that?" Nemain's tone was sharp as she huffed, exasperated with me.

"I guess I've read too many fairy tales." I swallowed hard and studied Macha. The sensation faded as her presence left my mind, more like sharp feline claws retracting and drawing blood.

"Only one with powerful magic can journey a living being from one place to another. Not even I have that ability. Who sent you here?" Nemain's eyes grew serious as she focused. "Was it Grandfather?"

This was the golden-haired princess who caused

chaos. Colm had once accused me of being a banshee, looking at the Faerie woman tasked with predicting death, and remarking, "Better that than the *Lianan Sidhe*, the Faerie lover who steals men's souls." Huh. I could see that.

"Nemain, be nice. Our guest is having a bad day." Macha smirked, her gaze settling on me.

Reading my mind? Oh, yeah.

"Who are you?" Nemain circled the conversation like a cat hunting its prey.

A bell chimed, and I shot upright on the sofa. Not just one but a million all at once, and based on Macha and Neman's reactions, the loud peals marked an important guest.

Nemain's facial muscles relaxed, her expression unreadable. Cool as a cucumber.

Macha cleared her throat and sat up straighter.

The great door swung open, and Finvarra entered. He looked the same, except for the archer's bow. He crossed the room with confident strides while Bran pounced, settled beside me, and laid his enormous head on my lap.

"Father, how are you today?" Macha rose from the sofa, embraced her father, and pecked his cheek.

"Will you be joining us for dinner, Father?" Nemain looked at me and then at the dog.

Finvarra's eyes sparkled as he greeted the two girls. He held Macha's hand, guiding her back to her seat, and then stood at the end of the sofas. The sunbeams washing over him in golden light made him appear more like a god than a man.

Bran lifted his head and woofed.

"Daughters, I see you have met Rioghain, your sister." He motioned toward me with an open palm.

"Father?" Macha's eyes grew wider.

"What?" Nemain's head snapped toward me.

"Macha, Nemain, you are one of three. We lost Rioghain at birth, taken from your mother's arms as a babe. She has now returned." He clasped my wrist and turned my palm to show the teardrop mark.

"My name is not Rioghain." I snatched my hand away, and my gaze darted to each girl's left hand. The same blemish darkened their palms as mine did.

"A sister? We're one of three?" Nemain's silver eyes sparkled. She glanced at me, then huffed.

"She looks like you, Father." Macha tilted her head, glancing at me from a side angle.

"You're from the mortal realm?" Nemain rose, her face flushing pink.

"That is a conversation the three of you can have together. Your sister is here now, and that's all that matters." Finvarra nodded once, as if the discussion was far from over. "Rioghain's training must begin. There is no time to waste. Macha will teach you the history of our people. Nemain—the ways of passage." He held my gaze. "We're leaving the castle tomorrow for our summer grounds. Nemain, take Rioghain to the stables and select a suitable mount." His low baritone voice demanded.

"What? You said I could come and go as I please." I stared into his shimmering eyes and felt nothing. Perhaps these walls also warded against enchantment.

"And that is true. But first, you must learn how to journey through other forms and how to use the *féth fíada* to your advantage. It takes time to master these skills. Tonight, the kings and queens of the realm will receive you. The celebration will commence this evening." He stood his ground, unwilling to bend.

"He means when you can change into another form and call upon the mist." Macha considered his instructions, nodding in agreement.

"You tricked me." I curled my fingers into the folds of my dress.

"Your Ciarán has returned to his people. I expect you to uphold your part of the bargain." His gaze softened, but his lips turned up into a satisfied smile.

"Ciarán's gone? He didn't say goodbye?" Nemain sprang from the sofa, her voice rising into a pained shriek.

"Nemain." Macha sent her sister a sharp glance.

"I have called upon a seamstress to fit Rioghain with an appropriate dress. Come. Come, my darlings. We have much to accomplish." He clapped his hands and walked from the room, Bran following in his footsteps.

"Appropriate dress? What does that mean?" I gazed at my sisters. I agreed to this. Part of me wanted this. There was no turning back now.

"That looks like something our grandmother would wear." Nemain scrunched her nose. "Father is quite particular about his 'celebrations.'"

"Huh. More like introducing you to the most available prince." Macha lifted her hand and nibbled on the fingernail of her left pinky finger.

"Arabelle can't finish a proper dress by this evening. Who does he think she is, a miracle worker? That's ridiculous." Nemain bounced toward me. "Ciarán said a girl named Calla could see him. That's you, of course. This is freaking amazing. You're from the other side." She cupped my elbow, steering me across the grand room and through an archway into the ultimate walk-in closet. Rows of skimpy satin dresses and breathtaking gowns circled the rainbow. Shelves loaded with matching slippers reached the ceiling. "Macha, come and help. I love dressing up, don't you?"

Nemain's attitude had flip-flopped from suspicious to welcoming in mere seconds. She tilted her head, dazzling me with her enchanting allure.

I chewed the edge of my bottom lip, consumed by doubt.

"What should we call you?" Macha peered at me through her thick lenses.

"Rioghain, I guess." Ériu gave me this name, the identity I needed to assume to escape this place. Sooner rather than later.

"Look, Macha. How stunning. Crimson is Rioghain's color." Nemain held a blood-red gown woven with gold thread, the neckline shimmering with onyx gemstones beneath my chin.

The hand-sewn and well-crafted silk slipped through my fingers. I contemplated the obvious: the crimson hue mirrored the rubies sparkling in Finvarra's crown, while the black cabochons reflected the darkness in his gaze. I was my father's daughter in every sense of the word.

"The black heels, Nemain." Macha spun a carousel of silk pumps.

"Jesus. Do you dress like this all the time?" My eyes widened. It was indeed a sight to behold.

"I think we're the same size." Nemain picked through a drawer lined with satin underclothes. "How about this?" She dangled a lacy-wired bra. "No. This one? This is so much better." Her eyes flashed as she flung colored slips every which way, settling on a one-piece black-satin corset with garter straps.

"Nice. When can you teach me how to journey?" I turned my head.

"It's the easiest thing ever." Nemain twirled into a cloud of mist and reappeared on the spot.

One thought popped into my head: I liked these girls.

"Wait until Balor sees you." Nemain gave Macha a mischievous glance. "He's only the Prince of Ulaid. Don't get your hopes up. He's a feckin' eejit."

"Nemain!" Macha's pale face turned as white as a bedsheet.

"Yeah, yeah." Nemain placed her hand on her heart. "His mother has journeyed from this world to another, which makes him King of Ulaid once Father agrees. Macha crushes on him. Oh, wait? Do you have a boyfriend? I'll bet you do. What's his name?" Her eyes shone.

"I do not crush on Balor. Stop saying such things, Nemain. We were children." Macha pinned her lips together, throwing a piercing gaze at her golden-haired twin.

The sisters shared a lifetime of memories I was a stranger to.

"Father would take us every *Lughnasadh*. We would

swim in the sea. And eat cake. It's pretty there." Nemain smiled, her gaze turning dreamy.

"Loo-nuh-suh?" I squinted at the foreign word.

"Why don't we leave Rioghain to rest? I'm sure she would like to bathe." Macha turned her head, directing her wrath at Nemain.

"A bath?" I touched my hair, and the sand fell like rain. "A bath sounds like a great idea."

"We'll have lunch in the garden, aye? Do you have any allergies, Rioghain?" Macha's voice was like Finvarra's, soothing but gentle.

I turned, drawn to her soft voice.

"No. I don't have any allergies. Can I borrow some, um, normal clothes?" I stared wide-eyed at the dazzling outfits I would wear for a night of clubbing. Was there such a thing in the Faerie realm?

"Oh, of course." She tucked her hand inside my elbow, ushering me from the closet into the sunlit lounge. "Now, this entire wing of the castle is our suite. If you need anything, ring this bell, and Lucinda will come. She's our lady's maid." She gestured toward a braided silk rope hanging from the ceiling. "And this is your room, Rioghain." She opened another door to an opulent room, decorated to the nines.

Braided rugs adorned a shining marble floor, and a stone fireplace crackled with burning logs. An uphol-stered settee in crushed velvet faced the stone fireplace, while a matching wingback chair with a leather ottoman dominated the opposing corner.

"My room? Were you expecting me?" I looked from one end to the other.

A four-poster bed in ivory chiffon sat between two gilded paintings depicting the windswept sails of tall ships sailing through stormy seas. I was too tired to wonder if those paintings held a hidden message.

I gazed upward at the same glimmering ceilings, painted a muted green hue, with intricate cornice work curling at the junction of the walls. Leaves twisted in a vine-like manner, and from each corner, an elaborate carved face looked down at me. Four green men, born of the ancient wood: one slept, another caught in wild-eyed fear, one serene-faced smiled, while the last raged in contempt.

I would think about them later.

"Our suites have always had three bedrooms. Isn't that funny?" She squeezed my fingers, leaving me on my own. "Take your time. There's no rush."

This sweet escape lulled me into believing I belonged.

Colm—I visualized our last moments and wondered if I would ever see him again. I swallowed hard, promising myself this was not the end, but the beginning. I had sisters, and I wanted to know them. I looked out the lancet window, gazing beyond the pine forest into snow-covered mountain valleys and shadowed glens.

It was, in one word, beautiful.

I left the window and warmed my hands by the fire, my gaze darting from one antique piece to another—nothing plastic in this place. I returned to the lounge with the gargoyle-like green men staring after me, only to find it empty. I cocked my head, listening to the silence.

The arched door that Finvarra entered from swung

open. I laughed, scolding myself for believing the two princesses were captives in an ivory tower.

That would be—crazy.

I gazed in both directions—polished ivory walls broken only by doorways that led to even more rooms. At the far end of the long hallway, stone steps spiraled downward. My heels clacked, announcing my arrival to anyone who might be around. I stood at the top of the staircase, my confidence fading with the flickering wall sconces.

I backed away, not ready to face the other inhabitants of this castle, and returned to the Princess Suite. The fireplace flickered, and sunlight streamed through the sparkling panes. I walked to the window and threw open the sash, gazing at the snow-capped mountains.

I closed my eyes, remembering what I had always known.

My thoughts reached out, searching for a gap in Colm's consciousness—the only way we could be together. His essence touched mine, the same yet different. My eyes flew open, and I lost the connection.

"Goddammit." I paced the floor, my focus wavering. Colm—our relationship had grown from our first meet-cute, when he saved me from the roadside, to a vow of eternity. And what had I done? I had moved toward that Otherworldly force. I had left him to the ruthless wind and turbulent sea.

I stepped out of the lounge and returned to the green suite—my room. Removing my shoes and shedding the ruffled dress, I left my undergarments on the floor as I entered a bathroom gleaming with five-star luxury, mirrored walls reflecting an immaculate space. A golden chandelier, lit with eighteen tapered candles—I counted —hung above a large pink stone soaking tub.

A white alabaster statue of a woman stood on a marble pedestal in the center of the room. I studied the woman from every angle, wondering who she was. Her eyes were closed, and her hair twisted into a knot. She held her breast in one hand while the other pleasured her sex. How provocative. The sculpture would rival Michelangelo Buonarroti's statue of David in every way. I wondered who the medieval artist was who created her.

Finvarra's voice lingered in my memory. *"Our people revel in pleasure, but pleasure is one thing. Union is another. A king awaits you, my dear. A proud warrior, a prince, at the very least."*

What was I supposed to do with that?

I closed the door, my fingers brushing against the plush terry-cloth robe hanging from a carved hook. Holding the robe to my nose, I inhaled the warm scent of goat milk soap. I turned and surveyed the room. Spa slippers with pink pom-poms sat underneath an upholstered bench. Fluffy towels, rolled in a spa style, filled the open marble shelves, while seashells decorated the counters, overflowing with bath bombs, heart-shaped soaps, and oatmeal scrubs. I dropped a violet bath bomb into the water, breathing in the sweet lavender fragrance.

Sinking into the steaming water—pure delight.

The real world faded away, and my hold on reality with it. It was almost too fantastical to believe that I, Calla Sweet, was not human. I gulped down the lump in my throat, Colm's face floating into my mind, the curve of his jaw, his shining eyes. Bath bubbles popped one after another.

"Tomorrow." I threw water onto my face. "I'll leave tomorrow. I can return anytime. I can visit. They can visit." When I opened my eyes, the solution revealed itself. I rested my fingers on the polished granite sides and stepped out of the tub, splashing water onto the floor. I stared into the foggy mirror, wondering who would emerge from the chrysalis and when the metamorphosis would occur. There were so many unanswered questions. How did one shift into another being? The hooded crow seemed to be my familiar, a sharp-beaked, black-throated grey crow with long black tail feathers. But how? I did not know how the transformation had occurred. I couldn't remember exchanging my body for the feathered bird, either. I rubbed the back of my neck, recalling the scratchy sensations and hoarse throat that haunted my dreams.

"You're a banshee." That's what Colm had said. His mother heard the keening cries of the scald crow moments before her husband died. And Breda, the white-haired Irish beauty with nightshade eyes. What was it Breda had said? I couldn't remember.

I stared at the teardrop stain on my palm, shared with Neman and Macha, feeling confused and nauseous all at once.

"RIOGHAIN, are you in there? Are you ready? The

stableboy has selected several mounts. We must hurry." Nemain pounded on the bathroom door.

My thinking slowed, my thoughts tangled in too many webs. Would I ever get used to this new identity? This new world?

"I'm coming." I wrapped myself in the plush robe and slipped my feet into the soft slippers.

"These are for you." Nemain bounced off the canopy bed, her long blonde hair chasing behind her. "I hope you like them?"

"They're lovely." I smiled, resting my gaze on the display of hand-spun silks, flowing tiered dresses, and hourglass corsets.

I ran my hand over the only pair of pants—caramel-colored deerskin breeches made from the finest hides, then chose a long-sleeved, green tunic with a leather-laced front. A hooded cloak of dense boiled wool in a soft claret finished the riding outfit.

"Father wants you to choose a horse. We should hurry before Macha calls us for lunch." She slipped out of the room, her grin mischievous. "I'll give you a minute."

"These are amazing." I eased into the silky undergarments, silent thoughts thanking Nemain for not choosing the lacy wire bra. I pulled knee-high silk socks over my feet, giggling at the vibrant purple color. Then, I slipped into the riding pants, the leather soft and snug on my legs. Loosening the leather strings, I pulled the tunic over my head. I sat on the bed, sinking into the soft mattress, and pulled the supple boots onto my feet. The entire ensemble fit like a glove.

"Why do I need a horse?" I found Nemain sprawled

on the sofa, reading the latest issue of a popular fashion magazine. I raised my eyebrows, curious about how a mortal publication entered the Otherworld.

"We're heading to Knockma in two days." She tucked her long legs beneath her, kicked off her stilettos, and slipped into white leather knee-high boots with a thick block heel.

I recognized the brand.

"You're leaving here? Why?" I followed her down the marble hallway and, this time, descended the circular stairs.

"For Bealtaine. We leave the north and return to regular castle life. It's very formal. Grand balls every evening. Macha hates it." She took me through the grand foyer, where two-story columns met a glittering domed ceiling, and ornate tapestries hung from ivory walls.

A man in a black tuxedo and a crisp white shirt bowed his head in respect to the Princess. He gave me a slight nod.

I followed her golden head through a gothic-style door embossed with the same leafy vine adorning my bedroom walls and into a courtyard shaded by a canopy of broadleaf trees. Honeysuckle climbed the castle walls —whorled clusters of purple blooms buzzed with bees. Sweet hyacinth scents wafted from the manicured borders, creating a breathtaking carpet of delicate pink. Sword-shaped leaves and chartreuse petals guarded the entrance, forming a striking display of irises.

Dappled in sunlight, a white marble table, veined with ivory, held a crystal vase bursting with lavender and lush green sprigs. Three housekeepers bustled back and forth from the outdoor kitchen, setting golden plates with matching cutlery on woven placemats. They spoke in low tones in a language I did not recognize.

"Why does she hate it?" I padded behind her, my doeskin boots soundless on the neat cobblestones.

"Because. You might as well know. Macha prefers her books to people. She hides behind those glasses and refuses to speak with anyone she might like. She hates me for it." Nemain huffed.

"I don't think your sister hates you." I felt the need to boost Nemain's confidence.

"Yeah, well. She hates me in Knockma. They fawn all over me...it's pathetic." She tossed her blonde head, disdain in her eyes. And sadness?

"You're beautiful, Nemain. You remind me of the Elvin princess in a blockbuster movie." I grinned, admiring her perfect features.

"What is this thing you call a movie?" Confusion flickered in her silver eyes.

"Oh, you don't have television. Of course, you don't. How could you? You don't have internet, either. Geez, girl. We gotta talk." I laughed. I laughed a lot. Talking to her seemed effortless despite our differences.

"What are these things you speak of?" She clutched my wrist, eager to hear more, but released me with the same suddenness.

"When I leave here, you and Macha can hang out at my place. We can binge-watch and chill." I met her gaze, a smile lifting my lips.

"Binge-watch? What does it mean?" She lifted her hands.

"Have you ever spent time in the mortal world?" I stopped in the path to admire what appeared to be an apple tree bursting with ruby-red fruit. It struck me as odd.

"A little, with Ciarán. Well, he didn't know. Only once, I showed myself to him." She shrugged her shoulders. "He's the only man who doesn't want me. I enjoyed following him. It was fun. But he's gone now, isn't he? Father released him?" She twirled her hair, humming a melodic tune, completely nonplussed.

I looked at her, more than a little confused, as we left the manicured courtyard,

"That was the deal. Why was Ciarán here? Why couldn't he leave?" I pressed for more details. I needed to understand the complexities of their world.

"He played a vital role." Her gaze met mine. "For the hurling team. He's grand. Well, he was grand. I don't know what they'll do without him. It's so sad."

Hurling? I slowed my pace, my voice rising. "A game? You kept him captive for all these years just because of a game?"

"We have won the championship for the past seven years. Winning is essential to the *Tuatha Dé*. Father wouldn't let him go unless the trade was worth it. I take it you were the trade?" She looked down her nose, judging me for losing her friend.

"Yes, I guess I am." I sounded apologetic, and I was.

"Hmm. You'll like it here. We have celebrations every night in the ballroom," her silver eyes sparkled. "It's such fun."

"I can't stay here. I don't belong." I looked into her eyes, wanting her to understand.

"We're the same, Rioghain. You. Macha and I. You belong just as much as we do." Nemain's sharp tone caught my attention.

A slate roof rose from a fold in the glen, and in view of the castle towers, a one-story building sat at the edge of rolling green pastures stretching toward a dense forest. The clang of a blacksmith's hammer broke the peace. Voices murmured as stable hands groomed bright-eyed, beautiful horses. The sharp scent of horse filled my senses as a man approached, his withered hand resting on a child's shoulder—a young boy, dressed in grey wool, a belted tunic, and finely woven breeches. A shock of brown hair framed a face on the brink of boyhood. The boy walked with easy steps.

Doubt nagged at my mind beyond this fairyland. Colm—I worried about what I couldn't see and what I could—our connection broken. Visions flickered in and out of my mind: bits and pieces.

Colm tapping his foot to an erratic beat, doves cooing, Eamon passing a file folder across a desk. My stomach turned sideways as I stared at the little boy. Colm's mother, her hair wrapped in a checkered scarf, her hand clenching Colm's shoulder. What were they looking at? A newspaper? A grainy black-and-white photo of a boy missing from his home, taken in the early hours when the rest of the world slept, nine days ago. "Where are you, Calla? How can I find you?" Colm's tortured voice whispered.

"Princess, how may I help you today?" The older man

tipped his flat cap. His face bore scars, and his eyes lacked sight.

The child's chocolate eyes widened. He seemed out of place, and yet he belonged.

"Hallo, John. This is my sister, Princess Rioghain. Rioghain, this is John, the stable master. Rioghain needs a mount—a suitable mount." She inclined her head, not only captivating those around her but also with unquestioning authority.

"It's nice to meet you." I looked into the man's eyes—hooded chocolate orbs unmarred by the expected black pupil—roaming saucers, unseeing but seeing all.

"John is a seer, Rioghain. Allow him to touch your face. Based on what he sees, he will choose an appropriate horse." Finvarra appeared from the shadows, dressed in more formal attire: a long, gold-fringed waistcoat, his regal head crowned with the same ruby diadem.

"Your grace." John turned at the sound of his voice. He bowed and greeted the King, seeming unfazed by his presence.

I studied the scarred man. He seemed familiar, and a buried memory clawed to the surface.

"You're home, child." Leathered hands cupped my face.

Cloaked in darkness, shadows swirled in those blind eyes.

My mind bled with memories, not my own.

"Rioghain, this is your grandfather." Mama knelt before an older man, love shining in her eyes. She held me, a pudgy child still in diapers.

"You need not be afraid." The man dropped his hood, his ebony hair shining in the moonlight.

"I am not afraid," I whispered into the night wind, drop-

ping my blue blanket—a child's blanket. I had been there once before. I cast my gaze around the underground vault. Sea spray. Salty brine. Another realm entirely.

"Do you know who I am, child?" He offered his hand, his fingers ringed with gold. Black flames swallowed the mist.

The castle, the stables, Nemain and Finvarra disappeared into nothingness. The mist swallowed me as it had so many times before. I walked through the watery world into the land of another.

"Why am I here?" I gazed at the cloaked man as a full-grown woman, not a child fraught with nightmares. The woozy sensation passed. I stood tall, shoulders squared.

"This is your home. This is where you belong." The scar slicing his face added to his evil charm. From my nightmares, I knew this was the Lord of Death.

"Why have you brought me here?" My voice sounded hollow. There was no fear, only a passing acceptance of the dark fire crawling beneath my skin.

The raven screamed, calling my name from a faraway place. The winds shifted, rolling over the seas.

"Death brought you here." The blind man lifted my hand and pressed his hard lips to my bent knuckles.

His darkness was part of me.

"She deserves a life beyond this valley." The wraith weaved through the shadows, past the proud figure, and took my hand in hers, her lithe form wrapped in a silver cloak of the finest gossamer silk—a diamond crown adorned her golden head.

"Mother?" I gazed at her heart-shaped face with eyes as blue as cornflowers.

"Hear me, daughter. You are my life, my love. Do not come

here again. Promise me." Ériu *spoke with anguish, her cooling touch dousing the flames.*

Sunlight broke through the clouds, casting warmth over the courtyard. The old man tipped his flat cap, his ringed fingers glinting in the light, and walked away, his limp more pronounced than ever.

"He's breathtaking, isn't he?" Nemain led the white stallion in a figure-eight pattern. The horse arched his neck, his silky mane flowing with each graceful step.

"Aye, he is a worthy specimen. Strong and swift." Finvarra gestured toward the magnificent animal.

I swallowed my confusion, gazing beyond the stone building. Where did the stable master go? And Ériu—I saw her. Had she always been there?

"Does he have a name?" I admired this Faerie horse, saddled in exquisite leathers jeweled with amethyst, its arched neck and bright eyes captivating. I had seen nothing like him before.

A gentle nudge from the stallion's soft muzzle showed its eager curiosity. The horse tossed his flowing white mane and whinnied into the wind, showing his exuberance.

"He is yours, Rioghain. He awaits a name." Finvarra rested his palm on the stallion's neck.

I took the offered leg up, settling onto the horse's short back. I slipped my fingers through the supple reins. One touch had the animal walking backward.

"What will you call him?" Nemain lifted her hand, shielding the sun's rays.

"His name is Resurrection." I rested my palm on the horse's strong withers.

His ears twitched, and the big horse stamped his feet.

"A good name." Finvarra nodded his head in approval.

My gaze left them, attracted to the dark forest looming on the horizon. The shadows called to me, urging me to embrace what I was, fully and completely.

Colm was wrong.

I was not just a harbinger of death; I was one of three, and we were greater than Finvarra claimed. He had toyed with me, whether he knew it or not, was irrelevant. Ériu didn't give these names to honor the Morrigan. No... we were the Morrigan—three aspects of the same entity, a phantom goddess who moved between realms, protecting her people by instilling fear in their enemies. What it truly meant, I wasn't sure. I burst into laughter as the truth came to light. Their gifts were clear to me: Nemain thrived on chaos, and Macha, dear Macha, had the power to travel unseen through someone's mind—the chaos she could unleash. And then there was I.

Lifting my arms to the whispering winds, I left the light behind.

5

———

C *olm*

Light pierced my eyelids as familiar voices called. Recoiling from the glare, I sank deeper into an uneasy sleep. I clung to the darkness, the black hole offering solace to a wasted mind. I lingered, finding comfort in an abyss where whispers of the past lived within the shadows.

"Colm. Jaysus, man, wake up." Ciarán's voice rang out, his fingers digging into my shoulders.

"Jaysus, Mary, and Joseph." Saoirse pressed her palm on my forehead, her touch sending stabs of light through my mind.

"*What fool bursts upon a battle without a plan? Have you learned nothing from me, man? You court disaster at every turn,*" Ruairi grumbled, ire in his voice.

"I saw her. The White Woman, the *Bean Fhionn,*" I mumbled, resisting the light, lost in the shadowland. I recalled The White Woman's presence, which was more spectral than human. She lifted her silken hood and looked at me through ink-black eyes, her facial bones translucent beneath dew-like skin. When she held my hand, my heart stopped. The darkness had welcomed me —the great divide, the twilight zone between life and death. How easy it was to stay.

"*Aye, ye tickled the fancy of that one. 'Twas I who defended your honor, mo chara, from the Bean Fhionn.*" Ruairi's soft chuckle soothed my mind. "*She was willing to take ye till she discovered ye were already spoken for.*"

An odd, foreboding sense lingered, yet I could not grasp the significance. It was a funny thing when darkness came. I walked through the shadow of death until I was pulled back, not so graciously.

"*Aye, ye heeded her call, drawn in by her beautiful voice. They tricked her, ye see, the Tuatha Dé—promised her life when what they wanted was something else.*" He spoke as if he knew her well, leaving me wondering what had happened to that poor waif.

"Are you all right, man?" Ciarán's voice boomed, a loud clap.

"What happened?" My voice burned my throat, my mouth washed with the coppery tang of blood. I clawed the plank floor—my vision blurred.

Lightning struck the sky, eclipsing the moon's glow. The fury battered my body, and the wind that took Calla rushed over me. Ruairi's incessant chatter faded.

The fever raged. What plague was this? What scourge laid open my soul?

"We need an ambulance. Jaysus fecking Christ, there's no cell signal." Saoirse's voice clanged like the bells on a church-Sunday.

The airy presence offered a refuge from their panicked voices. One long exhale allowed the chaos to leave my being. The noise subsided, and the boundaries blurred. The ether split, and the lines of existence dissolved, allowing passage through the veil and toward the realm I sought.

Shadows drifted across the night sky, and the land of the ancients showed itself: blue skies, primeval trees, and the air itself. A dark blue ribbon of water followed the chiseled banks of a wooded valley, and a waterfall flowed over the face of the vertical cliff.

The Devil's Chimney was the highest waterfall in all of Ireland. My brain failed to make sense of things during that shift in time. The dense forest I gazed upon should have been sloping green fields with man-made walking trails and viewing platforms, enabling many tourists to wander. Instead, age-old trees met the sky, leafy hazel, great ash, towering beech, and the mighty oak—stands unheard of today. And there, the immortal yew, a symbol of death, worshipped yet feared, flourished in the cliff's shadow.

Calla's silver-eyed gaze locked with mine, and her smile welcomed me, a noble air surrounding her. She was Other-worldly, one of Them, as I knew she was—the gold band crowning her head shimmered with rose-colored stones, a crimson cloak embroidered with gold threads shielded her from the evening dew. Leather riding breeches covered her long legs, and her feet were in finely stitched doe-skin boots. She was borne through the silent woods by a magnificent white stallion, a creature of breathtaking splendor, unlike any seen by mortal eyes. The golden bridle on the stallion's head sparkled in the moonlight. The eight-

point diamond on the horse's brow only confirmed my suspicions.

This was the Otherworld the ould ones spoke of.

I followed her gaze to the glacial lake, the peaceful scene bringing a smile to my face: a playful otter slid down a muddy bank, and a sea trout leapt, breaking the surface of the shimmering waters.

Blackbirds screeched, fluttering from branch to branch and disturbing the quiet. The waterfall stopped its descent, and the flume flipped backward. The rushing waters soared into the sky—streams of dancing water, swirling upon themselves, held back by the devil himself.

A branch snapped and fell with a thud onto the forest floor. Calla's horse flicked his ears, nostrils flaring red. Haze drifted over the valley—the death tree wept poisoned tears.

What force wielded its evil hand in this Faerie glen?

"Calla." I called her name, but she couldn't hear me. She was oblivious to my presence.

"He's bleeding. Ciarán, run the hot water. Get some towels. Colm? You're going to be okay." Saoirse's voice echoed far away.

"Enough of this lollygagging, soldier. Your ladylove is in danger, unlike any other. There's no time to waste." Ruairi's will hammered mine, demanding my return.

The O'Donnell—I called upon the spirit world, and he answered as I knew he would. My heartbeat pounded in my head.

"Blood is blood, laddie." My father's voice lingered—Da —gone from us so suddenly. The day we met, Calla had warned me of his passing, her dove grey eyes flashing,

her fear striking my heart. She ran from me then. It had struck me as strange.

The curtain rose. I was only somewhat aware of my situation: battered and semi-conscious, lying face down on the cold flagstones at Calla's entrance hall, a silver candlestick inches from my head. I peeked through heavy lids into the adjoining room at the chess pieces scattered across the floor. They arranged themselves into formation, one army against the other. The black king nodded his regal head, signaling his knight to attack. Enemy soldiers stood tall. Swords clashed. Soldiers fell. The king's bishop swung his shepherd's staff, with pale blue eyes calling me into the fight.

The thrum grew louder, and the shapes of people I loved formed through foggy eyes. I heard their cries. I grabbed the sidewall, heaving my broken body up onto my feet.

"Colm? What are you doing? Where are you going? Ciarán, do something." Saoirse's attempt to hamper my escape failed. She reached out, grasping my elbow as I staggered forward.

"Slow your go, bro. You need stitches. Let's get you to the clinic." Ciarán placed his hands on my shoulders, peering into my eyes.

"No. No time. There's no time. Calla's in danger." A wave of nausea swept over me. Lurching forward, I left a bloody handprint on the plaster wall.

"Colm, please, you need a doctor." Saoirse followed, holding a blood-stained towel in her hand.

"I have to go to her. I have to find her." I grasped the doorknob, startled by the sight of my bloody knuckles.

The pain shooting through my hand, my index finger bent at an awkward angle, meant nothing to me.

Twilight skies greeted me as I looked across the courtyard. Silver clouds hovered over the mountain's back, still and waiting. I trudged toward my truck, parked on an angle on the cobblestones. The driver's door was open, the headlights flickering. If that wasn't enough to ruin someone's day, the bastards had slashed the right front tire.

"What happened, Colm? What happened to you?" Saoirse's voice jolted me out of my thoughts.

"We were... I was ambushed." I brushed my good hand through my hair, which was matted and stiff with dried blood. What options did I have left? Hamstead's threat echoed in my mind. He was determined to find her. To what lengths would he go? I shook my head in disbelief. Would he dare enter the Otherworld in his search? My thoughts raced from one scenario to another. Hamstead couldn't be that far along in his plans. Could he?

And yet, if he saw the wind and the storm carrying Calla away, I was so captivated by her presence that I was blind to him. I wondered if I had missed something.

"*I cannot tell if you were followed, mo chara. Had you involved me sooner...*" Ruairi's voice carried an ominous warning.

"We'll find her, mate." Ciarán squeezed my shoulder. His heartfelt words meant something.

"The lights were on. The door was open. I thought. I thought Calla had returned." My thoughts drifted through the haze of last night's events. What was real and what wasn't? I leaned against the truck and, in a moment of clarity, pieced together the events leading up to this moment.

"*I won't say I told you so.*" Ruairi voiced his opinion loud and clear.

"Did you see them? What did they look like?" Ciarán's steadying voice calmed my racing mind.

"Yes—" I reflected on the incident. "—The muscle was about six feet four, dark-haired. The other guy looked like a schoolteacher." I knew who the schoolteacher was without needing to ask. I recalled the earnest look on Eamon's face when he pushed the classified file across the desk.

"*She's in grave danger, man. We need to move now.*" Ruairi's voice was piercing, his words hot with conviction.

"That's him then. He called himself a 'scientist.'" Saoirse threw the final death spear into my heart.

My thoughts drifted to Eamon, his rasping voice echoing in my mind. The townspeople thought of him as a retired soldier living a quiet life, not the head of Irish Intelligence. Sharing too much information could threaten his position. It was wiser to stay silent and let them believe the illusion he had built. I was one of many operatives under Eamon's command. My latest mission was to protect Calla Sweet from a mad scientist, a man determined to prove the existence of the Faerie Folk. It had only been days since I last sat with Eamon.

"How did they know where Calla lived? Dear gods, where is she, Colm? It's not like her to up and disappear." Saoirse's voice rose in panic for her friend.

Ciarán shuffled his feet, his gaze locking with mine.

He believed that his release from the Otherworld was because of Calla. I had no choice but to agree.

I looked at him long and hard. This was not the time for full disclosure.

"Saoirse. You said two men came to the pub, asking for Calla. What did they want?" I pressed my good hand against my forehead, stilling the pulsing throb.

"They had Calla's picture. They wanted to talk to her. When I told them she'd left, they pressed for a forwarding address." She steepled her fingers, her brows furrowed in thought.

"When? When was this?" The wind gusted across the courtyard, lifting wet leaves from the cobblestones and leaving tea-colored stains behind. Branches groaned overhead, and water droplets splashed down, the bitter chill snapping me to my senses.

"The other day. Yesterday. I didn't tell them anything, Colm. Nothing that could hurt Calla. I tried to call, but she didn't pick up." She lifted her hands.

"I believe you, Saoirse. What else do you remember?" I clenched my fists, payback filling my mind. I would bring Hamstead and his cronies down.

"I have his card. His name was Sean. Sean Hamstead." She dove into her satchel, pulling a business card from within. "I searched the internet, Colm. He doesn't exist."

"Did you try calling him back?" I studied the card— standard stock with clean print on a white background, no defining marks, no photo.

"No. No. I didn't do that." She jutted her chin, a muscle twitching in her jaw.

"That would have made sense, wouldn't it?" I seethed,

unable to hide my frustration. I regretted my wrath. Any fool could see she was guilt-ridden and distraught.

I pulled my phone out of my pocket and tapped Hamstead's number. The call didn't go through. I stared at the screen—no signal. I held the phone above my head —still nothing.

"Calm down, mate. Losing your shite is the last thing you want to do. She has an evil eye, this one. Take care," Ruairi whispered through the shadows.

My incompetence hit me hard. I looked at Calla's cottage, noting the red bicycle leaning against the front wall and the little bird flying in and out of its nest. I entered unprepared, making a careless mistake that could have cost me my life. Where would that have left Calla? At the mercy of a madman's sinister plan? Lost in another world? The image of the magnificent white horse, its eyes filled with fear, flashed in my mind—along with the location—The Devil's Chimney. It was my only clue to her whereabouts.

"She didn't look lost to me. The woman I saw looked high-born. A princess, perhaps?" Ruairi raised a good point.

Orlaith said Calla was the daughter of a king from the Otherworld.

"Pish Posh Applesauce." Calla sang songs only I could hear. I pressed the heels of my hands into my eyes, tottering forward on the balls of my feet. Too many voices. Too many voices.

"Colm? Are you all right?" Saoirse planted her hand over my forehead. "Ciarán, is he all right? He doesn't seem himself."

"Saoirse, what did this Sean Hamstead look like?" I

asked to confirm the man's appearance. I saw him for a fleeting moment before all went black.

"I don't know, average, not good-looking, not ugly. He wore glasses. Black horned-rim. Short hair, thinning on the top. He said Calla did one of those DNA samples. He mentioned irregularities. Something about ancient genomes. The suit? The big guy? He was the scary one. Got up in my face, insisting I was hiding something. Freaked me out." She confirmed what I already knew.

I remained calm, heeding Ruairi's advice. The last thing I needed was an angry witch raining down on me. I shoved my phone back in my pocket and gazed between Saoirse and Ciarán. They were involved, whether I liked it or not.

"Did you tell her?" I turned my attention to Ciarán, wondering how much he had shared.

"No." He dipped his head, his hair falling over his eyes.

"What? Tell me what?" Saoirse's gaze darted toward Ciarán.

"Look. We don't have much time, but you deserve the truth. They took Calla, Saoirse. The thing is, when Calla vanished, Ciarán appeared." A wave passed over me, freeing me from the secrets I kept.

"Who took her?" Her face paled, and her gaze moved toward Ciarán.

The wind lifted the wet leaves. I watched the swirling dervish at work. Even then, acknowledging the existence of an immortal race was mind-blowing. Eamon asked if Ciarán was sound and whether his mind was still his own after seven years trapped in their world. The Ciarán I remembered was never 'sound,' but he was never afraid. This Ciarán quaked under my scrutiny.

"Time is not your friend, mo chara. Whatever horrors your brother endured are of his own making. Let it be." His concise words left no room for doubt.

"I don't know. Finvarra. Maybe." My eyes flickered over Ciarán's tall frame, pronounced cheekbones, and jutting shoulder blades. I met Saoirse's confused gaze.

"Finvarra? The King of the Faeries?" Her mouth fell open. Her eyes widened, and within moments, she questioned the impossible. "Why would Finvarra take Calla?"

"According to Orlaith, Finvarra is Calla's father." I watched the tiny wren fluttering under the eaves, a worm hanging from its little beak.

"Orlaith? What does Orlaith have to do with this?" She lifted her chin, looking at me with obvious confusion.

"She was there, Saoirse. Orlaith was in the Faerie realm when Calla was born. She was tasked with taking Calla from the Kingdom and sending her away." I looked at my brother, at his horrified gaze.

"Jaysus, Mary, and Joseph. Orlaith knew this? And Finvarra, the King of the Faeries, is Calla's father? Why didn't you tell me?" She punched Ciarán's chest, her face white.

"I didn't know that part. Well, I was not certain of that fact." He swallowed hard and looked away.

"So, she's safe then, right? She's in the other realm with her family." Saoirse looked back at me. She had accepted the existence of the Other Crowd a long time ago.

"I think she's safe." I acknowledged her conclusion. I recalled seeing Calla dressed in royal finery, away from this world. Still, I couldn't squash the feeling that something wasn't right. The horse reacted to something. Worry consumed my very being.

"And Sean Hamstead? What is he after?" Her gaze pierced mine, always questioning.

"Sean Hamstead is the head of an organization called the Reconstructionists. He's suspected of hijacking Calla's DNA sample. The authorities are after him for that and other reasons." I shared with her what little information I could.

"Abducting Calla would give him a real-life specimen. He'll perform experiments, assuming he is a scientist. His findings would give him the evidence to prove the Other Crowd exists." Ciarán said what I had dared not.

"How do you know this, Colm?" She stared me down.

"It's my job, Saoirse. Keeping Calla safe is my job." Protecting the woman I loved was a foregone conclusion.

"What do you mean, your job? You quit the Garda. You moved to Canada. What do you do in Canada, Colm?" She clenched her hands, her lips tight.

"I am employed in the private sector of the government, Saoirse. The Irish government. My responsibility is to protect Calla from this man." I looked back and forth between them, caught in a web of deception I could no longer keep up with.

"*What are we waiting for, mo chara? Time is of the essence.*" Ruairi interrupted my thoughts.

His vengeance was true. I wouldn't rest until Calla was back in my arms.

"What do you think his next move is?" Her gaze held mine, her words deliberate. Her fear and any sense of panic had vanished.

Never underestimate a witch.

"Legends suggest the Faerie raths allow entry on festival days, and today is Bealtaine Eve. That's where I'm going. If I were a betting man, I'd say that's where Hamstead is headed." My breath left my lungs. I plowed my hand through my hair, exhaustion taking its toll.

"That's a stretch, isn't it?" Ciarán tilted his head, his expression changing from disbelief to horror.

"Her DNA proves to him that the Otherworld exists. He came here, didn't he? He's not giving up." I motioned toward Calla's cottage. "If I were in his shoes, that's my next move." I touched my head, jarring the scab that refused to heal.

"But he doesn't know where Calla is. Does he?" Saoirse swallowed hard, her expression shifting from hope to disbelief.

"But I do." My heart pounded faster than it should have, the ocean's roar drowning out my thoughts—that moment Calla vanished flooded back.

"Colm, tell me what happened. How did it happen? Ciarán won't." Saoirse touched my upper arm.

I revisited that moment—the startled horses, the flailing reins. The ocean's fury flipped me upside down, smashing my head against the seafloor. The wind howled, turning the sky into a tempest, and Calla—Calla had vanished. I buried my face in my hands, letting the dark waves swallow me.

Ciarán cleared his throat. Was he trying to tell me something? I was too tired to care.

"A fog came from nowhere, but it wasn't fog. It was a being. And whoever it was took Calla away from me." I fought to keep her, didn't I? I fought to stay alive.

"And this being left Ciarán in Calla's place?" she asked, turning to look at Ciarán, her face paling.

"She was there, and then she was gone. Please take me to Eamon's, Saoirse. I'm running out of time." I inhaled, quieting the demons.

"You need the hospital, Colm. You're concussed." She grasped my chin with one hand, pressing a towel against the throbbing gash with the other.

"She warned me of the danger. She told me it was there. I was too late." I ignored Saoirse's ministrations— my only concern was Calla. I remembered the promise made. By all that was good, I would find her.

"*What if she doesn't want to be found?*" Ruairi always played the opposite side.

"What? What did you say?" Saoirse lifted her chin, her eyes lighting up.

"Calla speaks to me—inside my mind. Or she used to. Something's not right. She's not with me anymore." Sharing our secret bond with my brother and Saoirse felt freeing, but had I betrayed Calla's confidence in doing so? Saoirse, of all people, would understand the Other-worldly.

"She speaks to you?" Saoirse's gaze pierced mine.

Ciarán shot me a sidelong glance. He sensed the change in my physical state, the subtle suggestion in my words. He understood what I had become. The fire burning in my soul belonged to the O'Donnell. Was Ruairi's presence shielding my mind from Calla's? Is that what was happening?

"There's no fae being wanting inside your wee brain, if that's what you're asking." Ruairi's voice, a hot poker fanning the flames, *"Let us get on with this, man. You've given these fiends a day's ride."*

"When did this start? She didn't tell me this." She bound my broken finger to the adjacent one with a ripping of cloth.

I studied the makeshift splint and then met her knowing gaze.

"How long has she been 'speaking' to you?" She poked my chest, demanding an answer.

"Since Da's wake." Sweat pooled on my brow. The thought of never seeing Calla again turned my stomach. "It was the oddest thing. She kissed me in the meadow, beneath the oak tree." I placed my fingers on my lips, as if that could bring her back.

The clouds opened, and raindrops fell from the grey sky. I lifted my face, allowing each one to pour over me. I imagined Calla's soft lips and her breath mixing with mine.

"Since the wake?" She looked at Ciarán and then back at me, her lips pinched into a straight line. "We'll take you where you want to go, Colm." She opened the passenger door and slid across the bench, settling into the middle seat.

"This isn't your problem, Saoirse." I planted my hand on the passenger door, gazing inside the wood-paneled interior. Pine scents wafted from an air freshener dangling from the center mirror.

"Calla is my friend, Colm. And you need all the help you can get. We're going with you. Aren't we, Ciarán?" She cast a soft look at him. Her pursed lips and forceful tone left no room for debate.

"You're not going alone, bro." Ciarán jumped behind the wheel. The engine backfired and then started up with a rumbling roar.

Ciarán nosed the vintage truck down the long drive, beyond the stone pillars, and onto the fog-bound road, heading east toward Ardara town.

"Hurry. Ciarán. I have to find her before those bastards do." I faced the obvious fact—getting anywhere in this weather would not happen quickly. I refused to entertain negative thoughts.

"Seems we have two opponents, no? One of the flesh, the other ethereal. This Hamstead has bested you once, O'Donnell. Take comfort, mo chara. Mortals are predictably the same, a race ruled by greed. If he's after your lady friend, it is not to harm her. It's to benefit his stature." Ruairi's sigh offered insight.

"I see your point." I rubbed my eyes, my thoughts racing. "Proving Calla's lineage would make him the most sought-after scientist in the world."

"But that's not what worries me. If she is what you say, your lady friend belongs to the Tuatha Dé, and they are indeed a race to be reckoned with. Don't think you can enter their world without consequences. They won't give her up easily if she is of royal blood. That is guaranteed."

"She was taken against her will."—I refused to give up hope.

"Redundant. Your lady friend looked well suited to her place. You know nothing of the Otherworld, O'Donnell. I have first-hand knowledge of many realms, the land of the dead and the realm of the Tuatha Dé."

"There are threats from all sides. I know what I saw, and nothing will deter me." I argued my case with Ruairi. My senses told me to forge ahead. If Calla wished to remain in the Otherworld, I would respect her decision. That said, turning back was out of the question. I would not leave her in peril.

"Colm? Who are you talking to?" Saoirse's gaze darted to Ciarán.

"What?" Did I voice my thoughts? I turned my eye toward the two of them, sweat pooling beneath my collar.

"I think we should go to the hospital." She shifted in her seat, her palm cooling on my forehead. She brushed the blood-coated hair away, almost tenderly. "Ciarán, he has a concussion. Maybe this isn't such a good idea."

My brother murmured words I could not hear.

I refused to acknowledge my irrational state and instead thought through the events that had occurred so far. Calla disappeared twelve hours ago at the hands of the *Tuatha Dé*. Violent abductions never ended well—at least not in my world. And what about the scientist and his henchman? They defeated me once. It wouldn't happen again. "Hamstead worries me," I murmured, more to myself than to anyone.

"Maybe he left the parish, Colm. He could be in

Dublin for all we know." Saoirse watched me and then looked at Ciarán.

I trusted my brother to do the right thing.

The skies opened, pelting the truck's windshield. Within seconds, rain lashed down. The wipers squelched, flying back and forth over the windshield.

"Eamon's rath is the closest entry point to Finvarra's castle. The portal opens in a glen behind the palace." Ciarán tapped his fingers on the steering wheel. He looked at Saoirse, his mouth drawn tight.

"What?" She turned to him, gripping his wrist.

"If it weren't for Eamon, I would have been forced to eat their food. I'd have been trapped forever in the Otherworld." He lifted his shoulders and swallowed hard.

"You were able to leave? It's true, then, what Calla said. She told me she spoke to you. That she saw you in the pub." Saoirse's eyes dampened, her voice hitching.

Ciarán pressed his lips together and then nodded. "Eamon left food in the barn, an offering to Themselves. For the last seven years, he never missed a day."

"I can't believe it." Her knuckles whitened. "You were so close, and we couldn't see you."

"I owe Eamon my life." He nodded, conviction filling his voice.

My mind drifted, unwilling to engage in further conversation. Ruairi refused to let up, hammering my thoughts with his.

"The Tuatha govern through cunning and deception—trickery is their calling card, their magical power unmatched. Consider yourself fortunate if they don't siphon the blood from your mortal bones. Whence you enter their ungodly kingdom,

remain steadfast in your purpose. Your resolve must not waver, lest they detect weakness."

"Colm, wake up. We're here." Saoirse tapped my shoulder, waking me from my unease.

Ciarán parked the truck and left the headlights beaming toward Eamon's cottage.

I gazed through tunnels of light into a shroud of darkness. From somewhere far away, a dog yapped and then howled. Or could it be a wolf? It couldn't be. This land was rid of wolves centuries ago.

"Where's Eamon?" Ciarán looked toward the cottage. All was quiet, even the rain had stopped its quiet patter.

The night lived, and darkness reigned. Soon, the Lunar Bealtaine Moon would dominate the night sky. I was sure of one thing: the Super Moon would penetrate the shadows and reveal the horrors that lived.

"Something isn't right." I led the way beyond Eamon's cottage and past the inconspicuous dovecote, the cooing and humming of the birds inside calming my mind.

A loud thump halted me in my tracks. Turning on my heels, I saw Saoirse squatting in the mud, a pained grimace on her face.

"Shite. Go on with ye, now. I'm fine. I stumbled, that's all." Saoirse rose and, with a pained grimace, hobbled toward Ciarán.

"Are you all right? Let me help you." Ciarán hooked his arm around her waist, his gaze filled with worry.

Wet drizzle clung to my skin, seeping into every pore —cold, clammy fingers gripping my heart and refusing to let go, a dampness penetrating through denim and wool, numbing my bones. I turned my head, drawn by the haunting sound of rushing water. Beneath a thin layer of peat lay an underground river capable of transporting one's soul to the underworld. I pushed aside the childhood memory and moved down the path, with Ciarán and Saoirse following through the darkness.

The twisted branches of the Faerie rath appeared before me. I tilted my head, listening for any signs of movement, an unnatural fog muting even the buzzing of bees. I moved around the thorny mound, wind racing through my shirtsleeves.

"Colm. Colm, it's Eamon." Saoirse's shrill tone caught my attention. "He's not breathing. Sweet Jesus, Ciarán, do something."

I turned from the Faerie rath, staring into the darkness, my sight lines so poor that it was hard to distinguish shapes from the landscape. I retraced my footsteps through the mud and found them crouched in the path.

Eamon, sweet Eamon, lay flat on his back, his neck bent, his fall cushioned by hawthorn branches. I walked right past him, unaware of his fading breath.

"Eamon, can you hear me? Can you talk to me?" I knelt beside him, pressing my fingers to his throat, and searched for a pulse. Faint but there. Relief poured over me. "He's alive."

"Should we lift him? Should we call an ambulance?" The panic in her voice struck fear in my heart. How did this happen? The possibilities were endless at his age, yet a foreboding sensation settled over me.

"Goddamn, this weather." I rested the back of my knuckles on Eamon's face, his skin clammy. His soaked clothing told me he had been here a long time. "Eamon? Eamon? Are you alright?"

"Arrah, laddie," he whispered, his lungs rattling. "On top of the ground, aye, and not below."

"Bless him, he's coming to." Saoirse hugged her arms around her chest.

"What happened, Eamon? Did you fall?" The cold in his bones seeped into mine.

"'Twas a man wandering about the forth. Could you give me my stick, laddie? Where's that dog got to? Finnigan, his name is. Barks at the moon in the middle of the day, that he does." Eamon's voice was weak, yet he struggled to rise.

"Eamon, you need a doctor," Saoirse pressed her hand to his brow.

"Nothing a draft of whisky wouldn't cure, lassie. Colm, help me up." Eamon drew his cold fingertips across my face, his eyes pleading.

"And this time, we're going." She glared at me while searching her pockets for her phone.

"Ciarán will take you into town, aye? Liam will fix you up." I nudged Saoirse, suggesting the most amenable solution to the older man. Convincing him to visit a proper hospital seemed unlikely. Most preferred the old ways, calling upon a healer—a last resort.

"Hugh Jr? Aye, that boy's a stickler, that he is. Such a good boy, made your da proud, that he did." His eyes closed halfway.

"Who did this, Eamon?" I grabbed his limp hand.

"They got me this time. Aye, they got me good.

Finnigan took a rasher out of one of them. Finnigan." Eamon called out, his voice trembling.

I locked eyes with Eamon, the intensity in his gaze speaking volumes.

"You take Eamon. I'll find my way." Together, we lifted Eamon from the brambles.

"Finnigan? It's not like him to run off. Finnigan!" He leaned on my shoulder.

"I've got you, Eamon." Ciarán wrapped his arm around the older man, and we half-carried him to Saoirse's truck.

"Ciarán, laddie. You're back. Well, it's a kind thing that the Faerie girl did, wasn't it?" Eamon limped ahead.

Ciaran murmured quiet words as Saoirse gasped.

I stood in the courtyard, watching the truck roll in the other direction. My course of action was clear as mud.

CALLA

Resurrection soared, his hooves barely touching the ground. My thoughts scattered with the clapping wind. The horse stretched into a full gallop, showing no sign of tiring. I doubt I could have slowed him. He was a wild creature, more magic than flesh and bone. It was over-whelming, and yet not.

I needed to escape from all that I had become. For the first time since arriving in this Otherworld, I could breathe. I found solace in that. I could stay or leave—eventually, once I had fulfilled my part of the bargain. I had no doubt Finvarra would keep his.

Lightning rippled, sending crackling bolts through a darkening sky, shards of light piercing the green canopy. The air softened into something malleable and alive. Shadows bled, and colors whipped by, blurred and iridescent, fiery shades of earth and sky. The wind found me first, buffeting my body with warm, caressing gusts. I closed my eyes, my mind racing with visions of muscled lines and sculpted edges—Colm. His thoughts reached mine, his voice calling me from a dark place I couldn't find. Yet, I could feel him. The soft brush of his lips, his tongue stroking mine, his teeth raking my lower lip. His hands drifted, igniting the fire. Hunger overwhelmed me, need coursing through my veins. I clung to him, his fevered kisses cooling. The forest was silent, except for those listening.

I loved him, and yet I was allergic to that word.

Resurrection raced onward, his ivory mane flowing with the wind. I don't remember losing the reins, but it didn't matter. It was liberating. The horse understood. My entire life had been a lie. It was no one's fault. It just was.

6

*C*alla

"What do you know about our mother?" I tugged at the loose thread linking the plunging bodice to the tiered skirt of the crimson ball gown. The puffed shoulders added a fairy tale charm, while the fitted sleeves brought sophistication. Dressing up had never been this much fun.

Macha turned her gaze toward the lady's maid, fussing with the scalloped hem of her gown, a fancy affair of satin and lace, the straight neckline framing her face. "Leave us, Betty."

"Yes, ma'am." The girl dipped her head, curiosity clear in her silver eyes. She gathered her sewing kit against her chest, obeying Macha's demand.

"Where did Betty come from?" I watched the girl leave the suite of rooms. "Is she *Tuatha*?"

"Yes, of course." Macha's lips peeled into a grin. "What? You think we steal mortals to work in the castle?"

"The thought crossed my mind." I dismissed that idea

and moved on to a different conversation, one of greater importance at that moment. I needed information, and Macha was the person who could provide it. I lifted the flowing skirt of the elegant dress, admiring the way the rich hues transitioned into an ombre effect, and followed Macha to a cozy nook lined with floor-to-ceiling bookshelves, my black stilettos clicking on the marble floor.

"Why would Ériu send me away?" I ran my fingers across the leather spines, inhaling the woody scent of vellum pages. The idea of reading all those books made my head spin.

"This is the first I've heard of it." Her hand rested on an ornately carved desk in the center of a braided rug. "Why would Mother do such a thing?" She pinned her bottom lip beneath her upper teeth and stared at me.

"I don't know." I studied her eyes. "Ériu was weak, dying."

Macha's face paled.

"She said they would use my dark heart against me. She told Orlaith to take me away." Her reaction sent an icy chill down my spine.

"Who would do that?" Macha gazed over her shoulder.

"I don't know. How would I know? I have to assume she meant Finvarra." I studied the purple petunias spilling over the window's edge, entangled with twisting tendrils of glossy green ivy.

"No...that's not possible. Your magic is your own. Another can't control it." She shook her head, denying my accusation.

"Hmm...well, it seems once Finvarra discovered my

existence, he stole me away from my world, just like he did Ériu. That's all I'm saying." I pressed my lips into a straight line.

"Hello, Sweet Thing." She smiled as the feline slipped through the open lancet window, disturbing the foliage creeping over the sill. The cat's purr followed it around the room. It stretched out on the floor, warming its belly by the fire.

"What's its name?" I lifted my chin, wary of the hissing beast.

"Sweet Thing." She giggled.

"Sweet Thing?" I stared at the cat, unsure of what to think of its presence. I had learned that not everything was as it appeared. "Do you know a little man named Seamus?"

"No." Her eyes shimmered as she considered my revelation. "Mother and father were together for a long time. He didn't steal her." She scooped up the snow-white cat into her arms, his long body nearly reaching her knees.

"I'm sorry, Macha, but there are things about Ériu you don't know. Things that Finvarra didn't tell you." I hugged myself and sighed.

"I guess you're right. You must be right, or you wouldn't be here. We didn't know of your existence. I don't think Father knew." She glanced up and placed the cat on the floor, rubbing its head for the last time.

"The bees told him, or so he says." My gaze remained on Sweet Thing. "I get it. You don't know me, but we are sisters." I enunciated the last sentence, charming her with my sincerity. Her raised brow told me one thing— she saw right through me.

"Hmph. What do you know of our people, Rioghain?" She turned, her gaze scanning the vast library of ancient tomes.

"Not a lot. Some. What are you looking for?" I followed her gaze up and up again.

"A book with pictures?" She glanced over her shoulder.

"I can read, Macha." I planted my hand on my hip. "I had a career before arriving in this Faerie kingdom. I was a newscaster on a major television network."

"What is that?" She crossed to the other wall.

"A career is a job—something you do daily to make money." I rested my chin in the crook of my hand.

"I know what a job is, Rioghain. We all have jobs of some sort. What is a *newscaster*?" She repeated the word.

"Huh...this is another world. Hmm, a newscaster speaks out to all the people listening and tells them what is happening in the world."

"Like a bard or a traveler or a dove." She nodded her head up and down, comparing ancient means of communication. "And a *television*?"

"A television is a screen that shows pictures. Sounds and voices come from it." I studied her.

"I would like to see a *television*." She seemed to float through the room, elegant in a simple white dress that rippled to the floor. "Let me see what I can find. We have many ancient works here." She looked at my raised brows. "Battles. Magic. The origins of our people." She grasped the side rails of a wooden ladder, gliding the wheeled legs across the marble floor. She lifted her skirt, climbing one rung after another in cloud-white satin slippers.

"Do you need help?" I held the ladder with both hands.

"Of all these manuscripts, this is my favorite." She released her grip and dropped to the floor.

"How did you do that?" I wondered what had just happened. Was it a trick of the hand? An illusion? Floating? Another ability I must learn.

"Do you know of Donn? The Lord of the Dead?" She held a yellowed manuscript in both hands.

"Donn? Yes, I've heard of him." I dragged my thumb across the soft vellum, and the air stirred, warmth caressing my face.

Beneath the waves, a barren rock broke the surface of the sea. The scarred man stared at me—his empty eyes hidden beneath a hooded shroud.

"Donn is Ériu's father, our grandfather." She pursed her lips, blowing a layer of dust in all directions, then offered it to me almost reverently. Leaving the alcove, she gestured for me to follow.

I hung onto the compendium for dear life, my stomach coiling. The vision swallowed me, coming to life in technicolor. I teetered back and forth, the ocean roaring in my ears.

Thunderous rolling waves reverberated through the tombstone. Even the seagulls avoided this place.

The island resembled a volcano, a jagged, desolate rock stretching toward a vacant sky. The vast central chamber glimmered with dark lumens, and four stalagmite pillars studded with black diamonds touched the upper vault. A corridor wound deep, twisting and turning into its dark heart, where an assembly of the dead waited.

Finvarra, ever young, sat across a low stone table facing the scarred man, Donn, the Lord of the Dead. The scar cut his smile in two, giving him a menacing appearance.

The Lord glared at his confident opponent, fury seething in his dark eyes. Between them sat a familiar marble slab—a chess board, the chess pieces fashioned from the bones of Donn's enemies, the Tuatha Dé Danann.

"My friend, it appears you've met your match. Our accord is complete." Finvarra's voice echoed off the gallery walls. He made his last move, a broad smile spreading across his handsome face.

Ériu, her long blonde hair cascading over her shoulders, stood behind Finvarra. She placed a congratulatory hand on his shoulder.

Oh my God.

I rested my hand on the ladder.

"Rioghain, are you all right? Would you like a jammy scone?" Macha's voice chased away the vision. She offered a silver tray covered with sweet delights: fluffy scones drizzled with vanilla icing and oozing with strawberry jam.

"How is that possible? Ériu was mortal, a human." She had confirmed my vision in the stable-yard. The wraith who spoke to me—Ériu, called The Lord of the Dead—Father.

"Yes, she was once." Macha lifted the gilded frame of Ériu and Finvarra. She stared into the photo, her eyes misty.

"Okay, I don't get it." I turned my head.

"Read the book from front to back." She pinned her lips together, unable to hide her smile.

"I don't have a lot of time, Macha." I knew how hurtful my words sounded. Macha, kind, sweet Macha, deserved a better sister than I.

"Have a scone." She held me in her pop-bottle gaze. Macha, the one who binds the threads, held this family together. Was she reading my thoughts?

"Don't look at me like that. I don't belong here. I need to go home." Home...the word rolled over my tongue. I had a home. And a man who wanted me—Colm. My toes curled, anticipating the moment we saw each other again. I closed my mouth over the sweet delight and hummed appreciation.

"Do you not want to stay? There is much for you to learn. I would like to get to know you, as would Nemain." Her voice softened, her words inviting agreement.

Wow!

"I want to know you both." I placed my fingers over her wrist, and she smiled.

"The Milesians came from Iberia, defeating the *Tuatha* for possession of this land. Some of our people left, but not all. Father negotiated a truce with the sons of Mil, and those who wished to stay remained. Banished to a world beneath the ground." Macha bent her head, focusing on the petunias climbing over the windowsill, pulling wilted deadheads from the flowering plant.

She gave me a history lesson, which I might have known had I tried to learn.

"How is this beneath the ground? The sun is shining in a brilliant blue sky. There are lakes and trees. I rode the most beautiful horse through those dark woods, the wind whipping my face. Over gully and vale and back to this castle. Fin has a dog, a furry, drooling beast. And that cat. Well, I don't know what to make of Sweet Thing. This is not beneath the ground." I sat on the cushioned window seat and crossed my ankles. There was no academic answer to this. It just was.

"Thousands of years have passed, Rioghain. Our people built great cities within this realm. We became the *Daoine Sidhe*—a spirit race feared by mortal beings." She turned to the credenza, glanced at the portrait, and poured tea into two pewter teacups.

"Thousands of years? Finvarra is thousands of years old?" I cocked an eyebrow.

"Aye. Father is one of the oldest in the realm." She gestured toward the painted credenza beneath the life-sized portrait of Finvarra and Ériu.

"I need more, Macha. What does this have to do with our mother?" I lifted the cup, noticing the blue sapphires embedded in the footed base.

"When Mil's sons sailed to Ireland, a great wave met them. Donn was the first to die. He assumed the role of the Lord of the Dead. His daughter was Ériu." Macha sat in the high-backed chair, her knees pressed together, her shoulders straight, clenching and unclenching her fingers.

"The Lord of the Dead is our grandfather?" I sipped the warm tea, letting the floral fragrance wash over my tongue.

"Father traveled to the underworld, where he bartered for Ériu's return. She left Donn's realm and lived as Finvarra's consort. They were lovers, Rioghain. They lived together in this castle where they made us." She handed me the gilded frame.

I gazed at the portrait of Ériu and Finvarra, his hand resting on her shoulder. Her explanation didn't sit well. Bartered? I knew differently.

"Not that long then, in the grand scope of his never-ending life." I mused. "How many worlds are there? Never mind, I don't want to know." I closed my eyes and then opened them. "What dark magic can bring a dead soul back to life?"

"Father is a powerful being, as is Grandfather." She smiled.

"So, Finvarra gets what he wants?" I wondered how many lives Finvarra had tampered with. "He brought Ériu back to life, to live within this realm? That's what you're saying?" I rubbed the gilded frame with my thumbs. Nothing. I sensed nothing.

"She was not dead, but yes. That's what I'm saying." She nodded her head, sadness dwelling in her eyes.

"Wow. I don't know what to say. Wait. Does that mean she's 'living' in the Underworld now?" I left the frame on the mantle and turned toward her.

"This is a lot for you to comprehend. But in time, you will come to learn all there is to know. Perhaps the Druids would be helpful. We could have a day out, a picnic in the forest." She twined her fingers, holding her hands against her chest. "There are others you should meet."

"I'd love to hang around and get to know you and Nemain, but I need to get back. Tell me more about this world." I gazed at my watch and inhaled a sharp breath.

The hands of time stood still. Since when? Yesterday? Was it yesterday? No, it was this day—this afternoon. I tapped the glass face with my fingertip. Two fifteen p.m. The exact moment the winds lifted Colm away. I gripped the windowsill, gazing over this Faerie kingdom.

Chickadees chirped, singing in unison within the branches of a nearby apple tree. A bold sun shone in a cloudless sky.

"Father is leaving the castle tomorrow for Knockma. He expects us to go with him. Did you choose your horse?" She looked sad.

"I did. Resurrection. I hate to leave him behind when I go." I turned toward her, refusing to acknowledge the obvious. How did I escape this underground world?

"You can't leave, Rioghain. There is much you need to learn." She placed her hand on my forearm. "Sit with me. Please."

"Show me how to call upon the mist. I can learn to journey later." I twined my hands together.

"Nemain is better to show you. I have no use for the *féth fiada*." She shrugged and looked away.

"Why not?" I said, my throat tightening as I watched the cat and its beaming eyes.

"I like it here." She gathered my teacup and walked away.

"What's that look for, Macha? What's wrong?" I said as I rose from the window seat and approached her.

"I don't enjoy Knockma. It's too big, too busy. Nuala lives there." She looked at me, her expression weary.

"Who is Nuala?" I inquired, taking a step back from the approaching feline.

"Father's wife, the Queen of the Realm," she said with a note of finality.

"The Queen...oh...I get it. Ériu was what? A salacious tryst? So, we're the love children of a sordid affair. Is that it?" I grinned, laughter bubbling inside me—the bastard children of a Faerie King.

Someone should write a book.

"Perhaps. Nemain steals the show, and Nuala hates her for it. I prefer lurking in the shadows." She smirked, revealing the true Macha behind those thick glasses—clever and smart.

"I'll bet. I wonder what she'll think of me?" I flinched. Why did I ask the question? What did it matter? Macha's furrowed brow left me guessing.

"Fin said we have great powers. Is that true?" I picked Macha's brain, searching for clues, hoping she would spill the tea.

"Nemain snares men's hearts. Toys with them. Destroys at whim." She sniffed, and yet her voice held admiration.

"She is a heartbreaker. Anyone can see that." I grinned.

"That's not what I mean." Her eyes widened.

"What do you mean?" I raised my chin, watching her every move.

"You'll have to decide for yourself. The last one was a kind gentleman, an artist. The poor soul pined away and died. She has no remorse. No conscience. Our sister leaves destruction in her wake." She tsked her tongue, her gaze fiery.

"And you hate her for it?" Silence followed my question. I tried another tactic. "And what about you, Macha? What is your extraordinary power?

"I have none." She pursed her lips.

"I don't believe that." I smiled, encouraging her to share more.

"I'm not beautiful like Nemain or you. I'm not good with people." She stood still, her facial muscles tense.

"Don't sell yourself short, sister. You've kept you and Nemain safe from this evil queen...she hasn't banished you from the kingdom, exiled you from the realm, transformed you into a white swan, or the teeny tiny fly you mentioned." I giggled. Macha's expression halted my laughter. "Not funny, huh?" I tried to understand. The bastard children of a high king. How many more of us were there?

In contrast, I lived an insulated life, loved by devoted parents who wanted me, haunted by fears I called my own. Somehow, those fears seemed insignificant now.

Bells rang across the castle grounds. I hurried toward the arched window.

Finvarra's dog sat on its haunches beneath the sprawling branches of a hazel tree, howling into the setting sun. I gaped at a candy-colored sky of purple smudges and soft pinks as day shifted to night. It was moody and magical.

"They're ready for us." Nemain burst through the arched door, her low-cut gown leaving nothing to the imagination. The gold circlet on her head sparkled with white diamonds. The metallic satin matched her eyes.

"Rioghain, this is for you." She presented me with a

golden crown embedded with red rubies. "It matches your dress." She set the gold band over my head.

"Let me see." Macha lifted her hand, taming my unruly locks. "There, you look amazing, Rioghain. Rubies for your ruby lips."

"A crown?" I touched the gold band, unable to pull my gaze from the reflecting glass. The regal woman staring back looked nothing like me.

Macha's smile urged me to follow.

"Is dinner always this formal?" I lifted my skirt, accompanying the two princesses. The marble walls glowed with gas light, golden sconces throwing bright flames.

"Father has invited the chiefs of every kingdom. A celebration to announce your arrival." Nemain looked over her strapless shoulder with an excited smile.

My mouth went dry.

Macha snapped her thumb against her index finger, and dancing lights followed us down the spiral staircase.

"My arrival?" My mind spun, absorbing this new magic. "How many kingdoms are there?"

"There are four: Munster, Leinster, Ulster, Connacht. Ulster shares its lands with Ulaid, where Prince Balor rules in his dear mother's stead." Macha shared her knowledge.

"Okay, I'm lost. I thought Finvarra was the king." I lifted my skirt and hurried after her.

"Father is the High King. The King of the *Daoine Sidhe*. Father rules over all the land." She stopped on the final landing, her gaze turning to Nemain.

"So, there are other kings and queens?" I gaped at Macha.

"Yes, but none as powerful." Nemain clapped her hands, buckling the air and sending magic in one particular direction. The single staircase transformed into something from a storybook palace. Three crystal flights spiraled downward, meeting on the marble floor below.

"How did you do that?" My eyes widened, and my mouth dropped open. I rushed forward, leaning over the glass railing and staring at the gathering crowd of unfamiliar faces.

White marble tiles veined with black flowed from one archway to another.

One particular arch stood out from the rest. Grounded by a twisting vine, eight mythical beasts stared in my direction, each more horrific than the last.

With a lion's body, a human face, and a scorpion's tail, the manticore, a creature said to swallow its victims whole.

A symbol of self-sacrifice, the pelican would pierce her breast to feed her young with her lifeblood.

A deadly stare from the basilisk, a rooster-serpent hybrid, turned men to stone.

I watched the harpy—her enchanting voice could lure men to their doom.

And the Griffin, who, with the wings of an eagle and a lion's body, would always serve as the king's protector.

I ignored the shiver running down my spine. I had seen this sculpture at a museum in France years earlier.

My gaze fixed on the remaining creatures: a two-headed, worm-like serpent coiled into a circle, the centaur drawing its bow, and the lion wiping its tracks with a sweep of its tail.

Mythical creatures, whom I hoped would never return to life.

"Things are not always what they seem, dear sister. We need to make a statement." Macha, the quiet one, spoke with a vehemence I wasn't used to hearing.

"Why?" Crystal columns twined with flowering garlands touched the domed ceiling, where translucent pearls reflected a pink sky.

My ears thudded, and I couldn't shake their screams. The mythical creatures cried out for freedom. Was I the only one who could hear them?

"We are the Triskele, and we will descend together." Her tight smile left no room to argue.

"That's what Finvarra said. I don't get it." I met her gaze.

"You will, once you learn how to journey. How to use your magic," Nemain piped up.

"It means you are not alone. Together, we are one." Macha pressed her lips together as a smile lit up her eyes.

"So, what are you saying? You complete me?" I giggled, reliving my other favorite movie. Macha raised one eyebrow. Nemain tilted her head.

I smiled, my heart torn and my thoughts conflicted. The mortal realm was the world I was most familiar with. I had never thought of leaving it until now.

Nemain squeezed my hand.

"How did you move the air like that? You realize, in my world...this...is an engineering nightmare. How did you do it?" I smoothed my palm over the railing and the lustrous display of twisted vines and crystallized flowers, unable to process this latest development.

"When you need your magic. It will come." Macha's lips curved upward.

"That's it? No secret? No magic spell?" I turned my head, taking in every detail of this enchanting place. Nothing was as it appeared. I told myself one thing: expect the unexpected.

"Think of something special to you. Picture it in your mind. Become one with your vision." Nemain sent me a knowing glance.

"You're serious?" I closed my eyes and imagined. One of my favorite places on Earth was the butterfly arboretum, where I would hide away from the world. I envisioned the lush foliage, the balmy atmosphere, and a kaleidoscope of colorful butterflies. I opened my eyes, and my imagination furled with fluttering soft wings, landing on leaf-covered tendrils—a million vibrant butterflies.

"See. You did that," Nemain smirked, gesturing toward the flurry of winged creatures.

"That's incredible." I extended my hand. Not one, but two black butterflies landed on my fingertips, bringing with them a premonition of death—shadows swirled, and my stomach twisted.

The dark duo soared upward, and I lost sight of them in the feathered greenery.

"It's time, Nemain. Father is waiting." Macha looked at me. With her hair pinned back, she couldn't hide her ethereal beauty.

That same sensation returned—a feather touch,

barely discernible. Most would pass it off as an imagined itch. Yet, I didn't imagine it. It was Macha, prowling through my mind. I detected no evil, only curiosity. I turned to her and smiled. "If you do that again, I'll kick your ass."

Her withdrawal was instant, like a breeze lifting leaves, and then she disappeared. Her cheek feathered, and she laughed—a hearty laugh that stayed with me.

7

C*alla*

Three trumpeters announced our arrival, silence falling over the crowd as we descended together.

My stilettos barely touched the red carpet as we arrived. Before entering the dining hall, I glanced backward—the fairytale staircase remained. I refused to question the extraordinary. I told myself it just was.

The King's table was more than impressive. A sturdy slab of whinstone rose above the dining floor, honoring the king. The marble pedestals showcased intricate scrollwork, while the tabletop featured striking black veins. Three high-backed chairs flanked each side of Finvarra's throne. To the right of the King sat three regal-looking young men, each beautiful in his own way. I wondered who they were.

My stomach filled with dancing sprites.

Three uniformed guards stood on either side of the King's table. All around the room, eyes met mine.

Servers, dressed in black, filled stemmed goblets with rich red wine while valets lit silver candelabras with white-gloved hands.

I inhaled a deep, calming breath and followed Macha toward the dais. Two of the three younger men gazed back, their silver-eyed expressions reflecting interest. Macha blushed, and Nemain tossed her head. My heart ached for Colm. I wondered where he was at that moment and wished he could be here with me.

I thanked the handsome valet, who ushered me to my seat, smoothed the folds of my dress, and waited for the spectacle to begin.

A man robed in white played a golden harp, filling the grand hall with sweet sounds and lulling the unsuspecting with peaceful notes.

"Rioghain, let me introduce Midir, Miach, and Cian, three of your brothers. You will meet the rest of our family when we arrive in Knockma." Finvarra motioned toward the younger men.

Midir raised his goblet, bowing his blonde head in acknowledgment. Miach's smile stayed steady. Cian, the only one with blue eyes, watched me.

"Brothers?" I tilted my head toward the trio.

Finvarra rose from the massive table and waved his arm. "Tonight, we celebrate a foretold reunion. Nemain, the beautiful. Macha, the wise, and Rioghain, the prophetess. Together as one. Raise your glasses, everyone. Let us honor the Triskele. Long live the princesses of the *Tuatha De*." Finvarra appeared regal, his emerald-green coat fastened with a golden brooch, and the crown on his head sparkled with diamonds. His voice echoed throughout the hall amid quiet murmurs and the clinking of glasses.

The guests from the four kingdoms sat at a half-moon table made from the twisted roots of a mighty oak, ensuring each guest had a front-row seat with an equal view. Their echoing responses filled the room. Golden goblets clanked as glasses lifted and drained. The wine flowed this evening.

I studied each handsome face and lithe body, reminded of another race of beings—ancient sea rovers from another time. Not mortal. All wore gold circlets—simple gold bands, some more exquisitely jeweled than others. One kingdom looked different from all the rest. Those folk had big heads and soft bodies. Quick to smile, their quizzical brown eyes met mine, yet I detected no hostility. I stared too long at their wide, long feet. Each kingdom, represented by a royal entourage of queens and kings, princes and princesses, and nobility of various ranks, except for one.

He sat alone. A wealth of copper ringlets spilled onto his shoulders, framing his narrow face, while the golden band crowning his head shimmered with black stones. Fitted to his lean frame, he wore fine silks in the darkest green. Silver gilt embroidered his collarless coat, while his waistcoat showcased a brocade of oversized yellow silk florals and silver threads. A formal black ruffled cravat embraced his long neck, illuminating the darkness in his sunken eyes.

His valet, dressed in matching velveteen livery, stood alone, his eyes wary.

Finvarra's guests gave the lonely man plenty of space

— no one dared to sit too close or start a conversation. I noticed.

He lifted his crystal goblet toward me, his gaze challenging mine. Unnatural darkness enveloped him. My senses urged me to look away.

Finvarra's deep voice made me turn my head. "Rioghain, these are your people—the chieftains of the realm and everyone present. All will see you as the daughter of Finvarra, a princess of the realm."

"Father, will there be dancing?" Nemain tilted her face, her ruby lips glowing in the candlelight as the servers set down golden bowls filled with fragrant lobster bisque before us.

"Yes, darling. The floor awaits your presence." Finvarra leaned back in his chair, a smile playing on his lips.

Midir chuckled, which earned him a scathing look from Nemain.

"Father, I would rather not attend the ball." Macha's bottom lip quivered as she shot him a dark glance.

"Macha, play nice. This is for Rioghain." Finvarra's gaze passed to me.

"Excuse me? Looky here, Fin. I'm not into meeting the tribe, if you know what I mean. Pass the buns, Nev." I murmured to Nemain. "This soup is fantastic."

The server, hovering within earshot, presented a silver bowl filled with dark bread and crusty buns. The aroma made my mouth water.

While the harp growled, filling the hall with resonant bass notes and angelic brilliance, I observed the distinguished figures engaging with occasional laughter. There was an air of familiarity or friendly rivalry. I sensed an underlying tension—each chieftain watching Finvarra with caution.

Respect? Animosity? A flicker of doubt crossed my mind. The chatter halted as the meal was served.

Seafood was the theme of the day. My stomach rumbled, stirred by the flavorful soup. Savory snow crab. Meaty lobster tails. Sweet mussels, briny oysters. The next course arrived, with servers balancing platters of king salmon and asparagus drizzled with whipped butter.

The sweet taste of wine, liquor, and desserts danced on my tongue. I looked at the variety of treats—honey cakes, honey-glazed fruit, and tarts filled with blueberries, peaches, or strawberries—all topped with dollops of honey.

"Rioghain, try the ice cream." Macha pointed to the crystal bowls of lavender-honey ice cream decorated with rose petals and a raspberry shortbread stick.

Dinner ended with the servants guiding Finvarra, Nemain, Macha, and me from the dining hall toward the grand ballroom. The brothers lined up with the guards, while the guests waited out of respect or fear—I wasn't sure which. "Stand with me, Rioghain. Meet the kings and queens of the realm." Finvarra offered his elbow, inviting me to the front of the line.

If the dining hall was spectacular, the ballroom took my breath away. Translucent walls of shimmering pearl formed a perfect circle, rising three stories high, with a floor of black obsidian. My gaze drifted upward—the domed ceiling looked like an ink-black sky twinkling with starlight. Archways invited lovers onto a balcony overlooking the ancient forest. A gentle breeze wafted through, filling the hall with the fragrances of jasmine, honeysuckle, and evening primrose.

Macha tugged at my sleeve, leaned in close, whispered her parting words, and left me surrounded by strangers. I watched her slip through the looking glass and disappear. See you later, alligator.

Finvarra greeted each guest by name, introducing me as his rightful daughter, the lost lamb who had come home. One by one, I met the kings and queens of each of the four kingdoms.

"Rioghain, let me introduce Prince Balor of the Kingdom of Ulaid. Please accept our condolences, Balor. It came as a shock to all of us." He nodded, sadness in his eyes. "We will miss Queen Etain. She was a lively spirit, and an accomplished chess master." Finvarra rested his hand on the small of my back, his fingertips guiding me toward the man whose gaze I held.

The prince, who stood six inches taller than Finvarra, undressed me with a fiery gaze, his lips curling into a lecherous smile.

Finvarra's attention shifted to the next guest, leaving Prince Balor in my capable hands. I pressed my lips together, my glance resolute in indifference.

"I'm sorry for your loss." I offered my sympathies and turned away. Surely, I could blow this pop stand soon. Dancing the night away was not on my agenda. If I had used my time more wisely and learned their ways, I could have shifted into another being. I could have *féth fiada'd* my way out of here.

"Thank you for your kind words." He took my hand

and pressed his lips onto my first knuckle. Was that respect? The niceties of the court? "You honor this realm with your presence, my lady."

Dismay filled my heart. I had hoped the handsome prince would disappear and crawl back to whatever cave he came from. Fuck.

As if on cue, the curtain fell, and darkness covered my eyes. Finvarra's voice faded, and the crowd dispersed. The vision appeared in vibrant color.

The wounded man toppled from his steed, landing inches from my hiding place. Blood seeped from a fatal wound, staining the rider's vest. His mouth gaped and his lungs rattled. Sorrow filled his silver eyes.

Prince Balor turned his wrist, lifted my hand, and took two steps forward. Taking Finvarra's place, he presented me to the dance floor and the waiting crowd.

The minstrels flourished their bows, drawing notes high and low. Ladies in flowing gowns curtsied, accompanied onto the dance floor by handsome partners.

"May I have this dance, Princess?" He tilted his head, his roaming gaze resting on my exposed cleavage.

"Of course." My voice trembled as the dying man's last words echoed in my mind, *"Why? Why, Balor?"* My gaze darted across the room toward Finvarra, alive and well—for now. My skirts whispered as I crossed the room, my hand in Balor's. I silently thanked my adoptive parents for teaching me how to dance. At the very least, I wouldn't embarrass myself.

He led me through the parting crowd, his long stride leaving no room for discourse.

With a quick bow, Prince Balor pulled me close. He

tilted his head, whispering in my ear. "We will rule this kingdom. We will share in the bounty."

The shadows receded, exposing the fierce stare of the person who murdered the High King of the *Daoine Sidhe* —Macha's childhood love.

I tore my hand away, searching through the sea of heads. Pretty women surrounded Finvarra. Nemain, lost in her pleasure, spun on the arm of a blond-haired man. Macha had left me. What happened to,' together, we are one'?

"Fear not, Rioghain. We share the same thoughts— the same abilities. My mother, gods rest her soul, gave me her gifts at an early age. I have awaited your arrival, dear one." Balor lifted my hand, taking two slow steps forward, moving with perfect precision in sync with the fiddler's strokes.

"I don't know who you think I am, but I'm not that person." I pressed my thumb into a solid pectoral muscle, my sweaty palm leaving an imprint on his fine silks.

"The time without you feels like eternity. My dearest love, how long I have dreamed of this moment." Two swift sidesteps, and he twirled me against his chest, his breath hot on the nape of my neck, too hot.

"I think you have me confused with someone else." Unease washed over me. I should back away. There were so many things I should have done at that moment. Instead, I followed his lead, performing a quick box step across the floor to the approving glances of those watching.

"The banners will rise in your honor, my queen. The giants will bow to your beauty." He lifted my hand.

"Giants? What giants? I'm sorry, but I don't even know you." I squared my shoulders, tearing my hand away.

"There is much to discuss. Come with me, please." He motioned toward the open doors that led to a balcony bathed in moonlight. The full moon shone over the dark forest, creating a magical glow across the land. If only it were so.

"All right, five minutes." I stared into his evil eyes, my mind racing. Lifting my skirts, with the Prince of Evil shadowing my every move, I crossed the expansive terrace and turned toward him, this man from my premonition.

"Let us converse where away from meddling minds." He clasped my elbow, lifting me onto my tiptoes, and guided me toward a more hidden corner shielded by fragrant vines.

"Excuse me? What are you doing?" I struggled, unable to loosen his grip, as the urgency of the situation revealed itself.

"I wish to taste what is mine, dearest Rioghain." He dug his fingers into the soft skin beneath my forearm, hemming me between his bulk and the stone balustrade.

"Ow! What are you doing?" Disbelief flooded my heart. I had heard and read about men forcing themselves on women. I was naïve to think it couldn't happen to me. I jammed my palms against his chest, breaking free from his grasp.

"You will know who you belong to." His voice rasped with rage, his lips curling into a snarl. His fingers tore through my hair, gripping the braided tendrils. When he twisted his wrist, yanking my head upward, white lights flickered behind my eyelids. The pain was almost over-whelming. Four long seconds passed, and I felt each one—blind shock, white-hot agony, flaming anger, and black rage.

What did I know about self-defense? Only one thing: the best form of self-defense was attack.

"I said stop." I locked eyes with my assailant, thrusting my arms toward him, kicking his shin with the pointed toe of my stiletto. He was unmoving.

He chuckled, his deep laugh instilling fear in me. His goal was total domination.

"Don't fight me—Finvarra's sweet princess. Do not think of screaming; no one will come to your aid, not even that foolish little dwarf. What was his name? Seamus? I took care of him, pet. The pesky servant no longer holds Finvarra's ear. He is now bound to the form of an ant." He pressed his forearm against my windpipe, cutting off my breath, his low snarl sending ice through my veins.

"What? Are you out of your mind?" I twisted under his grip.

"I've set the glamour, dear one. Should anyone venture forth, they would see a happy couple engaged in private conversation. Do not doubt me." He leaned close, taking a quick inhale.

"Let me go." I fought back against him.

"With you by my side, the chieftains will recognize my rightful claim as King of *Daoine Sidhe*. You will give me what I desire. You will understand your place." His eyes turned cold, and he struck me with a stinging back-hand across the cheek.

My jaw cracked, and tears filled my eyes. The weight of this moment went unnoticed. In the ballroom, the minstrels played beautiful melodies, the laughter and music blending into a wall of white noise.

He greeted my stunned gaze with a harsh cackle, jolting the horror back into the moment.

Stars danced in the sky above, swirling motes of mist rising from the ground below. I inhaled through my nose and exhaled through my mouth, the night air cooling my fevered mind.

"I know what you are and who you are. What's the plan? Have your way with me? Murder Finvarra? You think you will take my father's crown just like that?" My hands clenched into fists. Struggling was out of the question. I needed a different approach. Charm? Wit? I lost that battle a long time ago.

"My dearest one." He fingered the ruched bodice of my gown, a groan rumbling in his throat. "So beautiful. How long have I waited for this moment?"

"I'm not your dearest one, and take your fucking hands off me." I lifted my knee, thrusting my kneecap into his groin. He didn't seem to notice.

"I hoped to take you with your ready consent." He caged me against the stones, lifting his palm in silent warning. "Don't make me strike you again."

"I will never be yours. Not now. Never." I refused him, pressing my lips into a tight line.

"But you will, my lovely. Destiny wills it. Did you not come to me in your dreams? How many times have I satisfied your desires? Our union will be complete tonight beneath this moon. She shines for us." He yanked my head back, so we were face-to-face. "Smile, my princess, and do not let cross thoughts fill your mind. Tonight is for our happiness." That was when he drew his tongue along the seam of my lips.

"Are you crazy? You fucking piece of shit. I won't have you." I choked out an insult, bile rising in my throat, my heart shuddering within. The copper-haired man I dreamed of was Colm, only Colm. Not this psycho prince.

"What a vixen you are." He tore my bodice from its stays, leaving the silk in tatters, ripping my lacy brassiere and exposing my breasts to the night. "You will be a most worthy consort, I see that now. The enjoyment we will have. Imagine it, my sweet..."

"Let go of me. Who do you think you are?" Vanity overshadowed reason, and I squandered precious moments trying to hide my flesh from his hungry gaze.

"I will have you. This very eve. The prophecy foretold it." He pressed his arousal into the folds of my skirt, groping my breasts with heavy hands, molesting each swell.

My vision blurred, and my mind numbed. Mist fell over the shadowy timber wood, folding over the manicured fields.

"Tonight is just the beginning." He grabbed my wrist and, with one smooth motion, spun me around, my arm bent behind my back.

The balustrade offered some support to my wobbling knees. My heart fluttered like a little bird, white lightning shot through my mind, and rational thoughts stopped. I sank into him, resting my head on his shoulder— anything to ease the pain. I had no hope of escaping.

And in that moment, I envisioned the future—one of my own making. My ears rang with the sounds of someone else's screams as Balor crawled across the forest floor, his fine clothes muddy, begging for his life and forgiveness. But I was no longer who I once was. I had become something else.

"Don't fight me, dear one." He pressed my elbow into my lower back, contorting my arm and forcing my hips to collide with the stone railing. It was then that I accepted the inevitable. I was not strong enough. I was not enough. His brute force was greater.

"I will take you. Now." He shoved me forward, bending my waist over the railing. "You will be what I want you to be. And tonight, you will be my whore." He rutted against the fleshy curves of my bottom, his breath hissing with each burgeoning throe.

"Stop. You must stop." My mind wavered on the edge as I fought to free myself, but it was no use. The stone rail held fast. I was his prisoner. That's when my imagination took me elsewhere, where a peaceful lake shimmered beneath a tall waterfall. "You're going to die, Balor," I said in a gravelly voice, uttering a prophecy of my own.

Down below, a dog barked—Finvarra's hound.

"We're all going to die. But that day is not today. Now. Give yourself to your prince." He seized my skirt, tossing the folds over my back. He groped my inner thighs and, in one swift moment, tore my panties in two, exposing my most private parts.

The dog howled, yipped, and jumped into the air.

"Never. You will never have me." I trembled against

his might. I wanted to scream, but the lump in my throat made breathing too difficult.

"My seed is bountiful, Princess. Perhaps we will conceive an heir to my throne." He chuckled as he undid the buttons on his trousers. "But before we begin, we will shut up this stupid dog."

I watched him, my eyes wide, as he slipped his hand into his boot and pulled out a short dagger, its silver hilt covered with moving runes.

"No. No. You won't." I threw my hand back, knocking the magical dagger from his.

"Bitch." He wrapped his forearm around my neck, cutting off my breath.

"You fucking bastard." My voice shook. My throat strangled. I couldn't breathe. I couldn't swallow.

"They will not come for you. My powers are greater than even your king's—made of the blood of my enemies." His voice echoed through the woods, followed by a profound silence.

But then voices shouted out. Glass shattered. Chaos closed in on us. He looked over his shoulder, his blood-curdling scream matching mine. Magnificent and deadly, the serpent unfurled a snake-like tail, its arrow-shaped tip lengthening and stretching into a second snout—the two-headed dragon, born from Medusa's blood, had escaped its marble tomb—for me. The creature swooped low, slipping through the open double doors of the great hall and landing on clawed talons just an arm's length away. Battle-scarred and venomous, the twins took deep breaths, revealing a monster mouth filled with jagged teeth. I watched in horror as four tufted ears twitched, while four black slits surrounded by gold stared back at us. Awestruck, I studied the armored ridges along the creature's leathery spine, with turquoise wing feathers tucked against shimmering crimson scales. Had I imagined the beast in a moment of panic? Hell yes. It understood. It knew its purpose.

My throat tightened, constricting more and more than the serpent coiling around Balor's struggling frame, engaged in a game of tug-of-war, squeezing the life breath from the prince.

Balor's glamour was no match for this mythical monster.

"Leave her this moment." Cian was there, and the serpent had vanished, moonlight glinting off the short blade held to Balor's throat.

Balor dropped his arms to his sides, shrieking in defiance.

Was it just a figment of my imagination, or had I summoned the beast? The remains of the lavish dining hall, with overturned tables and shattered glass, told the story.

"Sister." My half-brother dipped his head, his soft murmur meant only for my ears.

Six uniformed soldiers appeared from within the castle's depths, each brandishing long swords, forming a protective arc around their king. Finvarra strode onto the balcony, his face red with rage.

"You hide behind your father's throne, halfling. Release me." Balor's hand shifted and went for a second dagger, strapped to his thigh.

"You dare eat at my father's table. You dare accost

Princess Rioghain." Cian disarmed him with a single blow, slamming Balor's face into the paving stones. "You worthless piece of shite."

Bran lifted his head and howled—a mournful, lonely call. From somewhere far away, an answer came.

The moon chased the stars across the night sky, and light flickered within the branches of the dark woods. I stared through the drifting clouds at the unfolding scene. Crows. Blackbirds. Ravens. Birds of a feather, a river of them coming to land within the branches. They spoke my name. They offered freedom. Escape. Was that not what I had wanted? To leave the hurt behind? Their cries cut through the dark woods—each, on their own, was striking, but together, they moved minds. I craved what they offered—the endless sky, the sweet aroma of the night flowers. The darkness spoke, loud in its silence, and for once, I listened. The wind lifted me, and the breeze swept me away. I was free, free from the human body that constrained.

I SPIRALED DOWN AND AWAY, the lacy greenery offering a brief refuge, a comfort for my fluttering heart. I spread my wings and floated through the tree canopy, my heart pounding against my chest. It was wonderful all at once, but there was no time to ponder. I landed on the forest floor and, with fire in my heart, became myself again.

"Holy shit. Sweet mother of Jesus, I did it." I hugged myself, rocking back and forth. Fear fueled this change. Was that what it took? I didn't like being scared. A shudder ran through me—a wave of nausea. I lurched forward, digging my hands into the ground, and retched, expelling the fear, shame, and disgust. It was all too real.

"Rioghain, my dearest. Did you think I wouldn't come for you? Where have you gotten to, little one? Your heart calls to mine, you see, as it always will," Balor whispered from somewhere deep within the shadowy woods.

My heart stuttered. No—I screamed inside my head. How could it be? How had he escaped Cian's blade? Was his power that great?

The pine thicket sheltered me, providing safety from my pursuer. I pressed against the rough bark, concealing myself within the greenery.

"I saw you soaring on such fine, silken wings, and it filled me with pride to see you return to your familiar form, flying with the wind. We will cross the currents of time, from this world to the next—as we will in Ulaid— no, what am I saying? The entire land. Do you hear me? Did you think that a halfling prince could fight my will?" His crazed rant sent shivers down my spine. He observed the quiet woods, tilting his head and waiting for my next move.

How did he find me? Oh, please tell me we are not the same. This was not the man who made love to me in my dreams. My chest heaved, and my lungs burned. I turned away from the confusion. I would not let him win this battle.

I exhaled a deep breath as the darkness lifted, giving way to blue twilight. The mist drifted through the old-growth forest, cloaking the ground with ghostly fingers.

"Let us begin our life together, my sweet Rioghain.

The shadows you call upon will not hide you forever," his voice rose in a smug retort.

I dared not move. I dared not rustle my skirt. I pressed my hands over my mouth, trying not to scream. What was once a beautiful ball gown was now torn and hanging in shreds. Denying him had brought me to this place. A storm of emotions surged within me. Blind trust had allowed this to happen—an illusion that persuasion held power. Who was I to believe that feminine charm could change the mind of a psychotic person?

I suspected my earlier vision would come true, and at any moment, I would see Finvarra's death. Balor planned to take his place as High King and ruler of the realm, and his sick mind had decided he needed me to do his bidding.

This prick had bruised my lips and stained my skin with his touch. He had instilled fear in my heart, and I was done with fear. I left the shadows and stood tall, my shoulders straight, "I am here, Prince A-Hole."

"Do you hear the horses thrashing through the glen? Someone is coming. To your rescue, perhaps? Your halfling brother will be too late, dearest one, for all his talents and the castle guards—none of their magic can match mine." He lifted his hands to his throat, adjusting his silk scarf.

"Oh? Why is that, Balor? Let me guess. You're the spawn of the devil. Is that it?" Conversation was a pleasant distraction. My mind searched for a way out. Rescue seemed unlikely. Shifting. Transforming. Traveling in the guise of someone else. Even if I could do that again, I wouldn't succeed. This bastard could follow me anywhere.

"Conceived in a hellstorm? Think what you like, dear one, but our children will rule this kingdom and the next. Let me take you to a place where you will be safe from meddling minds." His head tilted as he listened to the sounds of the forest, not a hair out of place on his wicked head, the silver threads outlining the flamboyant florals glimmering in the moonlight. He looked princely. He placed his index finger to his chin. "The two-headed beast was a nice touch, though. For one so young, your abilities are impressive."

"You have seen nothing yet, you bastard," I whispered under my breath.

"Hmm, I sense a mortal in the realm. Someone you know, maybe?" His laughter echoed off the shimmering water. "Your human is no match for this land. Did you call for him, my sweet? Now, that was not very smart."

"You have your own kingdom, Balor. Why would you want another?" My human? Colm? Big. Brawny. Sweet Colm.

"Are you daft? I want what every king wants. Power. Riches. And you are? What do your people call it? My ace in the hole." His eyes were two piss holes in the sand.

"That will not happen." I tilted my head and smiled. Cocky. Reassured. I had had enough.

"You refuse me? You, with your fiery address. Look at you. Ruined. So much like the others." He chuffed a quick laugh, his voice cutting.

I sensed something else in his tone—doubt in his ability to please a woman.

"And you're a dick. A real piece of work. What happened to Mom? Are you the cause of her demise? Did you murder your mother?" Rage burned in my heart. Still, fear lifted the hairs on my nape. They were related. The level of emotion was key. I saw that now. I understood.

"Arrah, a worthless woman with no expectations, content with the petty drops Finvarra handed out... Not me, Princess. No one can stop me. Should you escape, which you won't, not this time — I will spend all of eternity hunting you down. I've waited for your arrival, but maybe that was a mistake. I should have taken you sooner, yet there was much to be done in preparation. The politics of the court. My bitch mother and her sycophants. How easily I dealt with them." He curled his lips into a snarl, dragging his thumb along the edge of his jaw. "Of all Finvarra's cunnies, you hold the most promise. But maybe the plain one? Yes? She exudes a certain charm."

My mind exploded, my heart beating in my ears like ocean waves crashing on the shore. The thought of this monster doing to Macha what he tried to do to me pushed me over the edge. I saw what he was, where he had been, and what he would become. The time for talking was over. What kind of eloquent rebuttal could a monster offer?

He rambled on, spouting one psychotic sentence after another. Gods, he loved the sound of his own voice. I hugged my chest, hmm-ing and nodding like that sweet little dandelion I never was.

The mist rising from the ground caught my attention. Shadows appeared—the departed, those who had whispered my name in the dark woods. How many times had they invited me to join? This was my chance to make a change, for better or worse. What could be worse? I couldn't, no, I wouldn't wait for rescue. It was time to track some mud on the carpet. I left my physical form behind and followed the shadows into that watery realm, knowing who and what I was for the first time. A spectral? A scald-crow? I could be whatever I wanted to be. The possibilities were endless.

I soared with the wind, the ocean currents guiding me to a place where the dead gathered—Tech Duinn, the House of the Dark One.

My descent slowed, and I became myself again. I turned in a circle, scraping my foot along the stone floor, worn by salt and sea, my breath echoing. I ran my tongue over my bottom lip, tasting the ocean's brine. A chill numbed my mind and froze my heart. I wasn't sure if I was dead or alive. This realm of the dead was dark and foreboding, but beyond the great hall lay a labyrinth of passages lit by torchlight. Echoes bounced from afar: a woman's voice, a child's laughter.

The vault shimmered with a million facets of diamond light while stalagmite pillars glowed in the darkness. And yet, it was more. This was a gallery, a meeting place.

He stepped out of the shadows, the scarred man—my grandfather, Donn, the Lord of the Dead, a hooded cloak concealing his face. He appeared taller than I remembered, but he was still the same man who had welcomed me in Finvarra's stables. John—Nemain had called the stable master, John.

"You have gone against your mother's wishes." His unseeing gaze fixed on mine, those glassy orbs swirling with shadow spirits—this ancient one, who, in the world of disbelievers, should not exist. In this underworld, he was very much alive. Who would guide those dead souls into the next world other than he?

"I have. I wish to use dark magic, Grandfather. I ask for your blessing." My conviction rang true. I was, without a doubt, Finvarra's daughter. That was a jaw-dropping moment.

"Do you know what you ask?" For someone who could not see, he crept around me, moving with the stealth of a panther at night. This was not the hunched and fragile man I met before. This man, leathered and scarred, had been battered by the sea and lived. "There is no coming back from such a place. It is not without consequences." His voice was lustrous and deep, touched with iron.

I closed my eyes, feeling dizzy from his scrutiny. I should have asked what he meant, but I didn't. Whatever the cost, I would pay it.

"I believe you do." He offered his hand, his fingers ringed with gold.

I examined the gold rings, engraved with intricate swirls and runes that glistened in the light, those runes reminding me of the dagger Balor wielded.

"What will happen?" I thought to ask, but still, my hand slipped into his icy grasp.

I staggered as my joints loosened and those diamond lights went out, leaving me alone in the darkness. The three red horsemen, alive but dead, whispered a deathly omen of hunger, want, and a need so great that I fell backward. Only his grip kept me grounded through the time slip. My stomach tightened as the ball of heat exploded, burning a fresh path through my veins.

Shadows pressed down on me as I left my grandfather's house. I spread my wings, soaring through swirling clouds and stormy skies, the wind tearing at me, the moon casting painted light over dark spires. The waterfall, which flowed downward moments ago, funneled white fury upward into the sky above. Donn, the Lord of the Dead, had given his blessing, granting me the power to wield his dark hand.

I saw Balor as a crazed, vile creature. The bastard who had murdered his mother to serve his own gain. Was redemption even possible? Once done, it couldn't be undone. Whispering voices clamored for attention. The noise faded, giving way to clarity. I judged him without bias.

I denounced his existence.

Another spoke to me, her voice growing louder. I called upon her wisdom and ferocious nature. Protector of the People, the Guardian of this Land, and the Sovereignty Goddess of all that existed, she was the Morrigan, the Celtic Goddess of War. Bloodlust filled my soul, hers and mine—my mouth watered for retribution. I left the past and followed a different course.

Two crows, one deathly white and one shining black, joined me on my quest. Their magic became mine. Together, we were one.

I stood at the lake's edge, expanding my mind and reaching into the shadows. The edges blurred, and her image became clear—the legendary *Oilliphéist*, the Celtic Monster of the deep, dwelled within this realm. She had hinted at her presence the moment I arrived. Had she known the role she would play? I left the land, wading through the shallows, and met this reptilian queen on her terms. I had no doubt she would answer my call.

The lake shimmered with a crimson hue as the sea serpent emerged, slicing through the moving water and sweeping her horned head within inches of mine, contemplating my existence through slitted yellow eyes. Water cascaded over razor-sharp spikes and rippling scales.

"You wake me from my slumber, Princess Rioghain." Fiery flames licked her forked tongue, her hide shimmering rose-gold in the moon's glow.

"You know who I am?" I placed my hand on her armored snout and touched her magic.

"The land knows of you." She bowed to my caress. "I am Caoránach, the mother of all sea demons."

"I ask for your help, Curr-un-aah." I pointed to the animal on shore—Balor, with his mouth hanging open.

He wavered, then paused. His hesitation was almost funny.

"I have fought many enemies. I have lived long. My children dwell within the waters and rivers flowing through this land. We heed your call, Princess Rioghain." She bowed with a slight dip of her magnificent head, allowing me to live within her iridescent scales and to use her power as my own.

The air thickened, charged with a hum that crawled beneath my skin. It was a soughing hiss I knew well—a ripple that stretched skin, cracked joints, and lengthened bones.

The veil remembered.

My breath slowed as my thoughts intertwined with hers. Shaped by ancient magic, she had existed for millennia. I left my shadow behind and merged with a sea serpent—a full surrender to the wild. I unfurled my great wings, embracing the weightless strength of spider silk. The transformation was complete.

I turned toward the lost prince, the gurgling sound in his throat stirring my hunger—an instinct took over, a sharp and silent need. I was no longer the victim. I was the hunter.

I snapped my jaws, drooling venom through poison-filled fangs, gazing with glowing eyes, breathing Caorá-nach's fire. My heartbeat? Slow and steady. My mind? Clear.

The wind whispered in an ancient language, carrying memories and secrets—her secrets. Caoránach's kills became my own—giants, kings, lovers, and friends. I surrendered to the bloodlust, and it consumed me, drifting in the dark abyss, my mind slipping away, the tether unravelling. Lightning flashed across the dark sky, and the scent of the storm ignited my rage.

"No. No. Gods help me. What is this? This is not possible." The whites of his eyes showed his fear, his screams climbing higher.

"You will harm no others in hell, Prince Balor." Caorá-nach's fire danced before him.

"You speak of hell. Ha. Hell will not contain me." He

twisted his wrist, his fingers throwing lightning bolts in my direction.

My anger erupted. I roared, igniting an ash tree in flames.

Balor lifted his hands, shielding his face from the fury.

I battled with fire, one monster to another. Leaving behind my innocence, I embraced my fate—this time, with open arms. I swung her horned tail, lifting the waters and causing a tidal wave to sweep across the forest floor.

His eyes glowed, then the light faded, and his screams diminished to whimpers.

Thrusting those great wings, I soared into the moonbeam and spiraled downward, hell's fury showing the way.

"What say you, Prince Balor?" I zeroed in on my prey —the steam from my breath melting the flesh from his face.

"I wish to parlay." His voice screamed. His fingers reached toward the sky, asking for what? Redemption?

Flaring her wings slowed my fall. Perched on the mountain's black toe, I spewed blue flames in one direction only, leaving Balor's charred remains and his petrified bones on the lake's shore.

The moon cast a gentle, milky glow. The waterfall roared as it plunged from the cliff into the pool below.

My task complete, I sent Caoránach back to her murky home.

She lifted her golden eyes one last time as I whispered my thanks—firelights floating across the shimmering pool before vanishing.

I stood at the water's edge, fire touched with ice burning in my soul, teetering on the brink of madness, with oblivion still fresh on my tongue. My jaws ached, and my mouth tasted like desire. I lingered in it a moment too long.

War cries echoed through the pines. "O'Donnell Abú! O'Donnell to Victory!" Colm... guardian of the peace— my hero. The voice was his.

The leaves rustled, and the branches whispered—my name. How long had it been since someone called me that? Calla. Calla Sweet. That was another version of myself.

My senses awakened. I stretched my fingers and turned my neck, my gaze resting on the ancient oak tree bathed in moonlight. The wind sighed through her gnarled branches as images flashed by—Nemain and Macha and the laughter we shared—those fleeting moments flickered before my eyes. I brushed my fingers over the thorny blackberry bush, the ones that proved their blood was mine—immortal faerie blood.

The moonlit waters reflected a princess, a regal figure wearing a ruby-studded crown, with my hair flowing down my back, loose and wild as it should be. An apple-red gown with a full skirt brushing my ankles. Golden slippers replacing the strappy black stilettos, and an extra detail—a single strand of black sea pearls resting on my neckline. I searched for the clasp, but I couldn't find one. I knew where they came from.

It was Colm's melodic voice floating on the breeze,

calling my name and breaking the silence of the ether. This time, it was louder.

"Calla." Colm burst through the underbrush. "*Mo grhá*, are ye safe?" His clothes were torn. His face ragged, with stubble covering his jaw, yet his eyes burned with blue fire. He wrapped his arms around me, our breath mingling.

There was no fear. Only need. I caught his bottom lip, sweeping my tongue against his, tasting him. He was here. He was mine.

"Did you miss me, *mo ghrá*?" A slow grin spread across his face as he ran his fingers through my hair.

"You came for me." I raised my hand to touch his face. The man I loved stood before me, the same but somehow different.

He dared to smirk—that crooked grin that lifted one side of his mouth while his chin dropped and his eyelids shuttered. That movie star grin was my undoing.

When his teeth grazed my lower lip and his tongue chased mine, I responded with a hunger that consumed my soul, if I still had one.

I sank into him, feeling all that was wrong and all that was right. My hands slipped beneath his sweater, the same one he wore on the beach the night before, over rippling muscles.

His eyes shone with a mix of relief and agony. He cradled the back of my head, then leaned his forehead on mine.

"You smell different. You feel different. What happened to your face?" I placed my hands on his muscular chest and examined the gash above his eyebrow.

"I saw ye in a dream—I saw this." He nodded toward the lake and the waterfall flowing down.

"What did you see?" I held his face in my hands, delving into his thoughts. Something or someone slammed the door shut.

"There is something I must tell you, something you need to know." His eyes shadowed yet gleamed at the same time. Otherworldly. Supernatural.

Who was this being standing before me?

"What did you do, Colm?" I traced the curve of his cheek with my fingertips, while my mouth watered for more of him.

"I've realized so many things. How much I need you. How much I love you." He kissed the top of my head. "The force that took ye away. Was it the High King?"

"Yes, Orlaith was right all along: Finvarra is my father. Is Ciarán back? Did he return?" How could I explain all of this? Would he still want me after what I had become? I fingered the black pearls around my neck, my eyes drifting to the shimmering waters and the majestic sea serpent just a thought away.

"Did you do that, *mo grhá*? Tell me you didn't exchange your life for his? For Ciarán's?" His eyes darkened, and his hands clenched into fists. I watched him pace back and forth, his boots silent on the forest path.

"Sort of. So much has changed. I have sisters, Colm. Brothers, too." I reached for those happy thoughts, unwilling to face the monster I had become.

"Men are looking for ye. They ransacked your wee

cottage." He lifted his hand to his forehead, to the seeping gash. "They hurt Eamon."

"Eamon? Is he all right?" I gasped for the breath I had lost.

"I left him with Ciarán and Saoirse. The men hunting you have your DNA. They plan to prove the immortal world exists." He looked at me, his eyes cold, his face pale.

"Colm?" I recognized the familiar melodic lilt, now intertwined with a primal edge—a throaty voice rich with blood and bone. I lifted my hand to caress his face. I wanted to touch him.

"It's all right, I am here." He pressed my knuckles to his lush lips.

"My DNA? Oh, I forgot about that." I closed my fingers over my palm, hiding the teardrop mark. I remembered thinking that it would be fun, finding family through DNA. "Okay, but what is this, Colm? What did you do?" My gaze flicked over his defined muscles and the fury burning in his eyes.

"I thought. I didn't believe I could find you without asking for help, Otherworldly help." He cupped my face in his hands, his gentle touch evoking memories of the person I wanted to be.

"Otherworldly help?" The words hung in the air. I gazed into his eyes, so full of shadows. It couldn't be, could it?

"The O'Donnell's are an ancient clan, Calla. We, O'Donnell's, have deep roots in this land." He swallowed hard, his Adam's apple bobbing in his throat.

I remembered the day we met—the drive to Donegal

town with the rugged Celt, his haunted look when we passed Donegal Castle, and his words: "It's complicated."

Thunder rumbled across the sky, and a bolt of lightning struck through me. Colors exploded behind my eyelids—too many to count. Did the magic of this land have no limits?

"It was a long time ago. It was Samhain. My brothers and I agreed." He held my hands, his gaze begging me to understand. As if I wouldn't?

"What kind of pact? With whom?" I looked into the ancient within him: the proud young man I had seen once before in a vision. He was so filled with hatred that he set fire to Donegal Castle, his home, burning most of it down. My vision was real. All of it was real. Colm's warrior ancestor bore a striking resemblance to the man standing before me. It was he who gazed through Colm's fiery eyes. The same young man lived inside the man I loved.

"We were just kids, Calla. We didn't understand the consequences of our actions. We called upon our ancestors, inviting them to rise by the sacred fires. One by one, they appeared." Turmoil twisted within those baby blues.

"All right. A nice fireside chat, yeah? Nothing wrong with a bit of ancestor worship." My heart raced. He had committed the unthinkable. Conspiring with the dead? This was more than I had expected.

"The Dark Lady offered more—their insight for ours." He bowed his head, his voice wavering, yet the fire in his eyes burned.

"The Dark Lady?" Dread washed over me. What did I

know about the dead? Only what my grandfather had allowed me to see.

"They shared their souls, and we shared ours." He lowered his gaze before turning to me.

"Have you done this before?" I closed my hands on either side of his face and stared into him, willing the man I loved to return.

The truth had revealed itself. The land of the dead, the spirit world, was just a whisper away. But I already knew that, didn't I?

"Ruairi O'Donnell—the Chief of the O'Donnell's, breathes inside me," Colm confessed the impossible.

"You called upon a dead spirit? To save me? I'm flattered." I narrowed my gaze, assessing the specter lurking beneath Colm's skin. There was a stark difference between the two men. This Ruairi was a hostile force subdued by the passage of time.

"I saw ye in a vision. You were riding a white horse beside this very lake. You were in danger." He laid his palms on my upper arms, his gaze tortured.

"I was in danger." I looked up. The waterfall rushed over the cliff, flowing down. If it weren't for the smoking debris by the water's edge, I could believe that fairy tales had happy endings.

"Who hurt ye? Where is he?" His voice pierced the shadowy glen, filled with rage.

"I'm fine, Colm. It's over now." The last few moments blazed through my mind. I had transformed into another creature, a fire-breathing sea serpent, of all things. I inhaled its fury and let loose its rage, showing no hesitation and no remorse. I took someone's life, albeit a monster of a different kind. How did I share that revelation? How did I tell him what I'd become?

"I will rip this man from limb to limb. I will flay the skin from his bones." He reached for my hand. "Where is he?"

"Dead. He's dead." The memory of melted bones and razed flesh was all too real, too fresh in my mind.

"By whose hand?" His voice growled. His gaze scanned the shadows.

"Mine. I handled the situation." How did I untangle all of this? He didn't understand this world, and I was unsure how to explain it. Listen up, Colm, I became a fire-breathing dragon who defeated an enemy foe. Who would believe that? But hey, he had welcomed a dead soul into his bones. Were we so different?

"No, Calla. How?" He cupped my chin in his hands, his thumbs brushing away the tears as they fell.

"You came for me, Colm. Do you understand what that means?" I wanted to learn more about the ghost, Ruairi O'Donnell, living within. What promise could a dead man make to a living one? What did he want from Colm, and who was this Dark Lady? I kept my skeptical suspicions to myself.

"Calla, I'm sorry. I'm so, so sorry." He embraced me, wrapping me in his strength. "Are ye hurt, *mo grhá*?"

The thunderous sound of hooves breaking through the forest interrupted our talk. I turned my head as the branches parted. Finvarra, flanked by Cian, Midir, and Miach, and an army of uniformed sentries on silver-shod faerie horses, entered the glen.

"Rioghain, my child. Are you safe?" Finvarra's silver

eyes widened as he observed my pristine appearance. Or had he noticed the black pearls?

What had they seen on the palace balcony before I transformed and flew away?

I closed my eyes, my thoughts drifting to Finvarra's fairy tale castle, where Faerie folk filled the grand ballroom—extraordinary beings of various shapes and sizes, including mortals who stayed of their own accord or those, like Ciarán, who couldn't leave. My skin crawled knowing that I did not differ from the worst of them. My mind swirled as the image came to me through another's eyes: a stunning woman with hair as black as night, her crimson gown sweeping across the marble floor, on a man's arm. What had Nemain called him? The most eligible bachelor in the kingdom. How he twirled the beautiful woman across the dance floor before adoring eyes. To them, he was a handsome prince, an adoring son.

Thunder cracked in the sky. The ground trembled. My hand reached for the black pearls, this time, for comfort.

"I am quite safe, Father." I squared my shoulders and slipped my hand into Colm's.

The brothers dismounted from their horses, landing softly among the lush ferns. They whispered with Finvarra at the water's edge, speaking in hushed voices. Cian cast a curious glance in my direction. Midir gestured toward the embers drifting across the lake. Miach crouched on strong thighs by the smoldering ashes.

"The man was a beast. His kingdom belongs to

whoever defeats him. Who did this?" Finvarra's gaze pierced the glen, then settled on me.

"I did." I held my head high, unashamed. I tightened my grip on Colm's fingers, muffling his gasping breath. Embers flickered as the sea serpent's horned snout broke the lake's surface, then sank back into the depths. Was I the only one who could see?

"Princess Rioghain, the Kingdom of Ulaid belongs to you along with all its riches." Finvarra drew his sword, scattering ash in all directions.

"Father, what will I do with a kingdom? Shouldn't it go to someone who wants it? Macha, perhaps... she's much more qualified than I am." My throat tightened as I realized what I had done. But that's how things worked, right? Defeat the enemy. Seize their lands. Their wealth. That was Balor's plan. I looked at Finvarra, this Faerie king who had lived for millennia. My actions had saved him. That was something. Balor's remains drifted with the breeze, lost to the night. There was a finality in that.

Birds chirped, bursting into a symphony of song. The silver-tongued devil was dead. I shifted my gaze, looking into the dark branches. Moments earlier, the forest had been silent except for my rasping breath. But that was then.

"Mortal. Explain your intentions." Finvarra closed the distance between us and raised his sword, planting the tip at Colm's throat—a warrior among men.

"This woman is my intention if she'll have me, sir." Colm didn't flinch. He held Finvarra's gaze, declaring his wishes for the Faerie Folk to hear.

At any other time, I might have giggled. I might have

quipped back with teasing banter, but this was not that time. My mouth went dry as I stared at the sword. One flick of the wrist and it would all be over.

"Father, this is Colm. But you know that. You know who he is." I calmed my emotions and spoke with the same regal authority. "Hey, he's one of the good guys."

Okay, so I lied.

Finvarra lowered his shining sword, his steely gaze meeting mine. Then he gave Colm a slight nod, acknowledging his right to exist.

Cian let out a soft whistle.

I exhaled the breath I didn't know I was holding.

Colm knelt, holding both of my hands in his. "I love you, Calla. I will care for you with all my being and for all my days. I will honor you with every fiber of my soul. Will you have me? Will you be my wife?" His eyes shone. His voice sang.

"Marry you? What?" I stared at him, torn by so many emotions.

"Do you know who you're speaking to? You look upon Rioghain, Princess of this realm. Rise before the King," Cian declared, addressing the entire audience and drawing attention away from me. For that, I was grateful.

All I wanted was the way back machine, but it was nowhere to be found.

Colm rose to his full height, his gaze locked on mine.

My mouth watered. I stared at him. Couldn't stop.

"You are but a mere mortal." Finvarra sheathed his sword. "Unworthy of this kingdom and my daughter."

"I will do anything you wish, sir. To prove myself." Colm's eyes glimmered in the moonlight, Otherworldly.

My breath caught. He was Colm, but he was different. Another had taken residence within—a human possession—the shifting of a human soul. Amazing. I wondered if Macha had a spell book for such things.

"We will return to the castle. To win the hand of Princess Rioghain, Princess of Ulaid and the Realm, you must prove yourself before the eyes of the kingdom." Finvarra snapped his fingers, and Resurrection appeared on the forest path, accompanied by a magnificent chestnut steed. "Can you ride, child? After all you've faced?" He lifted my hand, guiding me away from the carnage.

Had the horses been there all along, hidden by the magic mist? Or were Finvarra's powers that great? I walked toward the stallion, resting my hand on his sculpted shoulder. He was as real as real can be.

Resurrection snorted, blowing hot air through his nostrils as a greeting.

"I'm fine." My eyes widened as Resurrection knelt before me, inviting me to climb onto his back. "Good boy," I murmured, stroking his powerful neck. I knew I would miss him when I left.

"We will accompany you to the castle, sister. No further harm will find you." Cian's blue eyes met mine.

I believed I had found a friend.

"You there. Mount your horse. When we reach the castle, we will decide what will be done with you." Finvarra nodded at Colm.

"Sir." Colm lifted himself onto the horse's back with the ease of an accomplished rider.

I couldn't help but notice Finvarra's scrutinizing

glance. I saw what he saw: a man who fought for those he loved, a man made of fire. A smile touched my lips as that shining curl fell onto his brow. My Celt—that big Irish lad standing in the middle of the clear blue sky. He was mine. That was my thought the day we met.

"We shall return without delay," Finvarra commanded, guiding the way through the moonlit glen.

The skies crackled, bolts of lightning slicing through the clouds. I took one last look at the tumbling waterfall and the shimmering pool as Resurrection moved through the forest, flanked on all sides by my found brothers, knowing that, come what may, I would leave this place with Colm. I had learned all the magic I needed or wanted—enough for an entire lifetime or two.

8

C*olm*

The horse beneath me moved through the glen as if on wings. The leather tack on the horse, decorated with jewels, revealed the great wealth of its owners. I watched the changing sky, sometimes electrified with lightning, other times shining with stars. The moon, a faceless orb, watched over this Faerie glen, witnessing everything. Calla rode two strides ahead, her shoulders squared and her head held high, surrounded by three Otherworldly beings she called her brothers. She glanced over her shoulder, her dove-grey eyes reflecting the moon itself. I tried to convince myself she was still the same Calla Sweet I had fallen in love with, but I knew deep in my heart she had changed. Halfling or not, an ancient magic simmered within her.

"What kettle of fish have you got us into this time?" Ruairi's deep voice growled.

He was correct in his account. I called upon him in times of personal crisis, knowing his sage advice would set me on the right course. He was the wiser man—fearless and calculating. His burning desire to fight the fight flared hot within me. I was ashamed to admit I relied too much on his guidance.

I studied Finvarra and the three men who accompanied him. Formidable and well-built, their eyes looked like molten silver, except for the one called Cian, who was lankier than the others and had a more telling expression. I observed the horse guards—twelve individuals, six men and six women—dressed in the royal colors of Finvarra's court: high-collared tunics in the deepest purple and leather riding pants of the same shade, with leather boots that reached their knees. Each wore a sword strapped to their side.

"*What did you expect? Shiny, mystical beings? Effervescent orbs of light? Did your brother not warn you?*" He exerted his thoughts.

Ciarán…I didn't give him a chance to explain anything. Had I even welcomed him back? It seemed so long ago.

I pondered Ruairi's question. What had I expected? A luminous space at the edge of time? Instead, I found an Ireland untouched by civilization, and a people touched by magic. I scanned the forest we had passed through, woodland unseen in the mortal realm, stands of trees extinct in my world. I let the air fill my lungs. It was unlike any other.

The brother, named Midir, turned his golden head and gave me a stern glare.

"*Don't be naïve, mo chara. These are the Tuatha Dé. Do not cross them. They may have lost the battle, but they won the war.*" His voice radiated admiration for this mythical race.

The horse guard slowed down, breaking formation to walk single file. Silence settled as each rider appeared to hold their breath.

I searched my mind for this location in present-day Ireland, but couldn't find it. Giant oaks grew thick, forming a grand circle, their twisted limbs weaving a canopy the moonlight couldn't penetrate. Emerald vines draped with violet petals hung from every branch. Beyond the sacred grove, I spotted a wooden structure with smoke curling from its chimney, likely where the Druids of this realm lived, in harmony with nature.

"*Stay vigilant, lest you become an offering to their pagan gods.*" Ruairi expanded his thoughts, showing me a man inside the wooden cage and four cloaked figures, one at each corner, carrying the caged man toward a crackling fire.

The riders left the ancient grove, following a well-worn path lined with white birch. Bathed in a silvery glow, the trees looked ghostly.

"*Nonsense. Druids are a peaceful lot. This is likely a gathering place for rituals and celebrations.*" I recalled the Druid gathering I had witnessed back home in a forest glen not so different from this one.

"*They are pagans.*" He spat, expressing his disdain. "*Fantastical beings blessed with the sight. Capable of dark magic.*"

My horse raised its head, its ears twitching. I followed its gaze toward a conspiracy of ravens perched in the gloom of a hawthorn tree. I took a breath, gauging the size of each raven and estimating their wing spans. The ravens watched the procession with unblinking eyes.

"*Hmm. We observe the same pagan rituals on Samhain. Do you recall the night your family showed up around our sacred fire? The oath we took as brothers? This ancient circle isn't so different.*" I steered the conversation away from this immortal realm and made it personal.

"*That is true. My mother did indeed heed your brother's call.*" There was sadness in his voice.

"*Your knowledge of the Tuatha Dé is impressive. Thank you, Ruairi, for responding to my call today and for offering your guidance and strategic advice. You are an invaluable asset.*" I praised him for his efforts and meant every word, "*And a loyal friend.*"

Calla looked over her shoulder, sending me an encouraging glance.

"*Hmph. No doubt her dark charms enchanted you.*" He huffed, his opinion damning the one I loved.

"*She's innocent in all this. She's from Canada, for crying out loud, a news anchor on television, a reporter,*" I snapped back, refusing to engage with his cynicism.

"*She is no bard, no wandering minstrel, if that is what you mean. She is a murderess wielding dark magic. Consider your actions, mo chara.*" He spoke with the ferocity I had grown used to. Still, I balked at his assessment of her. I refused to accept it.

"*I won't leave this place without her,*" I replied to his skepticism with determination.

Her lips trembled as she admitted her guilt, her pained expression seeking not forgiveness but understanding. I accepted what I could not change—Calla had sought retribution—and took justice into her own hands.

Would I not draw the life force from the man who harmed Eamon? In my society, a select few driven by greed held the power, twisting justice to favor criminals over victims. Was this world any different? I had no answers.

"Hmph... Your arrogance is admirable. You have not endured as I have. Let me tell you about my time in prison. Tricked by lechery? Held captive in chains?" He relived the raw wound bleeding in his mind. Cold crept beneath my skin, hunger gnawing at my belly as I experienced his memories. The annals of time could not forget such treachery. "Aye, 'tis what it was and no more." His voice gentled. *"Do not weep for me, mo chara. My life was well-lived."*

I asked myself, have I ever lived?

"You live every day, mo chara. It's the dying part that happens only once. I leave you with one last thought: do not fear the face of man, do not be swayed by their lies." His voice grew softer, offering wise advice.

"Have you ever been in love?" I had never considered asking this before.

"Aye, I have known love, though it was brief. My destiny called me elsewhere. I am O'Donnell, sworn to protect our land and our people." His thoughts drifted to another time. He showed me the boy, the young prince of the O'Donnell clan. His face was gaunt, but his gaze was firm. Surrounded by friends, flanked by the Dark Lady and an ailing king, young Ruairi stood proud on a rocky crag overlooking Donegal Bay.

Warm earth poked through a blanket of fallen snow, the air sharp, the distant mountains glistening in the morning sun. A boy succeeded his father, taking his rightful place as clan chief. O'Donnell. O'Donnell. The echoing cry whispered across the land as he circled thrice to the west, then thrice to the east, before facing his people, honor-bound to protect them.

"Perhaps I will find this love you speak of in another life." Ruairi's thoughts changed course—hope mingled with profound sadness, his failures paramount in his mind.

He didn't see the legacy he had left behind.

Rage simmered in my gut for all those wrongs I could not right.

"You possess a gentle heart, mo chara, yet you carry the courage of our clan within you. Noble blood flows in your veins. Do not doubt the man you are," he counseled me with an encouraging voice.

"And all this time, I thought you didn't like me." He could see the smile on my lips.

I waited for his response, but heard nothing. Instead, he watched Finvarra, a man untouched by age, who carried the weight of this world on his shoulders.

The horse beneath me moved unlike any other; its gait was graceful, and its hooves graced the ground—a horse, faerie-blessed.

We rode through a forest bathed in moonlight. I scanned the dense woodland, my eyes searching the shadows. A sense of unease washed over me. The wind was restless.

"Do you see the sacred treasure this king carries? Behold

Fragarach, the Sword of Light," Ruairi whispered—his voice filled with awe.

"*The Sword of Light?"* My eyes fixed on the magical weapon the king carried, shimmering with blue flames.

"*The one who wields the Sword of Light is invincible: protected by the Divine, master of the winds. Do you know what this means?"* Ruairi spoke of legend.

"*It seems the Shanachie's tales are true,"* I reflected on Ruairi's immediate concerns.

How vividly I remembered the stories about legendary heroes—the *Tuatha Dé Danann* and their migration from the four mythical cities, the magic taught to them by great wizards, and the magical talismans they received from each: the Sword of Nuada, the Spear of Lugh, the Cauldron of Dagda, and *Lia Fáil*, the Stone of Destiny—all legend.

What level of magic did Calla possess? Her confession was strange. My mind couldn't quite grasp what she had said. She sat on the magnificent steed with her heels down—posture perfect, glancing backward now and then with those eternal eyes. I wondered if she was reading my mind.

"*Your heart aches for this woman. Arrah, look beyond her beauty. The men you chase are motivated by greed. Think about what such a discovery could mean in your world."* He echoed my thoughts.

"*Aye.*" My mind had flirted with insanity, believing she was gone for good. I steadied my thoughts, controlling my irrational fears.

Yet my conscience bothered me, and I worried about those I left behind: Eamon, on the verge of his last breath, and Saoirse, shouting into her phone's speaker. Ciarán had whispered in my ear, "The portal opens one night only. You must go." While the bees slept, I had cut through the thorns and found what I sought. The opening to this hidden world revealed itself among the bracken, with the tunnel's entrance draped in vines. The silence deepened with every step.

I had followed the winding passage into the earth, with Calla's smile as my guiding light. I had raised my hands overhead, scraping at the earth's underbelly, wondering if, instead of finding the land of the young, I had buried myself alive. As I got closer, a sound had grown louder—the droning hum of bees.

The hairs on the back of my neck stood up as I inhaled the earth, filling my lungs with its scent and coating my tongue with its taste. Had I lingered too long, would it have claimed my soul?

The passage had narrowed, and the ground rumbled beneath my feet. The fracture between this world and the next shimmered just a hand's breadth away. I looked at it, watched it, and reached out to touch the swirling mass. It was nothing more than air, charged with an unknown radiance. I wondered if it was alive or just a trick of light. There was no time to think. I lunged through the vortex and stepped into a dark forest.

Lightning crackled through the night sky.

I arrived, but not at the spot Ciarán had specified. I hesitated, unsure which way to go, snapping a branch under my foot. The forest fell silent, as if listening for the sound of an intruder. A beast howled—a lonely, haunting cry. I searched the darkness for any sign of those bright yellow eyes. Wolves. Creatures like those no longer lived in my Ireland.

"Don't let a pack of wolves distract you. The Tuatha Dé are just as dangerous," Ruairi had whispered in my mind, leaving me to ponder the dangers of this mythical land, something I hadn't thought about when I started my quest. Wolves posed a genuine threat—dog-like creatures—and encountering such a pack could lead to my downfall. Or had he meant Finvarra himself?

My heart clenched in my chest as my thoughts wandered through legend and myth. I had come to the Otherworld for one reason only: to find the woman I loved. I hadn't thought about what other hosts of immortal beings might be lurking in these shadows.

I flinched in the saddle as the ground dropped away and the horse beneath me lurched forward. The path spiraled downward, with dense foliage parting to reveal a moonlit clearing.

"Arrah, mo chara. I will alert you of any demons or ghouls that approach. To be sure. To be sure." He chuckled, yet his words seemed to falter. "I advise you not to accept any challenges for a duel. God knows what this Tuatha king has in mind."

"A duel? Is that what you think this is?" I rifled through the last few moments—my conversation by the lake with Calla. I tried to replay those moments, but I failed. My thoughts felt muddled and unclear. It was strange not to have full control over my emotions, to blurt things out in a moment of excitement. I turned my head toward her and didn't doubt that her time in this realm had affected her well-being.

The wind sang a dark song, touching her, lifting the wispy black strands from her face, and holding her in a lover's embrace.

My mouth dried. There was more than magic at play.

The ramparts of Finvarra's castle appeared in view. The crenelated walls, protected by a wide moat, wound through the dense woods, stretching far into the surrounding hills. Turrets provided archers with a bird's-eye view of the surrounding land. Two sentries armed with long spears stood at attention as we approached.

"Pay attention, brother. Human blood cements these castle walls. This is no ordinary place. Look at the moat. Ghouls of a different kind live there," his usual teasing voice whispered warnings.

The waters swirled, but I saw nothing. Maybe his wits were sharper than mine. After all, he had lived in darkness for centuries.

My horse picked up its pace as it crossed the draw-bridge. I observed the counterweights used to raise and lower the massive structure. The portcullis, an iron grid designed to keep enemies out, sparkled like silver tines.

Moonlight shimmered on the grand residence. Nestled in a rolling stretch of green, the castle rose eight stories high, its gabled roofs flanked by four circular towers—spacious balconies protected by thick balustrades, the domed spires resembling gleaming pearls. One tower stood taller than the others, overseeing the vast kingdom. Was this a fortress or a palace? The archer's slits spiraling up each tower hinted at its true purpose.

They built a wide, water-filled trench surrounding

the castle walls to keep the enemy out, with the draw-bridge serving as the only visible entrance. One by one, the guards' horses crossed, their hooves clopping against the wooden bridge, the empty echoes bouncing off the water below.

With Calla by his side, the king entered his kingdom, followed by his princely sons.

Finvarra's nod signaled the horse guards to move forward. They turned left, following a cobbled path that led beyond the castle keep, leaving two behind me—one a somber-faced man and the other a stern-faced woman—both seemed timeless, strong, and in the prime of life. I dreaded the thought of tangling with either of them.

"*Do not forget from whom our island takes its name: Ériu, Fódla, Banba,*" Ruairi muttered in a low voice.

"*Pagan goddesses, Ruairi. Pagan beliefs persist.*" I reflected on my father and many like him, who held a deep respect for the old ways.

The myths tell how the *Tuatha* fought and defeated the Fomorians, a giant race believed to have come from beneath the sea. Then, centuries later, our ancient ances-tors defeated the Tuatha. It seemed...impossible.

He stated, "*St. Patrick introduced Christianity to Ireland, ending the era of pagan gods.*"

I reminded him of our earlier conversation. "*They say the Tuatha are the children of Danu.*"

"*Fallen angels or mystical beings—either way... There is dark magic here. I've toppled many castles. I know what this one is made of.*" His worries echoed through my mind.

"Guards, escort this mortal to the throne room. I will

speak with you, Rioghain." The King nodded toward Calla, his gaze passing over mine.

"*Look out, mate. It's your head now. Admit nothing. Keep your secrets close. You are not within the pale. They are not Saxon. The Tuatha Dé are much, much more.*"

Yes, he knew more about this Other Crowd than he admitted.

"Colm, I'll be right behind you." Calla smiled, landing on the cobblestones, her blood-red gown draped over golden slippers. My heart seized again. She was more beautiful than I remembered.

A guard reached for my horse's bridle, his silver-eyed gaze watching every move I made. I dismounted and stood with my hands at my sides. The pointed end of the guard's sword pressed into my lower back, pushing me toward the castle's grand entrance.

My eyes caught a sudden flash of light, a glimmer in an unexpected place. My mind froze. I stood prepared, expecting to face malevolence and believing Calla needed rescue. Maybe she did.

I turned away from my guards, searching the darkness for the human evil, and found him too late. The man who had assaulted me—dressed in the same black suit— stood beneath the eaves of the stone gatehouse, hidden in the shadows of the castle walls. He lifted a cylindrical weapon in Calla's direction. This weapon was unlike anything I'd ever seen before. Whether to wound or kill, his intentions were unclear; I didn't intend to find out.

I vaulted away from my guards, leaving them wide-eyed and reaching for me, but I was no longer there. Landing in a crouch, I lunged toward the attacker, but not before a thunderous boom sounded. A projectile launched a meshed net through the air, leaving behind the sharp scent of fired charge.

I dropped my shoulder and threw him backward, knocking the wind out of him.

His eyes narrowed too late, and his lips curled into a snarl.

Just revenge? I had only just begun.

"Who are you? Who are you working for?" I straddled his hips, pinning him to the ground. I threw my hate into my fist, cracking his jaw with a solid right hook.

Again and again, I pounded him. I made him pay for what he did, not to me, but to a defenseless old man.

"If you think you can stop us, you're a fool." Blood flowed from his lip. His eyes were sharp, too sharp. A crazed grin split his face, mirroring a reality I was intimately familiar with.

"Step away." Finvarra's voice rang out as he drew the mighty sword and swung Fragarach toward the attacker.

Blue flames surged over the blade, but he held the golden hilt loosely. The air quivered as the line of fire shot toward the attacker. Tendrils of flame curled around his legs, hips, and arms.

I waited for the man's screams, but they never came. The attacker's eyes were wide with fear, but he remained unscathed, only temporarily incapacitated.

"You. You didn't kill him." I looked at Finvarra in a new light. He wasn't the monster Ruairi made him out to be, at least not yet.

"This man will answer to the gods for his crime." The king turned away, leaving the man roped in blue flame.

I stepped back, and that was when my heart stopped.

The net had caught its intended victim. Calla lay on the hard cobblestones, curled up in a fetal position beneath what appeared to be fine chain-mail, trapped beneath the unyielding mesh. Her quiet whimpers filled me with fear.

I was only somewhat aware of others arriving: two women, a blonde and a redhead, who carried what looked like a white cat.

"Father? Cian? What is this?" The redhead's face turned pink as her gaze flicked back and forth.

"Bring it, Calla. Make it happen! You can do it." The blonde sidestepped between the three brothers, positioning herself at the edge of the net, then dropped to her knees and whispered to Calla. "Try harder. Remember what we taught you. Imagine your power."

"At the count of three. One. Two. Three," the one called Miach called out.

Beads of sweat formed on Cian's brow. The net seemed immune to their combined strength.

"What is it?" The redhead looked at me for an answer. She placed the cat on the ground and circled the net. "It's iron, isn't it?"

I saw they were powerless against this deadly weapon. Their effort to rescue Calla was unsuccessful.

"Get it off. It hurts, Colm. God, it hurts," Calla cried out, her eyes locking with mine.

My heartbeat slowed, her pain flowing into me.

"*The maiden is right, O'Donnell. It's iron-made. The only thing that can hold a Faerie or kill one.*" Ruairi informed me of the net's material and an interesting tidbit of Faerie lore.

I looked over my shoulder to make sure the attacker remained restrained. He stood, caught in flames, hate burning in his dark eyes, mixed with something even more sinister. He hadn't come up with this plan alone. Whoever sent this monster into the Otherworld was still on the loose.

The net proved weighty, but an easy lift for one of human blood. Aided by Ruairi's resolve, I lifted the net into the air. One powerful heave sent the fine chain-mail skittering across the courtyard.

"Arrah, your aid is much appreciated." Three brothers exchanged smiles. Midir slapped my shoulder in a friendly way. The redheaded woman smiled, and the blonde stared at me with her mouth hanging open. Sisters—they were Calla's sisters, the ones Orlaith mentioned.

"Calla, are you okay?" I knelt, helping her to her feet, and looked her over for any signs of injury. The crown was still in place, its rubies shimmering in the moonlight.

"I guess I needed rescuing, didn't I?" A pained smile lit her face, and then she wrapped her arms around me, burying her face beneath my chin.

"I promised, didn't I?" I whispered, inhaling her scent, my heart overflowing. I took her hands and pressed my lips to her knuckles. Her smile made my heart sing.

"There's someone I'd like you to meet." She took my hand and led me toward the two women. "These are my sisters, Nemain and Macha. This is Colm, Ciarán's brother."

"Where is he? Is Ciarán safe?" The blonde lifted her chin, her silver-eyed gaze expecting an immediate response. An icy wave washed over me, paralyzing my bones with complete control, similar to Calla's power.

"Nemain, stop it." The one called Macha placed her hand on the blonde's shoulder. "There's time enough for questions—later."

The sensation faded, freeing me from its enchanting grip.

"You." The king beckoned me forth. "What brought you to this kingdom is no longer of importance. Do you know what this is?" He placed his palm on the sheathed sword.

"*Tell the truth, mate. You can't hide from their powers. They see everything*," Ruairi warned.

"I do, sir. The *Claíomh Solais*, the Shining Sword." I nodded, my heart racing as I looked past the flames at the man in the black suit. Held captive in the Faerie realm, judged by their gods. My mouth dried.

"That is but one name. This sword is one of our sacred treasures. Once unsheathed, no one can escape or resist its power." He released the scabbard from his waist, offering me the magical saber.

"Thank you, sir, but I am unworthy of such a gift. I cannot accept it." I stepped back. "I only wish to return to the mortal world with Calla—with Princess Rioghain, if she will have me." I looked toward the woman I loved. Whoever she was, whatever she may be, for better or worse. I just needed to convince her that my love was real.

"We are in your debt, Colm O'Donnell. We will investigate the perpetrator's motives and identify his associates. Many mortals and others seek to harm our kind." His gaze exuded a quiet fury. "Let us not dwell on such unhappiness. Your courage and noble intentions confirm you are the hero the Princess spoke of."

"Thank you, sir," I replied, holding his gaze. Ruairi fell silent under the king's scrutiny.

"I grant you, Colm O'Donnell, the gift of sight. Wherever your journey leads, do not fear us. Our gratitude to you is eternal and unending. We are alike. We value bravery and honesty, and your strong moral sense is clear. You will always be a beloved friend of this realm." He waved his hand over my face, closing my eyelids with his royal fingertips.

A shudder ran through me, and as I opened my eyes, the world around me looked new—more...just more.

"I sense another living within these mortal bones. Who aids this man in his quest? Show yourself before the King." Finvarra spoke in a firm voice.

A lesser man would run and hide.

"I leave you now, mo chara. Perhaps my presence can be of some use in this realm." He informed me of his decision, leaving me with no time to argue. I must accept his will.

It was time to say goodbye. I feared the moment he would leave my body. The feeling was like pulling a tooth from healthy gums or tearing an eyeball from its socket, leaving a wide-open wound.

Calla's mouth dropped open when Ruairi took a corporeal form beside me. Undead, he towered beside me, embodying the essence of a lord. The *Tuatha Dé* seemed unaffected by his presence, as if the undead were a normal thing. Perhaps they were.

I had never seen him like that. I remembered a man scarred by war and consumed by rage.

He wore an Irish coat called an Inar, its shawl collar highlighting his muscular neck. The quilted jacket's design reflected the era's fashion, adorned with stylized vines and gilded leather accents. The pleated skirt ended at his waist. Striped sleeves buttoned at the wrist, with a split seam underneath allowing for the elbow-length bagpipe sleeves of the Leine—the tunic pulled up and bloused over a leather belt. He wore woven trousers and doe-skin boots as he stepped out of his world and into another.

I looked up again. He was taller than I remembered.

"Who are you?" Macha lifted her gaze, her brow crinkling. Raising her hand, she tucked a loose red curl behind her ear.

I saw what she saw. Proud. Defiant. A young man in the prime of his life.

"I am O'Donnell, chief of the name." He turned toward her, his fiery locks wild and untamed.

I had never seen him blush in a lady's presence. Then I noticed the tilt of his head and the intense fire in his blue eyes.

"Huh. Maybe now you'll stop cuddling that gods-damn cat and get with a real man." Nemain's snicker glided from her lips, low and sultry. She reached out, sending the redhead into Ruairi's path.

"My name is Ruairi, and you are?" He caught her elbows, holding her upright.

"Macha, I am Macha." She blinked once, then twice, meeting his gaze with the same smoldering eyes Calla possessed.

The blonde smiled, not at Ruairi, but at Calla. I wondered what secrets they kept between them.

"Excuse me, I'm so sorry." Macha stepped back and extended her hand in a regal gesture.

"I am honored, princess." Ruairi bowed at the waist, pressing his lips to her fingertips, then straightened up to his full height, his eyes locked with hers.

She turned her hand, curling her fingers underneath his, and guided him across the cobblestones, presenting him to Calla and the king. "And this is my sister, Princess Rioghain."

Calla's eyes widened as her gaze met mine, questioning the impossible.

"Princess Rioghain, it is an honor to meet you. Colm has spoken of you in the highest regard," his voice echoed throughout the courtyard, enhancing the ethereal atmosphere of this magical place.

Above, a pitch-black sky loomed over this world, just like it did over mine. A surge of emotions overwhelmed me.

"You have traveled a long way, young prince." Finvarra looked at Ruairi, questioning his statement. "Either way, I invite you both. You are welcome guests within this realm." Finvarra regarded him as a king might.

"My liege, King Finvarra, I have spent many years in the Underworld. I am eager to serve and ready to assist you in any way needed." He bowed again and then assumed his princely stance.

"I have warriors, and I have wise men. I see you possess the qualities of both." Finvarra nodded his head.

Ruairi held his gaze.

"Rioghain, it's time for you to take your rightful place in our kingdom. You have proved yourself a true queen." The King reached out his hand to Calla. Her sisters looked up, their faces showing surprise. Finvarra then addressed his two daughters, saying, "Amidst all this chaos, I must tell you, Nemain and Macha, that Prince Balor was not what we thought. Your sister, Rioghain, faced the most terrible trials. Balor is no longer alive, and the throne of Ulaid will pass to the one who defeated him."

Nemain gasped. Macha threw her hand to her mouth.

"Father, I don't know what to say. I'm delighted. But my kingdom? Macha will do a better job. I wish for her to rule in my place." Calla took a deep breath, a small smile forming at the corner of her mouth.

"What? No. I don't think so." Macha blushed again as her eyes met Calla's.

"If you are certain of your desires, I will not rule against them." Finvarra's gaze softened as he looked toward Macha. "Macha, my beloved, you possess a sound mind. Intelligence and wisdom shine in your eyes. Rioghain is correct in her assessment. I do not doubt your capabilities."

"But Father, I like it here." She held her head high and met his fiery gaze with one that took me by surprise.

"What did Balor do? What happened?" Nemain lunged forward and grabbed her father's arm.

"Nemain, we will discuss this later. Prince Balor committed a serious act of treason. That alone would be enough to strip him of his right to rule. Now, Macha, it's time, dear daughter, for you to spread your wings," he clapped his hands.

"But I am not a queen," Macha murmured.

Those present whispered to one another, each nodding in agreement.

"I can visit: birthdays, bank holidays, Christmas vacation." Calla cast a quick glance at her brothers, Nemain and Macha, who stared back.

"Calla, is this what you want? Are you sure?" Doubt weighed on my heart. She radiated the same Otherworldliness. She belonged among them. These were her people. Who was I to take her away from her heart's desire?

"I choose you, Colm. We can talk about the rest later." She tugged at my shirt sleeve, turning me toward her, her gaze shining like the stars above.

What dangers lie ahead? What evils would confront her each day for the rest of her life? A Fae creature living in the mortal realm left her vulnerable. I would do everything in my power to keep her safe. I would die trying.

"You have my blessing, daughter. Our story has no end, of that I can assure you. Trust in your heart. Everything you need lies within." Finvarra placed his palm over her chest.

"Sir, what about him? He's caused a lot of trouble in the human realm." I gestured toward the assailant—oh, how I longed to drag him by his flaming shackles from this world to the next.

"Retribution will be swift, I assure you. This beast will not harm the Princess or our kind again." Finvarra motioned to the guards escorting me through the castle gates. They surrounded Calla's attacker, unbothered by the swirling flames.

Calla's gaze swept over the castle grounds, lingering on the tallest steeple before shifting back to the two sisters. Her lips curled into a smile. "I will miss you. All of you." The wind clapped, carrying her words across the night sky, the meadow, and the forest.

"We are just a stone's throw away, dear sister. We shall meet again." Prince Cian's blue eyes softened. His words were unhurried, his voice resonating with Otherworldly conviction.

9

alla

Colm's arm stretched deep into the lion's throat, his fingers curling around the bronze handle of an oil lantern, the burning wick emitting a strong, fishy smell from the lantern's chimney. I knew the glowing light would lead us to the other side.

Together, we rode an emotional roller coaster, shifting with the spine of this sea cave. I sensed Colm's fear. I admired his determination. My awareness was almost overwhelming—my hearing was sharp, every sound intense.

I was no longer the person I had been. Faerie blood and the blood of my ancestors whispered through my veins. I was one of them, born from an ancient race, immortal and otherwise—a true halfling born of a mother who died thousands of years ago, brought back to life by a faerie king.

Every ten seconds—I counted—Colm turned, the

light in his eyes catching mine. My need for him thundered through my veins—an Otherworldly craving, amplified by a new sense of being. I wanted him. I hungered for him.

"Watch your step, Calla," Colm warned me of the next rock fall. We maneuvered sideways, squeezing through keyhole openings, pressing flat against the jagged walls, only to find a much narrower passage encrusted with shells and spiny vertebrae, remnants of the last tidal surge. We sloshed through foam-filled pockets, my gown's hem heavy with salt water.

The lion roared, signaling that our escape was close.

"I hear the ocean." He squeezed my fingers, his heart full of joy. I felt that, too.

We had said our goodbyes, with Finvarra acknowledging Colm as the man I loved. He touched my cheek and bid me farewell. When I closed my eyes, I could see it, feel it. What was once a quiet void danced with fireflies and hummed with an energy that hadn't been there before. That's how easy it was to call upon the magic, the creatures of both realms, and the elements.

"Let's stop for a moment, okay?" My voice echoed across the translucent pool of water. The smooth rock slab slipping into the depths provided an inviting resting spot.

"Are you all right? Are you hurt?" He turned toward me, his eyes searching mine.

"We need to talk." The smell of the sea and briny spray brought back memories of the Ireland I had left behind.

"I know. I know." He set the lantern on a rock shelf, lighting the cozy cavern in warmth.

"You don't know, Colm." I paced back and forth. "You don't know what I am. You only think you do."

"You make me the happiest man alive, Calla. I don't care about anything else." He rested his hand on the crook of my arm, calming my frantic pace.

"I used to think I was good. I'm not." I resisted the urge to throw my arms around him. Honesty was the best policy. Honesty was the ruination of my life. What happened to—keep your mouth shut, Calla Sweet?

He ran his hands down the velvet sleeves of the crimson gown, clasped my hands, and then released me.

"Do you know of the Morrigan? The Goddess of Destruction and Despair?" I needed to share everything with him—the one I could trust.

"That's not what the Morrigan is." He tilted his head, smiling that disarming smile.

"Well, she might as well be." I hung my head, tears filling my eyes. Not for myself, but for him. I could never be the person I was yesterday.

"What are you saying?" He lifted my chin with the tip of his index finger.

"Nemain, Macha, and I. We are the Morrigan reborn —the Triskele. That's what this is. Finvarra is our father. Our grandfather is Donn, the Lord of the Dead. Do you know who he is? We are direct descendants of an ancient people. Born of magic, Colm. Magic, and I don't know what else. My arrival in Ireland set the wheels in motion. This is unstoppable." I lifted my palms and stepped back, my heart throbbing. Light radiated from my fingertips, illuminating his face. What was I thinking about? Just then. If that was magic, I was in big trouble.

"You and your two sisters are the Morrigan?" He lifted his hand, resting his chin in the crook of his thumb. He blinked only once.

"When I touch someone, I see the future. I learned how to shift—to leave my body and journey in another." I visualized the scald crow, the gray and white bird with the long talons. "Remember what you said earlier. About the banshee. About the wailing screech when your dad died. I'm all of that, Colm, and so much more."

The truth hit home; I could see it in his eyes—the widened pupils and the pulsing jugular vein in his neck, beating with a quick rhythm.

"Before I came here, I saw through the crow's eyes. But now, there's no in-between anymore. I become something else, and when I'm finished, I return to this." I pinched the loose skin on my hand.

"That's expected, Calla." He watched me with a wary glance, as if waiting for the transformation to happen.

"I killed the Prince of Ulaid." My bottom lip trembled from everything I had been through. I would do it again. "Balor. His name was Balor."

"Did he hurt you? This Prince?" Colm's voice lowered, his demeanor shifting from wary to predatory. He seemed unaffected by my murderous revelation.

"He tried. He was going to. I saw his intentions, Colm. He planned to assassinate Finvarra, take his kingdom, and make me his bride. Well, that was his plan. He killed his mother to claim her kingdom. He poisoned her..." The image came to me of how he did it. How he took tea with that lovely woman every night, hers poisoned with hemlock... "For riches. For greed." My breath hitched. My skin crawled. "He confined me with physical strength. My panic held me captive—my fear. But Nemain—Nemain told me that pure emotion would allow my mind to escape this form and become something else. I had to learn how to harness my emotions. And at that moment, that emotion was fear. I used my fear to escape." I closed my eyes, inhaling a slow, calming breath...then there was the two-headed dragon...how could I explain that away? A mythical beast, carved into a marble arch... "I became what I am, Colm. A hooded crow is the familiar form of the Morrigan. I became that crow, wings and all, and I flew to the lake, where I became myself again. Oh God. I was so afraid."

"Will you let me make this right?" He cupped my shoulders, his voice wrapping around me.

"Make this right? There's no making this right. Are you not afraid of me? After what I just told you? I'm not human. I'm one of Them." Time fractured, and I could see my life left in splinters on the ground.

"One of my best friends is not human. Ruairi. You met him. This is Ireland, Calla. Strange things are not so strange to our people." In the lantern's golden glow, Colm and Ruairi blended together, the edges of one fading into the other—a doppelgänger of the man I love. "I'm not afraid of you, Calla. Do you want to tell me what happened?"

I rubbed my eyes. Maybe, just maybe, we weren't that different.

"A dragon lives beneath the lake, Colm. A fire-breathing dragon. Her name is Caoránach." The serpent spoke to me then, her gravelly voice rippling through my mind. My heart sighed in response.

"Aye? The *Oilliphéist*. Ancient tales recount the stories of many Celtic warriors battling the beast—a myth." Colm nodded, his lips lifting into an encouraging smile.

"Well, she's no myth. Balor could shift, too. I turned him to ash, Colm. I became one with a fire-breathing dragon and snuffed the Faerie Prince from the face of the earth. I spoke to the sea dragon in her language. I'm not just a simple Fae shifter. Oh no. I'm a weapon of mass destruction. That's what I am." I lifted my skirts and settled onto the rock.

"You're one of Them, Calla, and that comes with mysterious magic, both dark and light. I'm okay with that. I'm okay with everything. I'm not naïve and don't pretend to know what will happen in the coming days and months. You might be safer in Finvarra's realm. But I want to make you happy. I want to be with you. For the rest of my days. That's what I want." He spoke of a future, a future with him.

I wanted that more than anything else. I placed the pad of my index finger on his lips. He didn't realize what he was saying—he was good.

"I love you." He traced his fingertips along my jaw, sending a warm spark through my veins.

"I love you, too," I said, knowing the words were true.

When we touched, I saw a future filled with laughter and tears—tears that washed away the rain.

"Because of you, Ciarán is free. You achieved what no one else in the mortal realm could—negotiating his freedom with a Faerie King. You traded your life for his." His eyes welled with tears as he offered me his hand.

"I guess." My Fae-ness awakened, revealing the path ahead. Call it my inner eye, but I saw through the clouds for the first time. There was no right or wrong, even in this small chamber beneath the earth. I grasped his hand, clung to it, and held on for dear life.

"Don't sell yourself short, Faerie girl. There's a reason I love you." He lowered his chin and met my gaze.

"Hmmm...for my quick wit?" I threw him a smile.

"That, and many other reasons." His voice whispered over me, a throaty vibration of rough bass notes.

The lantern cast a golden glow over the transparent waters, revealing his destiny, which was connected to mine. I observed him, my brave Celt. I had questions. So many questions. Maybe now wasn't the right time.

Rage burned in my heart, a fury that threatened to consume me. Was it my conscience, or was it the mad prince? His final breath proclaimed hell could not contain him... Or was it guilt that came back to bite me?

My actions were irreversible, and justice in this world was absolute. Colm accepted this place for what it was, as I must. I had to let go. I had to accept what I had become. The stranglehold lessened, and the fury faded. I let it be.

The outside world was just a few steps away, confirmed by the ocean's roar. There was something about this night—something unlike any other. The spark grew, and my skin tingled, yearning for his touch, his heat warming all the right places. It was more than an ache. Fire burned beneath my skin, like the dance of fireflies and the hum of bees.

This was Bealtaine—the awakening of the spring maiden. The return of the Goddess to the earthly realm. A consummation of lust and love—the sacred union of earth and sky.

I recalled those times Colm gave me pleasure, unlike Balor, who thought he could take what he wanted and control through fear. I felt no animosity toward the dead man other than sadness.

I looked at Colm—his one demand—my pleasure belonged to him. I drew on his energy, needing him more than ever. I found my answer.

His power belonged to me.

"Can I kiss you now?" He traced the curve of my cheekbone with the pad of his thumb.

"I want more, Colm. More than your kiss." I slid my hands over his chest, smoothing the cotton placket of his buttoned shirt. An aura remained, the lingering soul of another. The spirit he called Ruairi—the spectral who stepped out of Colm's skin. The vibe was Otherworldly. And I thought I had secrets.

Colm's connection to his ancestors went beyond the limits of the mortal world. The timelines blurred, and I saw him for who he was—a fusion of the past and present. He was the O'Donnell reborn. I feared that forming a pact with the dead could enable his ancestors to come back. He was more than just a spirit host; he served as a conduit for the undead.

"Marry me tomorrow?" His warm breath tickled my ear.

"Tomorrow? Just like that? Don't you think we're rushing things?" I clutched his collar, a grin spreading across my face.

"A Bealtaine wedding. Do you know what that is?" He lowered his forehead to mine.

"No." I pressed my lips to his, tasting the salt of the ocean and beneath that his heat.

"A handfasting ceremony means we are husband and wife for one year and a day. If you're unhappy with me, we will part ways. We can repeat our vows or have a proper church wedding a year from now, if you still want me. If that's what you want." A smile ghosted his lips. He had guts. I had to give him that.

"So, like a taste test?" The pulsing in my veins intensified. I ran my hand past his belt buckle and cupped his growing erection.

"Yeah, just like that." He brushed his lips over my temple. That rumble in his throat was for me.

"Can we start now, Colm? I want to taste you right now." I stood on my tiptoes and nipped the underside of his chin.

My prince was so much more than a spirit host. He was a conduit for the O'Donnell undead and didn't even know it. This was a turn in a new direction. I thought my life was bizarre, but this took the cake.

"I thought I would never see you again, never touch you again." His eyes darkened, and he grinned. He was smiling, really smiling.

I needed to feel him. I slid his belt buckle free and,

with a flick of the thumb, unsnapped the button of his jeans. His cock sprang free of his underthings, thick and hot in my palm.

It was big.

"Calla." My name growled in his throat. He threaded his fingers through my hair and pulled me close, catching my bottom lip and nibbling the corners of my mouth. Then he kissed me like a man possessed.

I sank into him, drawn by swirling forces. The ache started low in my belly and grew into something more overwhelming, hunger rushing through my bones. It was not simple. The situation proved complicated and messy. I had always thought love was gentle, like a single leaf drifting on a breeze, falling from the sky. This was not that.

His cock throbbed for me, and I wanted to claim it. I wanted so many things.

The ocean's roar shifted into a gentle sigh of soft vibrations flowing over itself. The pressure change made my ears pop. That's when I realized something was wrong. It wasn't Colm's intoxicating scent making my head spin.

"What's wrong?" He ran his fingers through my hair and rested his lips on the top of my head.

"I'm not sure. Something. Don't you feel it?" I turned away from him, searching the sea cave for what I knew was there.

The heat coursing through me moments ago turned stone cold. I looked at Colm. His head lowered, his hands busy adjusting his cock and fastening his belt. I would have smiled; he was so darn cute, from the curve of his luscious lips to the lines etched in his brow. He was everything. And he was unaware of the Otherworldly presence.

The walls hummed, and the ledge beneath my feet radiated energy. The fireball followed the path of least resistance, flowing through my feet, surging through my limbs, and filling my soul with its life force.

"Magic lives in your soul, Rioghain," Finvarra's melodic voice whispered.

Water droplets fell from the domed ceiling, breaking the pool's surface in a rhythmic dance of tinkling notes, filling the chamber with song.

I noted the similarity to another vaulted chamber, one I witnessed through the eyes of another: the vast gallery of pitted stone, the winding corridor leading deep into the earth's core, the voices, the rumblings of the dead.

"What is it?" Colm gripped my elbow.

What had once been a peaceful pool had transformed into something else. The rippling water created perfect circles spreading outward from the center. I gazed into its depths, wondering what creature lurked beneath. Bubbles surfaced, bursting with a hiss.

"This place, it's a portal." I grabbed Colm's forearm, unable to look away.

Water swirled outward, whipping the cavern walls with frothy white ribbons. It streamed down the surfaces, filling every pore—feeding the monster within. The force hurled us back against the same wall. I dug my fingers into the hard basalt and forgot to breathe.

"We need to leave." He took my hand but paused, turning his head toward the maelstrom.

Water poured down my face, and icy winds stung my skin. The vortex switched direction, drawing life's breath from the abyss. Whispers rose in pitch, guttural moans screamed in response. Colm's face turned sheet-white.

"Calla." His muffled voice told me we had overstayed our welcome.

"Look." I pointed to the shadows emerging from what was once a shimmering pool. One after another, spectral forms took shape: ghouls, demons, and spirits, each leaving a faint scent—one I could not place. They followed the ocean's song, leaving the underworld and joining the mortal realm for one night only.

Bealtaine Eve—the night when the veil thinned and spirits roamed.

A hard lump formed in my throat. Would I ever get used to these worlds within worlds? Not knowing was so much easier.

Colm's grip tightened as dark matter emerged from the portal—ash particles mixed with silver pearls. The fragments clustered, binding, changing shape, taking human form.

Shrouded in dim light, the figure of a woman emerged. Tendons and bones hung loosely—silky threads draped her cheeks. Flowing strands of ebony framed a pockmarked skull, giving the macabre a new meaning. She turned her head from side to side as if awakening from a long nap.

She emerged from the water with faltering steps but didn't fly away like the other wraiths. No, this horror stood at the water's edge. The tattered remnants of what had once been an elegant black gown, riddled with wormholes, dusted the cavern floor. She turned her head from side to side, then snapped her long ivory teeth together. This was not a shadowy specter. No, this was a woman brought back from the dead.

"Calla. That's her—Ruairi's mother, the Dark Lady." Colm stayed close, keeping me in his shadow, protecting me from the apparition.

The remains of her face were turned toward Colm. She seemed to focus only on him. I wished I could say her eye sockets lacked life, but dark orbs flickered with both darkness and light.

This magic was powerful.

Colm's bargain with an ancient clan centered on allegiance, loyalty, and love. The same strings tugged at my heart in new ways. Call me selfish, but Colm was now my family—the one man I could touch. The bigger picture became clear: the Dark Daughter and the Red King—two ancients from another age. It's true what they say—time repeats itself.

She reached out her hand to Colm and then exhaled, filling the cavern with the putrid stench of death. I tasted her wicked past.

"Thanks to you, cousin Colm, my son lives. His essence glows within the ancestral lands of the *Tuatha*." Her dead voice rattled her hollow bones. She turned her skeletal face toward me, her fingers twitching, those eyes glimmering.

"Ruairi has found a place there. He's a good man, a good friend." Colm turned his head, his gaze sharp.

"Come with me, cousin, where they will welcome you as the hero you are." She directed her words toward Colm —her grating voice beautiful in its misery.

Colm's brow furrowed as he relaxed his grip on my arm, appearing captivated.

"What do you want?" I clenched my jaw. Maybe I would be prepared if I had taken the time to read the book Macha gave me. Ghouls. Spirits. Spectral wraiths. That was a topic of conversation we had failed to have. And there I was, negotiating with the phantom dead.

"What I want is none of your concern." Her voice screeched like nails on a chalkboard.

"You have no business in this realm." I shifted sideways, stepping in front of Colm. I would protect him to the death.

I reached out, anticipating the moment her essence touched mine. This time, I embraced the knowledge.

From the royal court of the Stuarts, the Princess of a Scottish chief crossed the waters to marry and become Queen Consort of Tyrconnell, reigniting the alliance between the O'Donnell's and the MacDonnell's. As the years passed, her husband's health declined. The wraith before me had ruled in his place, defending her family against internal threats from kin and the growing tyranny of the English invasion. With the heart of a hero and the mind of a soldier, she commanded her husband's army and a guard of Scottish mercenaries, riding into battle with those medieval warriors determined to destroy one man—her son's rival—for the clan chief's title.

She held my admiration until that point.

Hills clothed in trees watched the flight of red deer and Irish elk, the mist rising over the banks, the screaming war cries, and when Redshank arrows took steady aim, ending her stepson's life.

I saw the woman she was.

"I have every right to be here, just like them." She jutted her caved-in chin toward the wraiths still exiting the chamber. They paid us no mind and offered no help. "Come with me, cousin. Your ancestors welcome you. Your da longs for your arrival." She eased her bony fingers toward Colm.

"Da? What do you know of him?" He leaned toward her, captivated by her spell.

"Don't listen to her, Colm." I grasped Colm's wrist. Escape felt so distant. How did I go from here to there? What was holding me back? The ghostly figure of a dead Scottish Princess.

"I am Rioghain, Princess of *Tuatha Dé*. I demand that you return to the land of the dead." I twisted the black sea pearls between my fingers, a burning heat emanating from each one. Where was the magic when I needed it most?

"Your royal blood means nothing to me. You are a child." Shadows shot from her fingertips, enveloping the cavern in layers of blue ice, freezing our soaked clothing to our skin.

In that instant, I learned respect for the undead.

"Da? Is he happy?" Colm's eyes closed, a sigh escaping his lips. His heartbeat slowed—too slow.

"Colm, stay with me." I shouted, but he couldn't hear. His face was cold and clammy beneath my fingertips. "Don't do this to him." My pleas went unanswered.

"It is as I said." The Dark Lady lifted her palms,

summoning winter's force—stalagmites forming on the cavern ceiling.

How long would it be before the pointed spires split our skulls, leaving our bodies open for the taking?

"You can't have him. He's not yours to take," I shouted into the silent abyss, unable to locate her. The mist had wrapped around her, hiding her from sight. Where did this dark magic originate?

"But he is, little princess. One cannot break a blood oath." Her voice sent a shiver down my spine.

I spun around, scanning the mist for any sign of her.

I reached for Colm, tapped into his mind, and found only one thread left. Damn it. All this time spent debating semantics had given the Dark Lady the chance she needed to take what was mine. Yes, this giant Celt was mine, for better or worse. From the moment our paths crossed, our destinies became forever linked.

She was smart, this Scottish princess—I have to admit that.

If we stayed a moment longer, I would lose him, and she would win. There was no time for panic—only clear thought and logic.

I swallowed the scream rising in my throat.

Finvarra's lantern cast a yellow glow in the murky light. It sat where Colm had left it, on the rock shelf above my head. I contemplated the impossible. Finvarra had handed that lantern to me. Was he aware of the dangers we might face? Did that golden flame hold magic within? I sprang toward the shelf, pulling Colm along. I gripped the handle and swung the lantern in a wide arc, searching for her.

She showed herself, only inches away. Her arm shot out, drawing a razor-sharp, blackened fingernail down his face, leaving a long slice down his right cheek.

I wavered, unable to move, paralyzed. Drops of Colm's blood pooled and then seeped into her porous bones.

She extended her neck and cracked her jaw, guttering a single laugh from her rotted lips—more alive than a moment before.

I told myself she was only an apparition, but that wasn't true.

My thoughts connected to Colm's familiar. The man he called Ruairi looked almost alive within the *Tuatha* realm. Only a sideways glance showed a hint of transparency. How many times had Ruairi shared Colm's face? How much life force had he drained from Colm with each encounter?

"Our accord is not complete, cousin." Her voice moved like tendrils of mist filling the cavern. "My son will cross into the mortal realm before the moon turns. He will live again." She appeared a heartbeat away, the glimmer in her eyes piercing.

"Accord? What accord?" And there it was—a life for a life. If Colm left the mortal realm, her son would take his place. These were the words of a crazed mind.

"My accord is with Ruairi." Colm's voice carried conviction, his trust in his friend Ruairi unwavering.

"My pretty boy... You are born of my loins. You are an O'Donnell." She held the strings to his mind, and I was running out of time.

Whatever inherent magic I had seemed useless against her. I remembered the three horsemen who visited my dreams—they were not this. This woman was evil incarnate. The surrounding air grew thinner, making it harder to breathe.

The abyss roared, unleashing a storm of tiny, winged creatures, whizzing past and filling the chamber one by one.

"Calla, look." Colm wrapped his arms around my waist, holding me against his chest.

The Dark Lady lifted her skeletal arms. I wondered what force she summoned. But no, the light in her dark orbs faded as she tried to shield herself. She feared what was coming more than I did.

Bees.

The swarm grew larger, a million buzzing wings filling the chamber with sound. They descended on her ethereal form, each tiny creature clinging to sinew and bone. They crawled over her torn dress and into each other, forming a dense mat of fuzzy little bodies.

I threw my hand over my mouth, bile closing my throat.

The droning intensified, the sonorous hum rising in pitch, as the tiny bees paralyzed the Dark Lady with the natural anesthetic all honey bees possess. Their hunger transformed into contented sighs as they crawled and chewed the rotted husk until no distinguishable features remained. And then, inch by inch, the tiny creatures dragged what remained into the dark abyss.

The translucent pool returned to its original calm, leaving me speechless, unsure of what had happened. This was the ultimate bad dream. I lifted the lantern higher, intending to leave this place and never look back.

But the swirling mist had something else in mind. I backed into Colm's tall frame.

The mist rose and swirled in the middle of the pool, forming another apparition. I stared in awe as the golden-haired wraith took form—a woman I had seen before—Ériu.

"Who are you?" Colm whispered.

"I am Ériu, Rioghain's mother. It was I who sent the bees to recover their dead sister." Her voice held my attention; it was soft and meant no harm.

"How?" I moved closer to my mother, looking into her blue eyes for the answers I needed.

"When you touched the black pearls, I felt compelled to act." She nodded, her golden hair flowing over the high collar of a simple lavender gown.

"Is she gone? The Dark Lady. Is she dead?" Colm's eyes shone, his voice filled with life.

"She is still dead. She is less powerful than before, but the Dark Lady will rise again. You would heed my warning, Colm O'Donnell, and let the dead lie in peace." Her arms hung at her sides, her gaze knowing.

"I will." Colm's Adam's apple bobbed in his throat.

"Daughter. Beautiful Rioghain. I tried to protect you from Finvarra's madness, but failed. It is now impossible for you to stay distant. Your sisters need you more than ever." She reached out, her delicate fingers brushing against the ruby crown tangled in my hair.

I gazed into her deep, soulful eyes, swallowed the lump forming in my throat, and asked the question. "Why did you send me away? Nemain, Macha. They're my family."

"I wanted to protect you from the horrors of Finvarra's world—centuries of suffering and conflict—but I was too late. I couldn't prevent him from interfering in your life."

"It is too late. I've become what he said I am." I stood still, the blood in my veins humming.

"Trust me when I tell you this, dear Rioghain. Take this man and live your life free of Finvarra's realm. You will see your sisters again. They are part of you, just as you are part of them." Her voice wavered, softer and softer, leaving silence between us.

"Ériu, wait. Please. Will I see you again?" I feared I would lose her forever. This one moment would never be enough.

Mist swirled around me, caressing and enveloping me in warmth. Then, just like that, it vanished. She was gone.

"Ériu," I whispered her name.

"Calla, are you all right?" Colm twined his fingers with mine.

"I think so." I turned toward him, leaning into his strength. "We should go, don't you think?"

"Let's go home." He drew me into his arms and held me. Just held me.

My thoughts spun. Where was home? Where did I belong?

He stepped back, and I wondered why. "Look at the walls. Something is happening."

What was once hard basalt and jagged rock glowed with an iridescent blue, shimmering with ivory. I turned toward the glassy pool. The night was not over yet.

A deafening roar filled my ears, followed by a thunderous clap. The waters surged upward, and a wave of white foam rose from the depths—something magical in its own right.

Resurrection, the Faerie horse who chose me in the Otherworld, rose from the still waters. He tossed his enormous head, his silver eyes shifting to velvet black. He pawed the stone floor, water streaming from his muscular back.

"What is this?" Colm's grip on my hand tightened, his face stark.

"This is Resurrection. A wedding gift, perhaps? From Finvarra?" I rushed forward, wrapping my arms around the horse's neck and burying my face in Resurrection's flowing mane, inhaling his strength.

"He is the most magnificent creature I have ever seen." Colm trailed behind me, admiration coloring his voice. He stroked the horse's broad back and muscular flanks.

Resurrection twitched his ears, his nostrils flaring. Beneath a thick forelock, intelligent eyes observed his surroundings.

My heart trembled with a mix of emotions: happiness, hope, and resolve. I thanked Finvarra. He had given me the greatest gift of all.

RESURRECTION LED us through a scar in the rock face, bringing us back to the mortal world. I tasted the salty brine of the sea as the velvet night watched over us. Seagulls screeched, dive-bombing the moonlit waves. I turned my head, identifying the strand stretching into the nearby dunes, with rock outcroppings rising from the sand. I breathed a sigh of relief, content in the knowledge of our safety within the mortal realm. Yet, the world between worlds was always present. Resurrection tossed his head, embracing the warm night with a wild whinny.

"Jesus, is the whole town here?" I recalled Saoirse's invitation on my first day in Ardara town. "Good craic," she said. "Come," she had said. What began as an adventure of discovery steamrolled into another dimension.

Prevailing winds carried the pungent aroma of wood smoke and burnt pitch from the many bonfires burning on the strand.

I watched in awe as the cloaked figures, antlered men, and revelers celebrated an ancient pagan festival, moving in strange dances and circling each other. Were they spirits from another world? Fire torches flickered in the darkness, heightening the eerie mood.

Joe, the barber, juggled flaming bolas high in the air. The girl from the apothecary, her face painted with ancient runes, swayed beneath the bright star. Orlaith struck a shaman drum.

I tightened my hold on the reins, unwilling to lose my grip on Resurrection in the melee of celebrants.

Saoirse stood in the center of it all, wearing blood-red robes with whitethorn flowers woven into her auburn hair. Nine witches, all dressed in pure white, encircled her. She lifted her hands to the night sky, summoning the sacred to join her. The moon, a bright orb in the darkness, fueled her desire. The ocean shimmered beneath her gaze. Amid the whistling wind and crashing waves, her silvery voice stirred the crowd to madness.

She raised a silver blade while circling a roaring bonfire, her eyes scanning each cardinal point, calling the spirits to rise.

I inhaled a sharp breath, her intentions taking shape in my mind.

The pounding of the drum grew louder, and the moon's beams lifted the spirits of men. Her voice carried far, calming the revelers, her eyes shimmering with a lively glow.

Resurrection stamped his feet as she invoked the *Tuatha Dé*, inviting them to the party.

Colm seemed oblivious to the implications.

Shadows covered the moon, and memories of the day the *Tuatha Dé* invaded Ireland flooded my mind. They came from four great cities shaped by the wind, separated by ocean and sea, hundreds of miles from any mainland.

In Falias, snow whipped down, sleet freezing the ship's deck. The captain shouted orders, preparing the tall ship for the journey. Men and women cloaked in bearskins protected the Stone of Destiny, *Lia Fáil*.

In Gorias, the sweet breath of spring melted the icy remnants of winter. The golden hawk, talons extended, landed on the prow of the second tall ship. Four men stood guard over Slaughterer, the lightning-tipped magical spear.

The sun shone high in Finias. Leaving the safety of the thicket, the majestic stag jumped into the open, while in the harbor, a large ship rested at anchor, waiting for the small rowboat to approach. Uscias, the poet, offered an enchanted prize to the ship's captain—Fragarach, the

Answerer—the same sword Finvarra held to Colm's throat.

Saoirse's voice undulated with the wild rivers—salmon leaped, leaves descended, and cornstalks withered.

In Murias, wild ponies ran free, while predator birds circled overhead, orcas breached the surface of the sea. The locals honored the harvest with a legendary cauldron that never emptied.

Hidden among the clouds, four ships reached the shores of this land. A fierce people skilled in sorcery and magic, an immortal race of beings. And thus it began.

Saoirse called upon the Lord King to release his seed, and the Spring Maiden to receive him. She lifted a chalice with one hand and lowered the golden athame into the waiting cauldron, drawing energy from the male and female connection—the Fertility Rite, the Great Rite.

Colm took control, pushing Resurrection past the celebrants, white heat surging through his veins and into mine. Our connection was undeniable. I stayed focused on the present, the here and now.

Saoirse raised her arms, drawing strength from both masculine and feminine energies. When she lowered her gaze and pressed her lips to the rim of the chalice, she awakened the earth from winter's sleep.

"Take me home, Colm." I found my voice. I was his, and he was mine. Tonight, we would become one.

Saoirse

"With this Beal Fire, I honor Brighid, the Queen of the Faeries, the Goddess of Fire and Inspiration. Let us celebrate the awakening of the earth from winter's sterility." I gazed at nine witches, each entranced by the same Faerie magic, each swirling in a counterclockwise direction, holding court with the deity we served, each carrying a ceremonial branch from one of nine trees: birch, rowan, ash, alder, hawthorn, holly, oak, hazel, and willow, with colored ribbons flowing from each sacred twig, adding a magical element to their dance. Their faces drawn, their eyes glazed with the wonder they alone perceived, they whispered wishes into the flames. At night's end, the ceremonial branches would burn.

"Direct your intentions, close your eyes, and sink into the dark space behind your eyelids. Become one with yourself. Ask the spirits and the natural world for aid." I called upon Brighid's wisdom and healing powers to guide my quest. The white light surrounding my heart gave me courage, and her welcoming sigh brought me comfort.

When I was lost, she bestowed upon me my own talents of ironwork and smithing. Now, my path in life was certain. My energy flowed toward positive goals, and her skills moved through my hands. Ocean currents went through me, and beneath my feet, the land throbbed with energy.

I touched her power, delving deeper into my intentions than ever before. For seven years, I longed for a lost love: Ciarán, the boy who returned as a man. The Other Crowd had brought him back to this realm, answering my prayers. Questions burned in my mind—questions I was too afraid to explore.

My thoughts drifted to when Ciarán burst into the pub; my breath vanished, and my heart soared. He held me in his arms, but then his sturdy frame faltered. He said he loved me and wanted me. Yet there was uncertainty in his words. He seemed somehow broken.

They say those taken never come back the same, leaving part of themselves behind. I feared the damage done.

I cast my spell, channeling the fire's energy as my own. The ocean's roar drowned out the shouts and laughter of the lively crowd. Beyond the circle, partygoers celebrated this night. In true Bealtaine style, the mead flowed, and the land awakened in more ways than one.

"Tonight celebrates the union of the Green Man and the May Queen. Blessed be." I caught Ciarán's gaze, his spark igniting mine, his warmth filling my soul. Hope thrived where despair once dwelled. One day, our lives would end. The embers would fade, and like this fire, we would become something new. I accepted the inevitable for what it was.

The Goddess Brighid's powers guided me as I whispered my sacred vow. How naïve I was to believe? Tears streamed down my face as I dropped the coin into the chalice, completing the ritual. I murmured the words, my voice thick with emotion.

I circled the fire in a graceful grapevine pattern, my feet skipping, as I raised my arms into the starry sky, the moonshine reflecting in my gaze. I danced for Brighid, the daughter of the Dagda. I thanked her, and her energy flowed through me.

Who were these legendary beings we called upon? We both feared and admired them. History suggests that they would return when the world needed them most. Was this such a time?

The coven members cast their ceremonial twigs into the fire, exchanging smiles and hugs. As I packed the dagger and chalice into my bag, a gust of wind carried a fresh pine scent toward me. Sensing Ciarán's presence, I turned into his arms.

"You were wonderful." Ciarán dipped his head, catching my lips. Heat coursed through my veins, and my knees buckled.

"It's an honor to lead the ritual. It makes me feel light-headed yet warm at the same time. Do you know what I mean?" I searched his eyes, struggling to understand the man within.

"That's how I feel holding you. I'm so proud of you, Saoirse. You've achieved so much." He tightened his grip, pulling me closer against his chest. An aura surrounded him, an invisible shield I couldn't seem to break through. I focused my energy on my intention. Tonight, that shield would fall.

The ocean's thunder couldn't drown out the rising hoots and hollers of the crowd reveling at tonight's festival. The noise grew louder.

"Saoirse. Look." Ciarán whispered, his voice quick.

I turned my head to meet his gaze. A man and a woman sat on a magnificent white horse beneath the shadow of the cliff. I stared, bewildered by the mythical sight of a milk-white horse, its head held high, with a mane flowing nearly to its knees, moonlight glinting off a gilded bridle inset with emeralds.

The crowd parted, awestruck by the magical sight of the Spring Maiden and the Horned God, two ethereal spirits visiting the mortal plane on this Bealtaine Eve. I rubbed my eyes in wonder.

"It's Colm and Calla. They're safe." Ciarán squeezed my hand.

He was right. I could see that now. Colm, with his hair tousled, wore the same blue jeans and biker boots. But Calla? She looked like a Faerie Princess.

"Saoirse," Colm called my name from atop the magnificent horse. The wound on his forehead had disappeared, but a fierce cut marked his cheek. He was back, alive, and he had brought her home.

Calla sat before him, wrapped in an emerald cloak, while a golden crown studded with rubies glinted in her braided hair.

"Calla, you're safe." I hurried toward them, my heart racing, my words full of relief.

"We're safe." Calla bent at the waist and took my hand in hers. Her eyes flashed silver, then softened to pearly gray.

"What happened?" I gripped her fingers, sensing her rocketing emotions. Happiness. Trepidation.

"Eamon? Is he okay?" Colm's voice held worry, his gaze watchful as he kept one arm around Calla.

"He's okay, Colm. He's home." Ciarán rested his hand on Colm's calf.

"Thank God." Calla's gaze shifted to the blonde man

behind me, Ciarán, then back to me. She pressed her lips together but couldn't hide her smile.

I knew then that it was true. She was responsible for Ciarán's return. I met her smile, my heart ready to burst.

"We'll share a pint tomorrow, aye? Right now, we need to go home." Colm nodded toward Clonmara and looked at me. "Saoirse, one thing. Tomorrow morning, would you do us the honor of marrying us?"

"Marry you?" I couldn't hide my surprise. It rang out like a silver bell.

"Aye, a Bealtaine wedding. Something simple." He pressed his lips to the top of Calla's head, happiness spilling from his lips.

"Okay, for sure. Where?" That was a surprise I hadn't seen coming, but hell yes.

"Clonmara?" His head dipped, and he spoke in hushed tones to Calla.

"Clonmara." Her eyes gleamed, and then she smiled. "Thank you, Saoirse. You're a good friend." She urged the great horse forward, leaving me to wonder what had just happened.

I stared at the caves and swallowed hard. Those caves led nowhere, or at least that's what it seemed. The last person who thought they could navigate through had disappeared, leaving only their dog to return, emaciated and hungry.

"They made it." Ciarán's shoulders eased, a heavy weight lifted from him.

I then realized the burden he had carried. His thoughts were with his brother, as they should be. He would have understood what Colm faced when entering a place like the Otherworld. My heart rose in my throat, considering all he had faced alone.

"And they want to get married. It's wonderful, isn't it?" I squeezed his hand, feeling one thing. The butterflies in my stomach were for Calla—I shared her happiness. She was like a sister.

"It is." We walked across the hard-packed sand toward the distant dunes. The caravan was parked between two rising hillocks, safe from the ocean's tide.

"I can't believe you kept this old relic." He lifted his chin, a smile lighting up his blue eyes. He huffed a breath, inspecting the bumper stickers plastered all over the back of the camper van, each telling a story of a journey he wasn't part of. His brows furrowed, his lips moving up and down, questions waiting on the tip of his tongue.

I laughed, and it was freeing. It was effortless.

"We were going to travel the world, remember? Well, at least all of Ireland." I placed my hand on his upper arm. "Do you remember how we saved our pennies? We brought her home the day before. You know, the day before you left me."

"I'm sorry, Saoirse, for the pain I caused." His face tightened, and he lowered his gaze.

"You're home, Ciarán. That's all that matters." Concern filled my voice and my heart with fear.

"I was gone for so long. I've missed so much. I was so stupid." He hung his head, filled with shame, sadness, and grief.

"Did you know I left, too? I took the caravan and drove as far as I could. I stayed here and there, taking odd jobs in pubs. But I couldn't stay away. You were every-where, but I couldn't find you." I lifted his hand and traced my thumb over his palm, following the long life-line. I should have known he hadn't gone far.

"I tried so many times to talk to you. It was their magic, their invisibility, that passed to me. It was their way of holding me hostage." His voice carried only sadness.

"Why? What did they want from you?" I touched his face. He was so much the same.

"Hurling. I was their star player. They wouldn't let me leave, but they gave me the freedom to visit. Unseen. A silent visitor in my life." His whisper was filled with bitterness.

"Hurling? You're not even that good." I punched him on the upper arm, trying to lighten his mood.

"Hey, that hurt." He lifted his lips into a smile. The hinges creaked as he opened the door.

He extended his hand, helping me navigate the few steps into the caravan.

I gasped aloud. Candles flickered on every surface, casting a warm, golden glow over the small space, with sweet scents of vanilla and honeysuckle filling the air. "Did you do this? All these candles? When?"

"Come here to me. I've missed you so much." His hands slid under my cloak, resting on my bare shoulders.

"Me too. I didn't think." I swallowed the lump in my throat, my eyes filling with hot tears.

"Don't cry, baby. I'm here. I'm here, and I'm not going anywhere, ever again." His hands brushed my shoulders, dropping my cloak to the floor.

I wrapped my arms around him, taking a deep breath and inhaling a distant scent I always recognized. A hot flash of fire rushed through my skin. He was everything I had ever desired.

"You're so beautiful." His movements were unhurried. One by one, he slid the hairpins from the circlet of wildflowers in my hair. He ran his fingers through the loosened curls, and at the same time, closed his lips over mine.

That was when I realized he had never really left me. He had been there, in the ether, all along.

10

C*olm*

Twilight broke the dawn, casting a shadow over the sloped ceiling. The floorboards creaked, and my heart hammered. I shot upright, gasping for breaths I hadn't taken, searching the darkness for the unknown attacker I felt was nearby. A brooding darkness moved from one dormer window to the other, the ghostly figure leaving a trail of melancholy, its sighs barely audible. Someone else might have thought the wind rattled the windowpanes. I didn't know whether to laugh or cry.

There was a reason I disliked the garage loft, and now I see why. The ability to observe others was enough to make a man lose his grip on reality.

I remembered the night before when my mind abandoned me in that cavern. The Dark Lady kept my heart in another shadowy place. She failed to steal my soul, and I was thankful for that.

The gray sky showed no signs of relief. Rain lashed down, the patter washing away yesterday's wounds. The whistling wind pushed the branches of the old hazel tree against the shingled roof. My phone's screen lit up, and the chirping sound reminded me that life went on—my life with Calla.

I stretched my limbs and shifted sideways in the double bed. So much had happened, and I had only just begun to process the events that had transpired. Calla agreed to marry me, a Bealtaine wedding on May Day.

Happiness flooded my heart, filling my mind with hope for the first time in a long while. She was alive and well, and we were together. She slept on her side, a black halo framing her face. The sound of her breathing comforted me—the rise and fall of her chest. My Faerie girl. My superhero. That's what she was.

"Calla." Lifting the long tendrils from her neck, I dipped my head and kissed her nape. She murmured sleepy words and snuggled closer, spooning into my chest, warmth radiating from her skin. Heat, so much heat. My hand drifted, reveling in her beauty: her finely shaped shoulders and muscular back, her narrow waist connecting to strong hips, her sassy bottom, and her legs that seemed to go on forever. Perfection redefined.

I wanted her. Every muscle I possessed responded to her nearness. My skin tightened, the blood in my veins pulsed, my shaft throbbed. The pain was almost delightful.

I smoothed her hair with my fingertips. Something was captivating about those curling strands. Her ability to transform into another being made me realize one crucial thing—the impossible was possible. Her struggle had opened my eyes to a world of danger I had overlooked my entire life. I ran my hand over her hip, a perfectly human hip. Protecting her from the likes of Sean Hamstead and others who threatened her kind gave my life the purpose it had been missing. My previous existence felt insignificant by comparison.

The Faerie blood in her veins stirred, and the surrounding aura shimmered in the dim light. I watched, captivated by the glowing shades of black and gold, wishing I could hold her in my arms forever.

"Good morning." She turned toward me, a beautiful sigh escaping her full lips.

"*Mo grhá.*" I grazed the corner of her mouth with a soft kiss.

She offered the tip of her tongue, tracing and sealing the seam of my lips, fueling my desire even more. When she placed her hand on my shoulder, heat shot through my bones. Her closeness was like no other.

"I want you, Colm. I need you." She rose to her knees, straddling my hips with her hands braced on my chest, tendrils of black silk framing her face. She made my head spin.

"No regrets?" My cock sprang to life, thick against her heated pussy. I reached up, combing the wild strands away from her beautiful face.

"Regrets?" She ran her fingers along my jaw, the tender moment not lost on me. "You are mine, Colm. And I am yours. Do you remember your promise?"

"My promise?" My hands drifted, drawing her heat closer.

"To please me for the next three hundred and sixty-five days." Her rich laughter rolled over me, filling the quiet space, intoxicating my mind.

"And every day thereafter, *mo grhá*." I searched the hunger in her eyes, and my cock swelled.

"Those are only words, O'Donnell. I am a wanton woman needing a man." She took my hands, placing both over the swell of her breasts—her eyes heavy-lidded, her lips half-parted.

"Do you like that?" I stroked the arrowed nubs with the pad of my thumb, shifting my hips, settling beneath her heat. My cock throbbed, her need igniting mine.

Molten gold circled the grey in her eyes, a fire that was not there before. She left this realm and fulfilled her destiny.

"Hmm." She rocked, sweeping her pussy over my shaft, her whimpers a dark song that sang to my heart. Lightning split the sky, filling the loft with a wild strike.

"Come for me. Take what you need." I would spend my life trying to please her.

"I want something else, O'Donnell." Her lips were soft, her smile warm against mine. But her wicked tongue was lazily working my lower lip. And then she bit me. She fucking bit me. The sting was piercing, but then a wave of pleasure flooded my limbs. Hot and thick and laced with desire.

A groan rose in my throat, my whole body arching beneath her.

When she moaned, I almost lost it. My hands found her waist, and I held her, two live wires connected as one, as she drew the life force from my body. My life force. My blood. I would give. Everything. For her. To her. I already had.

She hissed then when I cradled her bottom. It was strangely erotic, her sex clenching as she ground against my hard cock. Needy. Wanting. And, still, she fed.

Only she could end this. Only she could save us. My need rose with hers as my hips jerked, my cock pulsing for release. Sparks shot through my veins, and blue flames licked the gates of hell. The sting of burnt copper and rust assaulted the back of my throat. Blood. My blood.

"Colm." She pulled back, her body trembling against mine.

"I didn't know you could do that." I brushed the wild strands of hair away from her face. I needed release, but to sully this immortal with my seed.

"Are you hurt?" I could sense her confusion as her attention turned to me.

"No. Never." An ache coiled in my belly. Pleasure. Pain. I tried not to moan, but I failed. The surrender thrilled me. My limbs melted as the ache dove deeper.

"You haven't come." She splayed her fingers over my chest, learning my body as if for the first time. She ground against me, taking me to the edge again and again. She was a seductress.

When she dragged her fingertips over my burning balls, my cock jerked, pulsing against her wet heat. The bliss was raw and all-consuming. I felt it in my spine.

"You saved me from the darkness." I gazed at the Faerie girl. She made me forget who I was. She knew how to wreck me.

"Last night?" Her face flushed the sweetest shade of pink as she lay over me, her long legs twined with mine. "You mean from the Dark Lady?"

I refused to admit that a lot of what happened remained a blur. What I knew for sure was that she brought me back to life. "Do you always sleep naked?"

"Does that bother you?" She trailed her fingertips over my chest, drawing lines and delicate swirls. I closed my eyes, lulled by her ministrations. She was a drug. She was my addiction.

"I enjoy being with you." I pulled her close, pressing my lips to her forehead. I breathed in the night's fragrance.

"I took advantage of you, if I remember correctly?" She swirled the tip of her tongue over her shining teeth and smirked.

"We didn't? Did we?" I walked back in time and recalled only vague flashes of memory. Why couldn't I remember?

"You needed sleep, Colm." She looked at me the way an immortal would.

I racked my brain. Was there something she was not sharing with me? My mind was a blank slate from when we arrived at Clonmara.

"I should have realized what the Dark Lady wanted. I should have known." Calla's hair flowed over her shoulders, shimmering in the same shade as the night pearls on her collarbone.

"That was something we did as boys. A pact made on All-Hallow's Eve. None of it was your fault." I touched her cheek.

"Do you know who I am, Colm? My father is the King of the Faeries. Our maternal grandfather is Donn, The Lord of the Dead. He lives, just like Ruairi." Her voice shimmered in the dark, and starlight flashed in her eyes.

"None of it matters, *mo grhá*. Not to me." I looked into those swirling silver orbs, and my blood ran hot. I could never get enough. I was hard before I could stop it.

"You saw Ériu. She brought those bees from the underworld, Colm. She drove the Dark Lady back to the grave. I don't belong here, but I want to stay. It's all I know." She rolled onto her side, gazing toward the wraith haunting the corner of the room. "Show me what it means to be a woman." She swallowed, her pretty lips quirking into a grin.

I played with her fingers, one by one, until the stress lines left her forehead.

"My woman, *mo grhá*." I planted my hands on either side of her bottom, lifting her hips, and positioning her pussy over my mouth.

"Oooh, what are you doing?" She extended her arms, thrown off balance, and settled her knees on either side of my face.

"Tasting what is mine." One long lick separated her luscious folds. I captured her clit, flicking the swollen bead with my tongue.

"Oh God." She rested her hands on the painted headboard, bracing herself.

Raindrops pummeled the slate roof, drowning out the rest of the world.

"Faster. Do it faster. Ohhh." She bowed her hips, rocking within my grasp, her moans rising into frenzied squeals. "Yes. Oh, yes." A quick tremble danced over her velvet skin—a shockwave over mine. Her eyes drifted open and shut as she climaxed hard and fast, flooding my mouth with a golden elixir, a taste of honey that filled my soul.

I drank my fill, lapping her tender flesh, cursing under my breath at the gut-churning revelation. I could not exist without her.

"So pretty, *mo grhá*." I gathered her onto my lap, my cock throbbing at her nearness. I cupped her breasts, scraping each arrowed nub between my teeth.

"I want you, Colm." She ground into me, her slick pussy stroking my shaft.

"Do you want to wait? To make love? To make our union official?" I brushed my lips over hers, pressing a soft kiss to her lips.

"You've made me wait long enough." Her thighs quivered, and her breathing ratcheted higher.

"I don't want to hurt you. This is your first time, no?" I dipped my head, tracing the curve of her throat with a wet tongue.

"I. Need. This." She whipped her head back and hissed, her eyes alight with fire.

"Every day?" I nipped an earlobe and pressed a soft kiss to her nape.

"Twice a day." She dragged the tip of her pink tongue across her bottom lip. "I will marry you, Colm O'Donnell. For better or worse, but I have waited long enough."

Her need sent me over the edge. Still, I squashed my desires. She was my queen. I would swear fealty to her alone.

"I know what you're thinking and don't. You're a man. My man and I want you to fuck me." The things this woman made me feel left me wondering how I had ever managed to live.

She took my face in both of her hands, dragging her tongue over the bristles on my chin, and then sucked my bottom lip into her mouth.

Lightning bolts struck, lacing the dark sky with white-hot heat. The crack following shook the window panes. Calla's eyes flashed silver.

"I want to taste you, Colm, and then I want you to fuck me." She walked back on her knees, swirling her tongue over the pulsing crown.

"Calla." I curled my fingers into the cotton sheets, quelling the rising storm. My heart jumped, watching her glide her mouth over the length. I waited for the moment she would bite.

She stared at me with devilish eyes.

"Does your cock have a name, O'Donnell? It's such an impressive toy. Let's give him a name." She drew her tongue from the base of the shaft to the crown.

My balls tightened, and my cock jerked.

"A name?" My eyes rolled back in my head when she slid her mouth over my length. When she hollowed her cheeks and suckled, sparks shot through my shaft. "Calla, you're making me come."

"Is it good?" She looked at me with a pleased smile on her face.

Cool air kissed my shaft, but did nothing to quench the fire.

"It's more than good." Light danced before my eyes,

and I wondered if I would ever get used to her magical ways. Her aura, once dark, glittered like stars in the night sky. Starlight. Moonlight. My mind floated between.

"Are you able to come more than once?" She sat back on her heels, my shaft pulsing within her grip.

"With you, yes." I chuckled, wondering what she was getting at.

"Good, because after I taste you, you will fill me with your seed." She lowered her chin, her darting tongue wreaking havoc.

"*Mo grhá*." I swallowed hard, understanding her meaning. Anticipation made my cock throb, my balls tighten. "Let's do this." I spun her sideways, repositioning her languid limbs. I lifted her knee and blew a cooling breath over her heated flesh.

"Hmm. I like this," she murmured as she drew her fingers over my hip, drawing lines with her fingertips.

"Hmm, me, too." I planted close kisses, one after another, along her inner thigh, making my way toward her heat.

When she closed her lips over the crown of my cock, I almost lost my mind. But when she cradled my balls, she commanded my complete attention.

"Calla." I reached for her, trailing my fingers through her dark mane. I gazed at her sweet mouth, her lush lips working my shaft.

She rested her cheek on my thigh, swirling the tip of her tongue over the crown of my cock. Lapping. Licking. Suckling.

When she pressed deeper, my cock jerked, my hips bucked.

I tangled my hands in her hair, unable to contain my lust, my need. When she slid those pointed teeth along my shaft, I forgot how to breathe. I caressed her heavy swells, her pebbled nubs, the gathering storm numbing my mind.

"Hmm." She took my cock to the hollow of her throat, bobbing her head faster and faster, her warm mouth inviting me to spill my seed. She was a demon in disguise.

"Calla, you don't have to do this." I planted my hand on her shoulders. In answer, she dug her fingers into my ass cheeks, pressing into me, shaking my very existence.

My head snapped back. My chest heaved. I wanted her to bite me.

I tore my gaze from that mouth and drove my tongue through her swollen cleft, matching her rhythmic dance.

She moaned low in her throat, and her thighs clenched. She trembled beneath my tongue, giving me another taste of heaven.

Fire ripped through my balls, a hot jolt pulsing through my bones. My cock jerked as I ground into her, flooding her mouth with seed. My mind floated in a world where pleasure and pain existed as one. She was fire, and I was rain. The sounds she made as she claimed my cock. Fuck.

I met her silvery gaze, searching for the right words. My thoughts jumbled, lost in a haze of lust. I trailed my fingers over her sinewy thigh. Wreaked. Undone.

A drift of air passed over me, morning light playing in the shadows.

"You're from a realm only the ould ones speak of." I combed my hand through her silken locks, my veins thrumming with want. Whether or not she knew it, she owned me.

"Yeah. In another dimension." She left me then, walking, her footsteps silent across the carpet, her curves a silhouette in the darkness. The plumbing squawked as she cranked the water taps.

CALLA

Steam fogged the enclosure as I sent him an inviting glance, my need for him heightening with every second. I wanted him. He did not know how much he thrilled me —this big brawny man with his cock thick against sculpted muscles. His salty, sweet seed, like the ocean and blackberry jewels, embedded itself in my soul. His blood...that was something else entirely.

I swallowed hard, my mouth aching, crowded with teeth that shouldn't have been there. My tongue grazed the dropping fangs, my mind swimming with unanswered questions. An explanation would have been nice —a warning of some sort.

He leaned on his elbow, his gaze following me.

"Are you going to join me?" I pushed those thoughts down deep—the need to ride the waves of pleasure with my husband-to-be clouding my mind.

He dreamed of me all night, and what he did to my body made me blush. I had crossed the line. I had tasted his secrets and taken his essence. What kind of monster was I?

"It's a wee bit tight." He slid in behind me, water

pouring over him. His hands were everywhere, caressing and stroking. Unafraid. Hungry. He had no idea how hungry I was.

"Yes. Yes. Oh, yes." I spread my hands on the tiled wall, my pussy aching liquid heat for him. My mind blurred. What came first? Lust? Love?

Jets of water flowed from above, hot rivulets cascading over his shoulders, dancing off my breasts, sparking so much heat. He reached for the body wash, filling the enclosure with the aroma of vanilla and honeysuckle.

"I need." My eyes closed, my mind expecting him to ram his cock home, to fuck me hard and fast. That was what I wanted. To lose my virgin status.

"You need to come, *mo grhá*," He murmured into the side of my face, squeezing the outer folds of my vagina with his big fingers. All the while, the heel of his hand kneaded my already engorged clit. The pleasure was agonizing.

"I can't. It's too much." I gazed sideways, through half-slits, at the man towering behind me. Chiseled lines and so much skin. His scent—winter frost and summer rain. There was no going back. I wanted this.

"You can." The tattoo behind his ear thrummed black. Fire danced in his eyes, and heat—so much heat. He was a man possessed. Had I done that to him?

He cupped my chin, exploring every inch of my mouth with a hard, demanding tongue.

The pulse between my legs, that insistent throb I could handle. But my mouth was on fire—a deep want that wasn't quiet. The hunger reached out like a lion in the night. His blood was more than an aphrodisiac; it held the world's light, and I had lived too long in the darkness.

"Do you want me, *mo grhá*?" He dragged his hand over my blazing skin, cupping my breasts, tweaking my heated nubs, sparks flying from each fingertip, as his cock, that velvet-wrapped shaft, throbbed against my backside.

"Yes. Yes. I want you." I gasped. My breasts ached, heavy and tender to the touch, heat swelling around my cleft.

"Here? Or would you prefer the wee bed?" His bristled chin scraped the side of my face as he nibbled my lips. He showed no fear, licking my teeth, tantalizing my lengthening fangs with a sweeping tongue.

My ears roared. I wanted this. I was more than ready.

"Here. Now." A blur of light danced in front of my eyes, and my breath left me as the broad crown sought entry.

He groaned, a rasping shudder that curled from his chest as he slid inward, one slow inch after another, stretching my inner channel until time ceased to exist.

I rid myself of any remaining doubt. He was mine, and I was his. I pressed into him, taking him deeper. I wanted more of this, more of his cock. All those imagined moments came to life.

"You're so wet, so tight." He planted his hands over mine, caging me in his arms. One thrust took him deeper than even I thought possible.

"More." My skin ached with a need, a desire, a lust that reached for my soul and took it.

"Calla Rioghain O'Donnell. Say it." His whisper rolled over me, his breath hot on my nape. He licked me then, drawing heat from my skin and cooling the flames.

I repeated my name with his, my throat thick with want. I widened my stance, making my intentions clear.

"*Mo grhá.*" His husky whisper set my heart ablaze as he drove deep once, twice, and then, with the wild fervor of a man possessed, he murmured into my ear, "Come for me."

It was more than I imagined. The connection. The need. My pussy wept liquid heat, flames scorching my skin.

"That's it. Yes, that's it," he murmured as water cascaded over us and around us.

The fire in my belly was for him.

"I need to come." He braced one hand on the slick tile, his heart beating in rhythm with mine, his cock buried deep.

The skies above thundered in answer.

He hooked his arm around my waist, his cock twitching as he came, each thrust deeper than the last. He was a lover proficient in pleasure, touching every pleasure point again and again. There was no going back from a place like that.

"I want you, O'Donnell. All of you." I turned my face into the crook of his neck. I was, oh, so very hungry. My entire being throbbed, his rich scent calling to an ancient part of me, one that teased me with its presence, one I had not fully met. I swallowed hard and gazed into his hooded eyes.

"Yes. Take it." His head snapped back, and he offered me his soul.

The black pearls burned as I sank my fangs into his neck. A jolt of heat slammed through me as his blood streamed, abundant, filled with his essence, his dreams, and his silent truths. I saw his fire.

He groaned, a deep rumble in his throat that spoke of need and lust. I tasted that too.

I saw the gates of hell and the place where souls collide.

"So wet. You're so fucking tight." He clutched my hips, thrusting hard again and again, and still I took from him.

In between there and then, I released him, his blood warm on my tongue, my body thrumming with pleasure.

"It's okay. Everything is okay." He held me, his soothing voice serenading another. A wolf cloaked in human form? Is that what I was?

When his seed spilled, he gave me something I didn't know existed—a sensation of being. It was wonderful. It was all that. But when he gave me his blood, the universe split open.

"*Mo grhá.*" His hands ran down my back, lathering body wash over my heated flesh, running soapy fingers through my folds, cleaning away our mutual release.

He left me beneath the pummeling jets as he stepped from the shower stall and into the bathroom. Drawers slid open, and doors shut. His voice sang to me, raspy and seductive in its roughness, as if everything was right with the world.

I closed my eyes and swallowed hard. How many

times had the wind screamed? Had the dead reached for me? I was neither human nor a goddess; I existed somewhere in between. Finvarra was right—darkness lived inside me... I leaned into the spray, but the stain remained. The throbbing hum had evolved into something more, like what the hell.

"Come here to me, *mo ghrá*." He stood outside the stall, his shaft thick against taut muscles. My Celt. My man. I had taken from him so I could live in the light.

"There's a towel here somewhere." He lifted his eyes and grinned as if everything was okay. Did he not understand? Did he not see?

I had only begun to discover who I was.

He returned with his find, wrapping the striped beach towel around me and then scooping me into his arms.

HE SAT in the captain's chair across from mine, wearing blue jeans with his leather belt unbuckled, a loose forelock resting on his forehead. His lips were moist and so kissable.

"*Sláinte, mo ghrá.*" He raised his lowball glass to mine, his eyes as blue as the ocean waves.

I sniffed the contents—liquid gold evoking the bite of autumn and another familiar scent: bog...or, as some might say, sweet peat. I took a tentative sip, letting the warmth wash over my tongue. I swirled my tongue around in my mouth. The canines had withdrawn.

"It doesn't make much sense. What about Ruairi? The

Dark Lady? You're a conduit for dead souls, Colm, whether you realize it or not." I ran my finger along the etched patterns on the tabletop. He initiated this conversation, diverting me from my immediate problem.

No one mentioned blood-drinking. Was I the only one afflicted with this desire? Desire? Or need? Questions remained. How much was too much? Would draining his life force leave him on the edge of madness?

I played with the pearls strung around my neck. They were a comfort.

My thoughts reached beyond the comfort of this cozy space to the magnificent serpent. I had left my skin and walked into another—Caoránach—the ground had bowed beneath her might. The ancients had whispered. I wish I could remember what... I wish I could cry.

Something inside me cracked as I stared at Colm. He was so at ease with what I had become and what I had done. Well, he had shared his soul with his dead ancestor. Maybe we weren't so different after all.

"Ruairi and I have a bond. He's a friend." He looked up into the corner alcove of the garage loft.

"And look what happened. He lives within the *Tuatha* realm. He breathes." My stomach churned. I rose from the table, searching the mini fridge for the goodies stolen from Clonmara's kitchen the night before.

"I've never seen The Dark Lady like that before. She was almost human." He shook his head, took the china platter from me, and removed the plastic wrap.

"She's evil incarnate. She would have sucked the life force from your soul. What bargain did you make?" I watched him slice the apple cake into four delectable hunks.

My mouth watered, anticipating the first mouthful of tart apples, cinnamon, and nutmeg.

We called to them, and they appeared. They spoke of ancient times." He picked up his slice, closing his mouth over the moist cake.

"Who did?" I dug in with a fork.

"Ruairi. His brothers, Donal and Colin. Their lives had meaning, Calla. They fought for freedom from tyranny. They died heroes." Three bites and his plate was empty.

"And the Dark Lady?" I picked at the crumbs on my plate, wasting none.

"She offered a trade. We walk in their shoes, and they walk in ours. I didn't think, Calla. I didn't know what it meant." He touched my fingers, his thoughts far away.

"She wants to raze the dead, Colm. Resurrect her sons in a breathing form." Dread tingled down each vertebra of my spine. How did I not realize this?

"Ruairi knows nothing of this. He's not evil." He stood, taking the plates to the sink.

"She cut you, Colm. Your strength flowed into her and made her stronger." I recalled the moment the blood drained from his face, and his eyes dimmed.

"I don't know what to say." He washed the dishes efficiently, quickly stacking each plate into a yellowed strainer.

"Tadgh. Killian. How frequently do they summon the O'Donnell clan?" I intertwined my fingers, resting my forearms flat on the table.

"I don't know." He turned toward me, the dishes forgotten.

"They need to stop. There's a long game being played. She means to steal your souls."

He returned to the table and refilled my glass, adding a few drops of water to the mix.

"You realize now that the dead live. They possess an Otherworldly power, maybe not like the *Tuatha*—but enough." I was only beginning to understand. To him, this ancestor worship was a way of expressing respect and love.

His forehead creased with worry lines. "We met as young boys, Calla. You have to understand...it wasn't like that. Not then."

"I know." I placed my hand over his and calmed his mind. My heart hummed, Faerie magic prowling under my skin. I wanted to unleash it. I wanted to explore the remnants Ruairi O'Donnell might have left behind.

"Stop that, *mo grhá*. I am tasked with keeping you safe, and I intend to do so." He lifted my hand, pressing his lips to my knuckles. His gaze held a warning.

I knew, then, the power I possessed.

"You're going to marry me today, Calla Sweet. Or should I call you Princess Rioghain?" His grin was disarming. I could see the future in his eyes.

"We need to talk about what happened." I sat back in my chair. "What I did. What I am."

He chuckled. He dared to pin his lips together and choke back his laughter. "I've known all along. From our first kiss, what those pointy canines were all about."

"What?" I looked at him. "You didn't tell me."

"I kind of liked it." He ran his thumb over the pulsing vein in his neck. "Now, let's talk about what's important. You're going to marry me, Faerie girl. Today." He placed his hand over mine.

"You don't give a girl much time to think. I have nothing to wear." I glanced at the crimson gown, at the ocean salt riding up the long skirts.

"Tell me what you need. I'll drop by your cottage." He twirled a lost lock over my ear, the skin around his eyes crinkling.

"I'll go with you." I studied his worried expression.

"Safety first, *mo ghrá*. You'll stay right here until I get back. There's a wee bit of chaos I need to clean up." He touched the wound on his forehead and noticed it was gone.

"What am I going to do here all alone?" I tapped my fingers on the table, unable to hide my grin.

"Stay out of trouble?" His lips curved down, but then he leaned forward and whispered a kiss.

IN THE MIDDLE of the meadow, there was an oak tree. I once stood beneath its towering canopy and kissed Colm for the very first time. In a vision, and in that ethereal moment, our lives intertwined. Like that ancient tree, our love was rooted in both worlds. In a simple ceremony, we would promise each other tomorrow and declare our love.

I lifted my hand to the budding branches, filled with the knowledge that I was home. My gaze followed the bees' flight among the purple heather as I embraced the reality that they were a part of me. Deep within my soul, the hum grew louder, the magic in my veins stronger than the day before. The black pearls around my neck reminded me I belonged to my grandfather's realm, just as much as the others—the underworld. Only time would reveal what that meant.

I had watched Colm walk away. He glanced back, his smile that of a fortunate man. He believed the worst had passed, but I knew differently.

He had come clean, sharing the truth he had tried to hide to protect me. I reminded myself that others had entrusted him with my protection. His heart was in the right place—he was my hero, risking his life for mine. Calling upon an ancient ancestor was his quest; that was a revelation.

But what about me? I had ended a man's life. My stomach twisted and then settled. There was no turning back, and I knew I would do it again if faced with a similar situation.

I could taste Balor's charred flesh, his screams piercing the barrier between this world and the next, echoing in my ears. I wondered if that encounter was a test of my true abilities.

Colm's confession made me smile, his anguished words echoing in my mind. I had become the target of a fanatic's quest because of a foolish DNA test.

"I have a stalker. Well, it wouldn't be the first time." I spoke to myself and the bees. I rubbed my temples, gazing at the horses grazing in the meadow. I had expected the idyllic scene to calm me, but the humming wouldn't stop, and my mind wouldn't shut off.

I held my head in my hands.

I was no longer the same Calla Sweet who had arrived in this land. I was someone and something different. Magic lurked beneath my skin. It had been there all along, waiting to emerge. I embraced it. Longed for it. I wasn't afraid.

Yet a weight bore down on me, and it wasn't the threat of discovery. It was something else. I closed my eyes, searching my memory, but the thought eluded me.

"What is it? What is it?" I played with the black pearls around my neck, searching the surrounding lands with my gaze: Colm's childhood home, the barns, the meadow, and the wild ocean.

Resurrection pawed at the ground with his head hanging low. The herd stayed far away, as if waiting for the volcano to erupt.

The memory haunted my mind, hidden deep within the shadows, an image flickering through my thoughts and then disappearing.

The ocean surged, flipping up and over itself. I had seen that before—the waterfall—the Devil's Chimney, Colm had called it. This was the same: the waves rose into curling sheets of white foam that crashed upon themselves and then rolled onto the shore. Oh, how furious they were.

I walked toward the big horse, intending to calm him. I stroked the white flair running down his face. He tossed his head back, the whites flashing in his eyes.

I replayed the moment Resurrection appeared. The blind stable master's hand rested on the shoulder of a young boy. It was the little boy who didn't belong. My skin tingled with knowing. The humming wouldn't stop.

This creature from the underworld was born from the dead and resurrected for a purpose, given to me by the Lord of the Dead—my grandfather. Finvarra didn't send Resurrection through the portal last night; my grandfather did.

"What is it, big boy? What's wrong?" I stood a foot away, studying his glazed eyes, his muscles roiling beneath a crushed velvet. There was no doubt in my mind. He was that magical horse who could traverse both land and sea.

But what of me?

"It's okay, boy. It's okay." I ran my fingers through the horse's tangled mane and moved closer to him, a plan forming in my mind. Resurrection could take me to his true home beneath the sea, to the land of the dead, to my grandfather.

Was that his goal? The more I thought about it, the clearer it became.

I gazed at the wild waves. White horses—that's what the Irish called them. The white horses were calling Resurrection home, and I had questions that needed answers.

"Take me to the House of Donn." I grasped his thick mane, leaping onto his broad back.

He stood on his hind legs and whinnied.

I swear the waves answered back.

I tightened my grip, straining every muscle to stay on

his bare back as he galloped across the meadow. Wintry winds whipped against my face as he leapt off the cliff and into the curling waves. I closed my eyes and prayed to whatever god might be listening that I would not drown. My fears were unfounded—whatever magic surrounded Resurrection enveloped me as well.

He dove into the turquoise sea, deeper and deeper, until no light remained. It was as I suspected—the oceans were a gateway to another world, and Resurrection was going home.

At last, the entrance showed itself to Donn's watery world.

I loosened my grip on Resurrection's mane as he entered the cavern, his hooves clattering on the hard basalt floor. Fire-burning torches cast a golden glow over smooth walls, and the arched ceiling loomed inches above my head. It felt ominous—Donn's House, the realm of the dead.

I swept my tongue over my bottom lip, tasting the ocean's salt. A chill froze my heart. I wasn't sure if I was dead or alive.

The horse stopped at a maze of passages that led deeper, with only one winding upward. No one arrived. No one waited.

I slipped off his back, facing the beautiful boy who had shown me so much, and landed on the smooth basalt. I pressed my lips to the side of his face. "I won't be long."

I walked alone, my clothes soaked, my feet squelching in my wet running shoes. Each step brought me closer to the vaulted halls where souls gathered on their way to the underworld. I was drawn to the glow across the smooth stone floor, and at the end of the long hall, an ancient wooden door awaited.

I placed my hand on the door, sensing the presence within.

"Come in." A deep rasp of a man's voice curled the air, finding passage through the many cracks in the weathered wood.

I lifted the brass latch, and the door opened not into a cavern shining with diamond-like light, but into a rectangular room with coffered ceilings in a warm mahogany tone. The recessed panels lined a long hallway decorated with portraits, leading to doors that opened into other rooms. At the end of the hall, there appeared to be a kitchen and dining area. This was the captain's suite.

The reception room was both austere and cozy, filled with the personality of the man sitting at the far end behind the ornately carved desk. A braided carpet warmed the wormy planks of reclaimed hemlock. A dog I recognized lay curled in a tight ball before a blazing fireplace. Bran rose to greet me, his pink tongue lolling out of his mouth.

"What are you doing here? You didn't die on me, did you?" I crouched on my heels and spoke to the dog, petting his wiry coat. He whimpered in response and licked my cheek.

"Grandfather." I met the hawk-like gaze of a man in the prime of his life, unexceptionally human. A seafarer, living in his earthly form, the same man who perished thousands of years ago in a shipwreck through Druid magic. This was neither the withered man from Finvarra's realm nor the one from my visions.

"You've come for the boy." Night-black waves fell over a strong forehead, the torchlight catching his swarthy complexion. His heavy accent was not Irish.

"I have." I rose to my feet, with Bran hugging my side, and studied the Spaniard. By his admission, my assumption was correct. The missing boy Colm had mentioned in passing was the same child who had accompanied the blind man in Finvarra's realm.

His wide lips curled into a pleased smile.

I held his gaze while noting my surroundings: ancient artifacts and delicate ornaments, upholstered barrel chairs surrounding a card table made of petrified wood, and a ship's anchor repurposed as a coat hook hung on the wall.

"I admire your tenacity." The warmth in his brown eyes reassured me.

"Should I be afraid? You are my grandfather." I held the Spaniard in a sharp gaze.

A round shield hung on the wall, painted with an emblem: a dark house on a cliff, surrounded by spirals of smoke. Or were they the spirits he commanded? A richly ornamented sword, with a bronze pommel and a hilt etched with Ogham inscriptions, was mounted beside the shield.

He appeared immense, not a man you'd want to mess with, exuding a badass sea warrior vibe. His fingers bore rings of bronze, silver, and gold. His clothes were layered, beneath a sleeveless vest of hardened leather laced with blackened rawhide, he wore a linen tunic dyed a muted shade of blue.

"You enter Tech Duinn uninvited." He planted his ringed fingers on the desk, rising to his full height. His voice held soft tenor notes of a language spoken by kings.

"I don't think so. Resurrection was the invitation." I cocked my head and studied him. Every twitch of his lips revealed secrets he had yet to share.

"He is a magnificent animal. As quick as the wind." He paced the room, his hands behind his back, his leather boots clacking on the plank floor, salt-weathered and perhaps stitched too many times. He carried the burden of fate on his shoulders.

Lines formed at the corners of thick lips. He was a charmer, this younger version of my grandfather.

"And the three fiery horsemen? The ones who haunted me for years? That was you. You've been calling me home for a long time. Does Ériu know?" I placed my hand on my hip, realizing my clothes were bone dry.

"Your mother's decision to hide you in the mortal realm was foolish. Have a seat, child." He gestured to one of the two chairs facing the desk.

"I prefer to stand, thank you. It was you who orchestrated my return. You sent the bees to Finvarra, and he looked after the rest."

"The king is easily influenced." His icy stare sent a shiver down my spine. Charming and calculating.

What did he desire from me? How many kings was I destined to serve?

My eyes drifted away from his stormy gaze to the large sheet of vellum spread across the intricately carved desk, the kind a sea captain would treasure as his own. I examined the tricolor web of lines over what seemed to be a world map, with place names written at right angles to Europe's coastline.

"What do these lines mean?" I asked, pointing to the red, black, and green lines, each radiating from a central point.

He stood at the end of the desk, his hands braced on each corner. "The lines show the wind's direction, charting our ships' course to a destination."

"How did you create all of this?" I gestured toward his depiction of a world map, curious about how he learned the lay of the land, or the world for that matter.

"It is a hobby of mine. I ask questions of those who pass through. They are happy to share the details of their worlds." The light in his eyes locked on mine as he smoothed his hands over the map.

"It's beautiful." I examined the bottles of ink and the quilled pens. "This isn't quite right, though. Newfoundland is missing." I pointed to the Canadian coastline.

I wanted to know. I needed to know. I touched the black pearls around my neck. I was standing before the dark one himself. "Who are you?"

"I am Éber Donn, son of Mil." A smile ghosted his lips.

Macha's history lesson came flooding back to me—Donn, the Lord of the Dead, left Spain to avenge the death of a beloved family member.

"A Gaul? From Spain? No. You're more than just a lordly seafarer seeking new lands. You're an immortal. How is this possible?" I gestured toward the artifacts around the vaulted cavern—the wine barrels and the wooden shelves filled with books. My gaze settled on the hooded cloak hanging on the anchor and the bronze clasp shimmering in the soft light. I focused on the engraving of a Triskele, each spiral rolling into a crashing wave.

"We came long ago, my brothers and I, to seek revenge for our uncle's death. We claimed these lands from the *Tuatha Dé Danaan* for our people." His eyes, a warm shade of roasted chestnut, hardened.

"And you? How did you end up here? You pissed off the wrong goddess, didn't you? Was it she who banished you to this underground hellhole? Why?" I should have felt sorry for him. Or should I? Here he sat, dispensing justice on unsuspecting souls.

"Women are sensitive beings," he sighed, his eyes sharp. "In her anger, the goddess condemned me to death, and the sea shattered my ship. In the end, the great goddess got what she wanted. My brother bowed to her wishes, naming the island after her. And I," he spread his hands, "live an internal life without sons to carry my name." A muscle twitched in his jaw as he shared what he wanted to share.

"Sensitive beings? Do you realize how misogynistic that statement is?" I huffed, slid into the bucket chair, and rested my hands on the leather seat; a faint scent of cacti wafted through the air. Cochineal—an insect that thrived on prickly pear, harvested by the Spaniards and crushed to produce the vivid red dye. "And you denied her that simple request. Seems rather short-sighted, don't you think?"

"I would thank my gods and the might of my men—the sons of Mil. The demands of a pagan were an insult to my people." He paced back and forth, the burden of fate weighing on his shoulders.

Bran watched from the shadows. He whimpered and lay his giant head on his front paws.

"A pagan? Huh. Did it matter what the island was called? She offered you safe passage, didn't she? Sounds like a rash decision on your part. And now? This is your fate?" I extended my legs and crossed my ankles.

"The goddess and I understand each other." He lifted his hand to his throat and, in an almost hypnotic gesture, stroked four faded scars—four distinct markings, made by a goddess.

The goddess—her whispers struck me like a storm, her starlight flowing through my veins. That thrum was hers, had always been hers, this Goddess Ériu, my mother's mother. The light I craved was as ancient as the giants who lived beneath the sea. And it was okay. It had to be.

"An understanding?" I laughed. "You're an old, withered man in Finvarra's realm. Why do you look different here?" My mind spun with possibilities. This place was timeless, but so was Finvarra's. "You died, and they haven't. You stay forever young here beneath the sea. And what does she get out of it?"

"There are worse fates." He lowered himself into the chair behind the desk and smoothed his hands over the map, refusing to answer my question.

My gaze dropped to the golden ring on his index finger, etched with runes and glimmering with a single black pearl. I resisted the urge to touch the string around my neck. I ignored the knot coiling in my stomach.

"You're her whore? Is that it?" Yes, that's what I said to the lord of the dead, without hesitation, and with eyebrows raised. My anger flared. I had gone from the crazy girl who foresaw death to a shapeshifting, blood-drinking murderess in a single day, like WTF.

"I have daughters and granddaughters. My life is as it should be." His fingers steepled.

"So you're saying that my grandmother is the Goddess Ériu, the sovereign goddess of Ireland? And you and she? Well, I don't need to know the sordid details." I stared at him, imagining what that DNA sample might reveal. "And she named every girl child after herself? Well, that's vain, not to mention confusing as hell. So, how many cousins do I have?" This only got better and better. I leaned back in the chair, shutting my eyes. When I reopened them, I found his gaze resting on me.

"The fire in your eyes belongs to her." His smile softened the hard planes of his face.

"She turned the seas against you, banished you to the realm of the dead. Yet you admire her." I motioned to the remnants of his life scattered here and there.

"She stood against my people, and yes, you are correct in your summation." He chuckled, his gaze lifting to an unseen spirit. "She is the whisper in my dreams."

"Oh my God, you're in love with her." I hugged my arms around my chest, gazing into each corner, expecting a ghostly apparition to appear. "Have you ever heard of Stockholm Syndrome?"

"She is the hush in the forest." His voice turned dreamy. "Wild and untamed."

"Okay, too much info." I planted my hands over my ears, took a deep breath, and focused on the reason for my visit: "What have you done with the boy?"

"You think I sacrificed the child to stay, as you say, forever young?" His head snapped back, and he chuckled, a deep, dangerous laugh that bounced off the balls. "You know nothing of our ways, Granddaughter. The White Woman honors her agreement between this world and the next. Every seven years, she delivers one living soul to me, and thus she remains living.

"The White Woman? She took the boy?" My adoptive parents were taken from me, but they died. There was closure. Still, my throat thickened, as their faces flitted through my memory.

Bran crossed the room, lowered his massive head, and drank from a cauldron on the floor.

"The child was on his deathbed. He would have passed in a few days. The White Woman settled her debt, for now. And this place? It's better than the death the child would have faced." I detected a glimpse of the man he once was.

"But his parents. Can you not imagine their pain? Not knowing where their child is? What terrible fate has befallen him?" I tried reasoning with my grandfather.

"She saved the child from imminent death." He tapped his ringed fingers on the desk.

"To live an eternal life in the land of the dead?" I tapped mine and raised my eyes.

"Your empathy is commendable, given your dark nature." His eyes narrowed.

I refused to take the bait. I looked at the chessboard on a weathered wooden slab and the two stools facing one another.

"His people are frantic. The police are searching everywhere." I thought of Ruairi and his mother, the Dark Lady, living between worlds. Still, I had a hard time feeling sorry for the Lady in question. "Suppose the boy returned to the mortal realm. Would he then die?" That thought broke my heart.

"That's a big if. His time here has saved him from imminent demise, but he will carry this place within him. He will have...changed." His eyes shadowed as he studied me, a slight smile feathering his face.

"Changed? How?" My heart raced. Had the boy died? I looked at Bran, so full of life. But how? Why was he here?

"These stones hold many within their pores. Although some pass through, others live and breathe within the many caverns. Would you like to see him? The boy?" He ignored the stunned look on my face and my question, rising from the desk, and walked down the hallway. He stopped in front of the second door.

I trailed behind him, my footsteps hushed on the plank floor, into a cavernous room bathed in torchlight— a boy's bedroom furnished similarly to the great room, functional and austere. Left in its natural state, the arched ceilings sloped to the floors, cave-like in every way. Smooth ordinary stone, veined with white quartz that glittered in the light. Carvers created a settle bed from one wall, swathed it in sheepskin, and added drawers beneath; bookshelves scribed to the contoured walls surrounded it.

A tow-haired boy lay flat on his stomach, immersed in a game of search and rescue with little toy soldiers and fiery dragons; real-life fiery dragons flitted around the room, flames shooting from their horned snouts. But that was not what made my heart race. A hellhound, the famed three-headed dog of legend, panther-like, with undulating muscles of shadow and smoke, protected the boy. The beast gazed through smoldering coals, fangs glistening, wet with saliva. It stared in our direction and then lowered its many heads to the floor.

"What do you want with him?" My voice hitched. I kept my eyes on the hellhound, meant to keep intruders out? Who was Donn, the Lord of the Dead, afraid of?

Bran stood at the doorway, his hackles raised and his lips curled back. I placed my hand on his rough fur. Dead or alive, he was no match for such a creature.

In your father's realm, the boy acts as a guide for a blind man. Here, he finds amusement, learns new things, and will eventually leave this place. He will become knowledgeable and skilled in the art of magic. He is now protected from those who might try to claim his soul," he said, gesturing toward the hellhound. He moved across the room, the hellhounds' eyes tracking their master. "Dónal? It's time for your lunch. I will call Marta," he added softly.

The boy nodded, ignoring the hellhound and our presence. I searched for any sign of discontent and saw none.

"You said he would live here for eternity. Which is it?" I questioned his earlier statement. Which one was it?

"The freedom to choose lies in his heart." He looked at me, his eyes dark.

"You will give me the boy. And in turn, I will keep your secret safe." I swept my thumb across the black pearls, wondering what kind of hold he held over me. Had my soul already been claimed?

"You know nothing that could jeopardize my existence. That the goddess is your grandmother poses a greater threat to you than I." He watched me with guarded eyes.

I could feel his anger, his fury—I had no leverage, or did I?

"Let's play a game." I gestured toward the chessboard. "If I win, you send the boy back with me."

"And if you lose?" The corner of his mouth lifted.

"I never lose." I sat in the chair and examined the carved pieces. The set was identical to the one in Dermot Sweet's cottage, made from the bones of enemies. How many did this man have?

"You speak boldly." He clenched two opposing pawns, extending his closed fists toward me and offering me the chance for the first move.

"I'm not afraid of you." I pointed to his left hand, which revealed the white pawn. Game advantage.

I made my first move, advancing the pawn to the first position. I waited and planned my attack, following a proven strategy. However, he had me in ten moves.

He sat back in his chair, chuckling. I thought I would scream.

"Your attack needs work, but I will negotiate and offer you a compromise." He poured wine from a clay jug decorated with a flying duck into two silver-rimmed animal horn cups.

"What kind of compromise?" I inhaled notes of pine resin and berries, sharp scents of home, and then sipped from the unique vessel. I studied it, stared at it, and wondered how old it might be.

"You will visit me once a fortnight. We will work on your game." He set the men back on their squares with the precision of a master.

"And?" I swirled the wine, watching angel's tears form inside the cup.

"I will give you the boy." He gazed over the silver rim, those dark eyes shaded by thick lashes, and then he held his glass to mine. "What is it they say in your country? *Sláinte*?"

"*Sláinte*." I tipped my glass to his and then let the wine wash over my tongue. A deal with the devil? Is that what this was? No...this man was my grandfather, the gatekeeper, not...not the devil. "Every two weeks? For how long?"

"Until the White Woman fulfills her next contract." He rubbed his chin, those dark orbs glittering in the half-light.

"Seven years?" I thought about that. In seven years, another soul would be taken. "And then?"

"The terms can be negotiated. The days are long, child. The visits will be good for you. Your game will improve." He snapped his fingers, and Bran rose from the floor. "You may take the dog. He likes you."

"And the boy?" I looked from Bran to my grandfather. "Why is Bran here? Are they? Am I...dead?"

"The boy will live a mortal life. The dog goes where he pleases." He turned away.

"And me? Have I changed?" I touched the black pearls. I already knew what he would say.

"Your mother hoped to keep you from all of this. It is why she sent you away." He stretched out his arm and cupped my chin, skimming my upper jaw, exposing the canine with his thumb. "Do you recall the day you came to me, when you asked permission to end a life?"

"You. You did this?" I snarled, snapping my head from his grasp. Horror filled my mind. My need to drink blood... There had to be an explanation. Only he could tell me why.

"I am a sailor, who deigned to bid farewell to my people when they journey to the other side. However, you, my dear, are immortal by blood. Your father belongs to the *Tuatha Dé*, and your grandmother is a Goddess. That celestial lineage courses through your veins."

"And my mother?" I whispered, my breath caught in my throat.

He shook his head, his eyes brimming with tears. "Your mother lived a long, long life, but her death came to pass. But not before she blessed the Other World with three daughters—Finvarra's immortal three, the Triskele."

"But she was a princess, the Princess of the Dead," I thought of my mother standing up to Finvarra and the words she spoke, that fateful day she left the mortal realm, one of my first visions after arriving in Ireland.

"Your mother walks the halls of death, as lively and vibrant as she once was. She speaks to me in my dreams as she does you." He tipped his chin, his gaze thoughtful.

I swallowed the lump in my throat. My mother was gone, just as Finvarra had said.

"This." He drew the back of his knuckle across my cheek. "This occurs in your kind. The goddess and your father. The darkness must find the light."

Bran whined.

"My kind? My sisters? Are they?" I lowered into the barrel chair, lost for words, and patted Bran's head.

"Your sisters possess other abilities, other needs. You are the dark one."

"The dark one." Huh. I had heard that before.

He stretched out his hand, and I took it.

I HELD the boy against my chest as Resurrection rose from the depths, breaking through the curling waves and surging onto shore.

Seagulls left the rocky crags, swooping low and screeching their anger. What a strange sight it must have been. The sea had released us from her grip. I had survived. The boy had survived. The whole encounter seemed surreal.

The boy chuckled, opening his arms wide as Resurrection tossed his head and galloped into the sunshine. He, too, seemed happy we were home. I glanced at the boy. The transformation occurred when the foamy waves welcomed Resurrection, Donn's prediction proving correct. The boy's brown hair was now white like the ocean's froth, and his eyes were black obsidian, glimmering like the walls of Donn's Rock.

"Are we home?" The boy looked across the dunes, his eyes shining bright, his cheeks rosy.

"Yes, we are." I slipped off Resurrection's back and helped the boy to his feet, my gaze locked on the man shuffling through the loose sand with the help of his shillelagh.

"Princess Rioghain." He lifted a withered hand to his flat cap.

"Eamon." I tilted my head, unable to hide my confusion. "How did you know?"

"I received a message." His gaze drifted to the boy, showing no sign of surprise at the boy's appearance.

"A message?" My gaze narrowed. "From who?" I watched him. This was Eamon, Colm's mentor and advisor. I searched the jagged cliffs and the empty beach. Why did this encounter seem off?

"I'm assuming an agreement was reached?" Eamon's rheumy eyes fixed on the black pearls strung around my throat, his face paling.

"Eamon, who told you to come?" I swept my hand through my hair, taming the wild strands.

"This isn't the first time, Princess. Years ago, a young girl was returned. You would know her as Breda." He looked away. "Donál, come with me, laddie. Your Mam is waiting." He took the boy's hand.

Breda, Colm's cousin and Saoirse's friend—the stunning white-haired beauty with nightshade eyes. OMG.

I followed his gaze to the car park where a dark-haired man stood behind a woman, his hands resting on her shoulders. Her face was tight, and the man's eyes brimmed with tears.

"Eamon, who brought Breda back to you. Do you remember?" I clutched the pearls warming my neck.

"Aye, it was a golden-haired lass by the name of Ériu. You'd best hurry, luv, or you'll be late for your wedding." Eamon tipped his flat cap and smiled as he walked away.

I watched the boy break into a run, and his parents' waiting arms. They hugged and kissed and cried—just as it should be.

11

———————

C*alla*

Colm returned with a list of items from Dermott Sweet's cottage: my flowy dress with satin buttons, white running shoes, and a bouquet of yellow Calla lilies. There was nothing else I needed or wanted.

I returned from the strand to find Clonmara buzzing like a hive. A little bird had shared the news of our impromptu wedding, and everyone flew in. The six brothers wore full formal attire, sporting the O'Donnell tartan. I later discovered that the sky-blue tartan, accented with green, red, and yellow, symbolized the historic county of Donegal, once ruled by the O'Donnell dynasty. I imagined Ruairi O'Donnell would smile if he were here today.

The Clonmara mares roamed, grazing on spring grass and flicking their tails at the bees in the sunlit meadow. Resurrection galloped along the fence line, kicking his hooves and tossing his head. Jack ran with him—best pals. Neck and neck, they put on a show for the onlookers. People stood far back, chatting and pointing at the proud stallions.

Beyond the white house, a peaceful ocean stretched out, its choppy waters now calm. Sunbeams sparkled over the turquoise water, and I wondered if the Goddess herself had caused it.

Colm took my breath away. His Celtic-sized frame was poured into a tailored waistcoat and vest, paired with a black bow tie and a white tuxedo shirt. The bow tie concealed the healing bite marks. If this need of mine continued, I would have to find a more discreet location somewhere else on his luscious body to satisfy my hunger. That thought made me blush.

"Look at you." I traced my knuckles along the sweeping lapel of the double-breasted waistcoat, pausing on the bronze buttons shaped like Irish harps. I raised his hand above his head, urging him to spin. The kilt swirled as he humored me, the laces of his Ghillie Brogues dancing over the tartan-matching ribbons of his knee-high socks. My hand drifted to the shamrock embroidered into the rabbit fur sporran. "I adore the socks."

"Touch me there, lass, and we won't make it down the aisle." His fingers splayed over my ass, drawing me close, his deep voice sending heat spiraling through my veins.

"I have a confession to make." I stood on my tiptoes, planting a kiss on the corner of his lush lips.

"What have you been up to, *mo ghrá*, whilst I dressed?" He studied me. The way his lips moved made my blood turn hot. The way he touched me sent delightful sensations tingling over my skin. He ignited a spark, one glowing brighter every moment.

"Who set up all these chairs? Where did you get them?" I smoothed the skirt of my 1940s party gown I had bought years earlier from a vintage shop in Toronto's Kensington Market. I hooked my hand through his and gazed over a smiling sea of faces.

Yellow bouquets with white tendrils decorated the grassy aisle. A circle of bonfires burned brightly, while picnic tables draped with lovely tablecloths waited for a later reception. I turned to where he was looking, toward the oak tree shimmering with red ribbons, where Saoirse stood waiting.

"Ciarán and Tadgh borrowed them from the community hall. Breda helped." He lifted my hand, escorting me down the aisle, accompanied by the whistling of flutes, the clacking of cowbells, and spoons rattling off the sides of soup cans—a cacophony of joyful noise to celebrate this Bealtaine wedding.

"Are you sure you want to do this?" I gazed into Colm's baby blues and saw no sign of his spectral double. He lifted my fingers, pressing his lips to my fingers in answer.

"Are we ready?" Saoirse's face glowed like the morning dew, her navy robes complementing her pale skin, which deepened the flecks in her hazel eyes. Around her neck, she wore a Brighid's cross on a corded black rope. She smiled, the corners of her mouth lifting.

"We are. We're ready," I smiled. There was so much I

wanted to tell her, but time had not been my friend. Racing back from the meadow, I dove into the shower. I had to wash my hair three times to get rid of the salty brine.

I glanced at Ciarán. I couldn't help but notice the pink flush rising on his neck. He answered me with a sheepish grin, as if he knew.

"Welcome, friends, family, and loved ones. We are here today to witness Colm and Calla join hands and be bound by their love. Calla and Colm have expressed their love through the ancient traditions practiced by lovers of centuries past. Many such traditions originate from ancient Celtic cultures. Handfasting is one of those." Saoirse looked beyond the two of us to the people gathered to witness our special day. Her gaze scanned the O'Donnell brothers, who stood as ushers, and Ciarán, the best man.

"Today is Bealtaine, a time to celebrate life, the earth's energies, and the sun's blessings. Many consider Bealtaine a magical time for weddings, a sacred time for sensuality and joy, and a time for new beginnings. This is the perfect time in the calendar to speak vows to your beloved.

Today is a day to celebrate Colm and Calla's love. They are two people who are the halves of a whole—two souls coming together to form one being, two hearts beating in a single rhythm. Today, we support them as they offer themselves to each other. We celebrate their love, their joy, and their expectations."

A warm wind touched my face. I locked eyes with

Breda; her ebony eyes mirrored the night sky, and her snow-white hair was intricately braided into a crown—the boy. I wondered if the boy would remember his time in Tech Duinn. Did Breda?

"Bride and groom standing left to left, ring hand to ring hand, represent the binding nature of your vows. The left side aligns with the heart, symbolizing that your feelings unite you. Facing each other from left to left signifies that you will always keep each other in mind. This position allows you to watch each other's backs, prioritizing one another's safety above your own."

The ground moved beneath my feet. Butterflies danced in my stomach.

"Many religions customarily create a sacred space for ceremonies, such as weddings, when they are not held in traditional spiritual buildings like churches or temples. Let us create a sacred circle for this beautiful ceremony."

An unnatural darkness spread across the sky. Was I the only one who could see it?

"The circle itself embodies infinity. It is magical, eternal, unchanging, yet always flexible—a ring without beginning or end. True love is infinite, transcending boundaries and limitations; it thrives in both light and darkness, imposing no ultimatums and making no demands. Love, in its boundless nature, cannot be forced or removed. It is a gift we grant ourselves and an honor we share with others from the depths of our hearts and souls." She spread her arms wide, embracing the circle.

I followed her gaze, thunder ravaging my heart.

"When two people come together and give one another this most sacred gift of all, the universe sits back and smiles upon us, laughing and showering us with every blessing. Let us now establish ourselves in the consciousness of the gods and goddesses as we pray."

A shiver ran through me as she summoned the *Tuatha Dé* to unite with the divine beings of their ancestors.

"We acknowledge your presence and power, blessed spirits. We pray your blessing will encircle Calla and Colm's marriage. Surround them and us with your love as we witness this sacred ceremony." Her hand found the Brighid's cross hanging around her neck.

"We give thanks that divine appointment has united these two souls, and the power of divine love will sustain their union. We rejoice that through this mystical union, these two have now become one. They will experience soul satisfaction and fulfillment. You, dear gods and goddesses, bestow your blessing upon them; your love is expressed through them, now and always. And so it is." She sighed a soft breath and then smiled at me and Colm.

"Dear Ones, you are entering a relationship that reflects the unifying, harmonizing power of divine love— the joining of two souls already in harmony. We gather here to witness your commitment to a deeper connection, and we believe you are already one in spirit."

Her smile was for us alone, and then her gaze flickered over the brooding sky, and her voice reached outward into the beyond.

"Today, we ask the infinite light of the divine to shine upon this union. In that spirit, I offer my blessing for this ceremony." She dipped her head in reverence.

"Blessed be this marriage with gifts from the East—new beginnings that arrive each day with the rising sun, communication of heart, mind, body, and soul.

Blessed be this marriage with the gifts of the South—the light of the heart, the heat of passion, and the warmth of a loving home.

Blessed be this marriage with the gifts of the West—the exhilarating rush of a raging river, the gentle and pure cleansing of a rainstorm, and a commitment as deep as the ocean.

Blessed be this marriage with the gifts of the North—a solid foundation upon which to build your lives, abundance and growth for your home, and the stability found in holding one another at the end of the day."

Saoirse clasped her hands together, closing the winds.

"Bride and groom, these four simple blessings will guide you on the beautiful journey that begins today. However, they are tools—tools you must use together to nurture the light, strength, and boundless energy of a love you both deserve, now and forever."

She asked each of us the same questions, and during that time, we admitted our love for each other, shared our desires, and promised to be honest, supportive, and temperate in all things.

"These commitments you made to your partner before this company, the gods, and the goddesses. May you always remain aware of them and strive to uphold your promises." She glanced sideways at Colm's best man. "May we please have the rings?"

Ciarán stepped forward and presented Saoirse with a beautifully carved wooden box. Inside lay two striking gold rings, bold yet elegant, long treasured by Colm's family. Two Claddagh rings—featuring a lover's hand cradling a crowned heart, nestled between intricate Trinity knots. The rings shone as if they had been polished to perfection.

"Let air, fire, water, and earth bless these rings for hopes and dreams, the spark of love, harmony and healing, and strength, respectively."

The circle represents the sun, the earth, and the universe. Let these rings symbolize the unity and peace that joins your two lives into one unbroken circle. Wherever life takes you, always return to one another and your shared togetherness. Now, I bid you look into one another's eyes and hearts.

Colm, please place the ring on Calla's finger."

He took my hand and gently lifted my fingers. His gaze moved upward, slowly tracing the line of satin buttons from the fitted waist to the ruffled collar of my ivory gown, stopping at my parted lips.

Even his gaze sent heat pulsing to my core.

"Do you promise to show Calla your honor and fidelity, to share her laughter and joy, to support and stand by her in times of difficulty, to dream and hope together with her, and to spend each day loving her more than the day before?"

"I do." Colm's voice was husky when he said those two words. He slid the tiny band onto my finger, pointing the golden heart toward mine, promising love and so much more.

One Claddagh ring remained.

"Calla, please give Colm the ring." Saoirse's voice

twinkled with laughter as she patiently waited, a smile lighting up her face.

Colm's heart drummed in sync with mine.

A song played in my head, lyrical notes that didn't belong. Lightning tore through the sky, with the clapping wind announcing the storm and whipping the red ribbons hanging from the old oak. The air felt electric with a mystical force. When I lifted the gold band from the wooden box, time seemed to stand still.

Colm's brows slashed downward. He, too, could sense their presence.

Spirits from the past gathered, joining the circle: my adoptive parents, Colm's da, and a few unfamiliar, ethereal faces.

Finvarra stepped out of an elegant carriage pulled by six black horses, followed by a mottled dog—Bran—who leapt ahead, wagging his tail and joining me at the front of the altar, pressing his enormous head against my hip.

Cian, Midir, and Miach lingered behind the last row of chairs while Nemain, her golden hair decorated with baby-blue satin ribbons, gracefully walked down the center aisle to take her place next to Breda. Macha held our father's arm as they settled into the front row.

I could swear Finvarra nodded at Eamon as he walked past.

They had arrived.

I grabbed Colm's hand and shoved the band onto his ring finger.

"Do you, Calla, promise to show Colm your honor and fidelity, to share his hopes and dreams, to laugh with him and share endless days of joy, to stand side by side with him in times of trouble, and to spend each day loving him more than the day before?"

"I do." My voice trembled as I looked from one extraordinary face to another. My adoptive mother, her eyes glistening with tears, shared a loving nod with the man who raised me.

"Exchanging these tokens of your love interlaces your lives. What one experiences, so shall the other; as honesty and love build, your bond strengthens and grows. I ask you now to cross your hands over each other and take one another's hands."

Saoirse wrapped a cord of wine red, royal blue, and ivory silk ribbons braided with organza ribbons and charms–silver trinity knots around our wrists. She bound them loosely and tied a knot.

"Bride and groom, as your hands are bound, so are your lives and spirits joined in a union of love and trust." She looked into our eyes and smiled. "Above you are the stars, and below you is the earth. Like the earth, your love is a strong foundation to grow and thrive through the seasons. Like a star, your love serves as a constant source of light. Like a flame, your union radiates warmth and glows with love in your hearts. Like the wind, may you navigate life safely and peacefully. Like water, your relationship remains pure and soothing, so it may never thirst for love."

In the branches above, an owl hooted.

"May the gods and goddesses bless this union; may all who encounter it be filled with love. May your lives be abundant, and your pains be few; may you draw forth the highest and best from each other. May you be receptive to divine inspiration and guidance. May you display poise, patience, and understanding with one another. May your lives blend in harmony and joy, and may your days be good and long upon the earth. By the winds that bring change, by the fire of love, by the seas of fortune, and by the strength of the earth, I bless this union." She smiled.

"Your two hearts now beat as one, your two souls now deeply joined anew—walk forward together, forever hand in hand. May your lives be filled with love and laughter.

As we leave this space, may the circle be open yet forever unbroken, and may the love of the gods and goddesses be forever in your heart. And so it is." She closed the circle and then tilted her head, her gaze resting on Colm. "You may kiss the bride!"

To the hoot and holler of the crowd, Colm dipped his head. His lips were soft, like velvet. I wanted nothing more than to be with him, for always.

But we were not done.

Saoirse clasped our hands, undoing the cord and pulling the ends together. She looked again at Breda, who placed the bouquet of wildflowers in my hand.

Nemain gave Breda a cold glare. Macha giggled.

Colm's gaze met mine as we intertwined our left hands and faced the crowd.

"It is with great honor that I present to you, Mr. and Mrs. O'Donnell," Saoirse said with a grand gesture.

Guests hurried forward all at once, leaving chairs askew, shaking Colm's hand, and slapping him on the back.

"Welcome to the family, luv." Colm's mother took my

hands in hers and then kissed my cheeks, followed by Breda, who hugged us both.

The wave swept over me once more as lightning lit up the clear blue sky. A raven screeched from the branches above. When I looked back, they were gone.

EPILOGUE

Cian

Lampposts, decorated with fluttering banners, added to the festive spirit of this year's May Day Festival. The sound of a tin whistle drew the townspeople under the flapping sails of a beer tent to enjoy a pint or two, while the dancing fiddles encouraged both young and old to hit the dance floor. I kept a close eye on my sister, who wandered the grounds with her new husband, their giggling laughter reminding me of two love-struck teenagers.

With the ghost by his side, Colm promised to be an impressive ally to the Tuatha Dé.

I thought of Eamon, who had proven his loyalty again and again. At the King's request, I gave him a silver chalice imbued with enough magic to grant him the long life and happiness he deserved.

I lagged behind the beautiful Breda, enjoying the view and avoiding Rioghain's gaze. Now was no time to bother my sister or share the information I had with my new brother-in-law.

I swirled my fingers over my face, painting it green and yellow with the Adara team colors, blending in with the lively crowd. I kept going, following Breda through the thick throng of Ardara fans and rival fans from the nearby town of Glenties, who traded good-natured insults back and forth.

Rioghain and I were alike; halflings fathered by a king. Our human connection gave us an edge over most faerie folk, allowing us to rise to positions of power in the mortal world, infiltrate the upper levels of society, influence intentions, and sway minds.

The true Fae cannot blend in quite the same way. I credited my father. He was right in his assumptions, mixing bloodlines for the sake of both humanity and the Faerie realm.

The *Tuatha Dé* walked a fine line between good and evil. Rioghain learned firsthand that not all Faeries were virtuous. Greed. Corruption. Base human instincts. My chest swelled with pride as I saw my little sister conquer her fears, adapt to our ways, and rise to her rightful place.

"Shite. Shite. Shite." Breda's sweet voice woke my mind to her predicament, knocked sideways by a young hallion rushing past. She steadied herself, holding the unwieldy stack of books in her arms.

"Let me help you." I lurched forward, unable to ignore her plight, making my presence known.

The slight smile flickering across her face acknowledged me as a fleeting acquaintance, a familiar stranger. She might remember me from the times I looked out for her or when I rescued her from almost a disaster. I smiled. She had no idea who I was or that she held my heart. That in itself was a bittersweet revelation.

"Where are you taking so many books?" Walking away seemed the right choice, but I could not.

She held me in thrall.

Those snowy strands would cascade over her shoulders if not for the elastic holding them back. Her wide cheekbones framed deep-set ebony eyes, carrying all the world's pain. Most would shrink back in fear, intimidated by her unusual appearance. I saw her, a mortal being touched by something otherworldly.

"Oh, thank you so much. We're having a book sale, mostly free." She gestured toward a white tent, her lip piercing catching the sunlight. "I'm sorry, I didn't catch your name."

"Cian O'Cleary. And you are?" I shuffled the stack onto my forearm, resting my chin on the top book.

"Breda. Just Breda. It's nice to meet you." Her gaze swept over me, and my heart pounded.

"Likewise, I hope we meet again." I placed the books on an old wooden table, one of many lining the tent.

"Hmm." She smirked.

"The O'Clearys are distant relatives of the O'Donnell clan." Captivated by her piercing gaze, I shared the first thought that came to mind. It was a half-lie.

My mother, an Irish queen eager to secure a legitimate heir for her husband's throne, tried for years to conceive a child. Conspiring with a Faerie King led to my birth, her husband believing he had spawned a legitimate heir. Her prayers went unanswered, and the title was given to my half-brother, the famed Niall of the Nine Hostages.

Memories flooded my mind of the mortal life I had lived—an Irish prince doted on by a caring mother, unaware of the Faerie blood in my veins. Brash and reckless, battles marked my mortal life—fought and lost in the fight for freedom. I yearned for a hero's death, surrounded by friends, but instead, wounded and alone, I waited for angels who never came. At that dark moment, Finvarra appeared, revealing my true identity. I have spent the last five hundred years drifting between realms, waiting for this moment.

"Oh?" She raised her pretty eyebrows, stopping me in my tracks. "How would you know I'm an O'Donnell?"

I tilted my head, a smile spreading on my lips.

"Would I be knowing you, Cian O'Cleary?" She turned my hand, her eyes widening as she ran her index finger along my long lifeline, her smile faltering as the air grew heavy, thick with foreboding.

"I would like that." An otherness surrounded her, a prickling sensation that flowed through my fingertips, tugging at my mind.

"What? What are you?" Her eyes widened, her face white. My heart stopped as death's hand brushed her shoulders, her gaze shadowing with understanding. She had faced death before.

"Breda?" That otherworldly sensation I knew so well gripped my heart. I clasped her hands, holding her to this world, refusing to let another take her. Not now. But the sensation only grew stronger—pulling her life force away.

"Breda? Breda? What's wrong, luv?" A volunteer rushed forward from the back of the stall, but it was already too late. Her limbs trembled, and her pulse raced. She was slipping away.

"Do you hear it? They've been calling me for days." Her voice faltered, the shadows in her eyes searching for answers. I felt it too, sad whispers, something ancient and born long ago.

I should have stayed away. I shouldn't have approached Breda today of all days, when the daemons rose from the underworld seeking souls to take. I would lose her if I didn't act.

"Breda? Breda?" I gripped her elbows as her knees buckled, falling with her to the ground. I brushed my hand across her brow—her white hair soft as silk, her alabaster skin frozen in time.

"The faeries took her." The volunteer brought her hand to her mouth, gasping. "Swept away, just like that. It's plain to see. Plain to see."

Breda's eyes fluttered, the weight of that unseen world calling her. I knew then, this was only the beginning.

GUIDE TO NAMES & FOLKLORE

Names:

Balor — *BAL-or*

Breda — *BREE-da*

Caoránach — *KEER-an-akh*
—*Mother of all Sea Serpents*

Cian — *KEE-an*

Ciarán — *KEER-awn*

Cillian — *KILL-ee-an*

Colm — *Coll-um*

Donn — *Done*

Éamon — *AY-mon*

Ériu — *AIR-eeu*

Finvarra — *fin-VAR-ah*

Macha — *MAK-ha*

Maimeó — *MAM-oh* — grandmother

Miach — *MEE-akh*

Midir — *MID-ear*

Nemain — *NEV-en*
Oisín — *uh-SHEEN*
Orlaith — *OR-la*
Pádraig — *PAW-rig*
Rioghain — *REE-in*
Ruairi — *ROOR-ee*
Saoirse — *SEER-sha*
Séamus — *SHAY-mus*
Tadhg — *Tige*

Terms & Folklore

- **Aos Sí** — *ees SHEE* — supernatural race; people of the fairy mounds

- **Arrah** — *AH-rah* — an expression of surprise or frustration

- **A stór** — *ah store* — my love / darling

- **Bean Feasa** — *ban FASS-a* — woman of knowledge / walker between worlds

- **Bean Sídhe** — *ban SHEE* — woman of the sidhe; a spirit who announces death

- **Clonmara** — *clon-MAR-a* — meadow by the sea

- **Donegal** — *DUN-ee-gawl*

- **Faerie Rath—Rath** — *rah* — fairy fort / ringfort

- **Féth Fiada** — *fay fee-AH-da* — magical mist or enchantment

- **Fomorian** — *foe-MOR-ee-an*

- **Geas** — *gass* — magical binding vow or curse

- **Is tú mo rogha** — *iss too muh ROE-a* — you are my choice

- **Leannán Sídhe** — *LAN-awn SHEE* — fairy lover

- **Mo chara** — *muh KHAR-a* — my friend

- **Mo ghrá** — *muh GRAW* — my love

- **Na Daoine Maithe** — *na DEE-na MAH-ha* — the Good People

- **Seanchai / Shanachie** — *SHAN-a-kee* — storyteller

- **Shillelagh** — *shil-AY-lee* — wooden walking stick or club

- **Sídhe** — *SHEE* — fairy mounds

- **Sláinte** — *SLAWN-cha* — cheers / good health

- **Sluagh Sídhe** — *SLOO-ah SHEE* — the
fairy host

- **Tuatha Dé Danann** — *TOO-ah day DAN-an*
— the People of Danu

Hey there, lovely reader,

Thank you for walking with me through *Resurrection*. The Faerie realm is vast, and while Calla and Colm's part of the story pauses here, other voices are waiting to be heard.

I'm thrilled to announce that the next chapter in the *Beyond the Faerie Rath* series is almost here:

Book Three—*Tides of Treachery*

This time, the spotlight turns to Macha and Ruairi, and to Breda and Cian—characters you've already come to know and love. Their paths are fraught with danger, desire, and a treachery that runs deeper than the tides themselves.

The bees have more secrets to reveal. Are you ready to follow them once more?

With all my best,

Hanna

P.S. Turn the page for an exclusive sneak peek of *Tides of Treachery*!

HANNA PARK

TIDES OF TREACHERY

A BEYOND THE FAERIE RATH NOVEL

Mist rose from the Underworld, tinged pink with the blood of many, tasting like salt and iron, curling over the shadowy hills of the Sidhe. Ancient yews, impossible in size, twisted into the night sky. Gnarled and thick, their great roots crushed through stone and earth, marking the boundary between the Underworld and the Fae realm.

I stood at the crossroads, where the dead whispered, and the Fae ruled, reaching out to my ancestors, whose wandering spirits offered comfort for a tortured mind.

Too stubborn to cross, I had drifted for centuries, until that day in the Fae realm when, within the guise of another, I was summoned by the Fae King to rise again—not as a revenant or undead, but as a living, breathing man.

"The mortal world claimed you no more, yet you chose not to move on." Finvarra's eyes reflected the betrayals I had endured and the wounds I carried—for those who had long turned to dust. My men. My kingdom. But that time was gone.

Shadows crept around my ankles, whispering my name and reminding me of something left undone, a wrong unburied, but only a fool would turn their back on the High King of the Daoine Sidhe.

"I was there a long time." I refused to admit the truth, the truth this Fae King would use against me if he could.

"Your refusal to cross over was admirable. You were loyal to your clan, your country." His voice lifted the wind —that was the magic he held. "I need a man who understands what loyalty means."

Finvarra—I willingly swore my allegiance to him. Even that was better than what lay within the shadows.

"What do you wish of me, my liege?" I lifted my chin, meeting his hard gaze.

He drew a blade from the air, long and slender, shimmering with runes that sparkled in the moonlight. The hilt was wrapped in silver and gold, intertwined as if the metals had fallen in love. I studied the etchings, refusing to acknowledge the whispers in the wind.

"This sword answers only to someone who has truly accepted who they are—mortal, Fae, reborn. Only then can you guard the one it awaits."

"How will I recognize this man?" I stared into his glowing eyes, their reflection echoing the terrors within my mind.

"The heir of both our worlds will come for it." His lips curled into a thin crescent. "The sword will serve her hand, and your heart may follow."

His words struck deeper than steel—cryptic, ominous, threaded with a destiny I could no longer outrun.

"Love has never found me, my liege," I admitted to the king of trickery. The wind sang in answer, hollow notes of blood and stone, pain and loss.

"Do you claim it willingly, Ruairi O'Donnell?" His voice, terrifying in his darkness, rippled through the dark wood.

"Steel like this comes from men—not spirits." My resolve hardened as I turned the blade. The weight was true. A master smith, a Norseman, or a Spaniard could have hammered this steel, not the magic he would have me believe. I raised the blade high, letting the runes catch the moonlight. I gasped as they moved, like stars shimmering on dark water.

"Yours is not to question its birth." He flashed me a smile, his mouth full of feral teeth.

"I will question what I please." My gut twisted, a sense of foreboding sweeping over me as the blade hummed, its vibration settling deep in my bones.

"You think the iron in your churches fell from the heavens?" Finvarra twirled his hand, manifesting a leather scabbard no mortal could have stitched. "All craft begins in mystery."

"A trick of light meant to deceive?" I slid the belt around my waist and fastened the last buckle. If I named it magic, it would give them power.

"Keep telling yourself that, Christian." His smirk almost hid his disdain.

I rested my hand on the hilt.

The sword thrummed. Alive. Waiting. Watching. And from the depths of the Underworld, something old and vengeful turned its gaze upon me—and smiled.

THANK you for journeying this far—when the tide turns, the bees will guide you back.

Thank you for following Calla and Colm on their journey into the faerie realm in Resurrection, book two in the Beyond the Faerie Rath Series.

If you enjoyed exploring the magic, mystery, and danger of Ireland's hidden worlds, I'd love to hear your thoughts!

Your review helps other readers find their way to Resurrection and means the world to me as I continue crafting the series. Whether a few words or a full reflection, your voice makes a difference.

Thank you for being part of this adventure!

—Hanna Park

ACKNOWLEDGMENTS

My heartfelt gratitude goes to my family, who support my writing obsession with humor and grace, and to my editor, Judi Mobley, who whips my words into shape.

ABOUT THE AUTHOR

Awards:

The Scald Crow

Literary Titan Book Award 2025

Readers' Choice Award 2025

Mary Christmas, a Steamy Small-town Romance.

N.N. Light's Book Heaven 2024 Book Awards

First Place for Best Holiday Romance

Unwrapped in Roros

Passionate Ink - 2023 Passionate Plume - Finalist

Finding Tiegan

American Book Fest Awards 2023

Winner - Romance Erotica

Paranormal Romance Guild

Second Place 2022 Reviewer &

Reader Choice Award

Contemporary Romance Writers

Stiletto Contest Winner 2022

N.N. Lights Book Award 2021

Best Erotic Romance

Sorrento Seduction

Passionate Ink - 2022 Passionate Plume - Finalist

N.N. Lights Book Award 2022 - Finalist

Hanna's Story:

I began my writing career in the pre-dawn of a winter morning while my husband snored like a train. We could call my husband the catalyst. If not for him, I would never have gone to the kitchen to make coffee, feed the cat, and sit on the loveseat in front of the fire. In those moments of wondrous quiet, it was there that I did something I had never thought possible. I opened my laptop, and while the coffee went cold, I wrote a story. My husband had no idea that these sojourns to the loveseat in front of the fire would become a daily occurrence, that writing would become an obsession, but the cat knew. She knows everything.

I write stories that make you laugh, make you cry, and make you love. Thank you, friends, for reading!

In the beginning, there was an empty page.

I am a writer who lives in Muskoka, Canada, with a husband who snores, a hungry cat, and an almost perfect canine—he's an adorable little shit.

Visit Hanna Park at

https://www.hannapark.ca

ALSO BY HANNA PARK

Novels

The Scald Crow, Beyond the Faerie Rath, Book 1

Finding Tiegan

Novellas

Mary Christmas

Unwrapped in Roros

Sorrento Seduction

9 781068 997587